Stay PRESENT

KINCAID BROTHERS BOOK SIX

NEW YORK TIMES BESTSELLING AUTHOR

KAYLEE RYAN

Cover Design: Book Cover Boutique
Cover Photography: Wander Aguiar
Editing: Hot Tree Editing
Proofreading: Deaton Author Services, Jo Thompson, Jess Hodge
Paperback Formatting: Integrity Formatting

Stay
PRESENT
KINCAID BROTHERS BOOK SIX

NEW YORK TIMES BESTSELLING AUTHOR
KAYLEE RYAN

Prologue

Jordyn

I can't breathe.

The world around me is muffled, and all I can hear is my pulse pounding in my ears.

I don't want to go.

Not like this.

My hands tremble as I sit beside my mother, waiting to board our flight.

I don't want to be here. I'm not supposed to be here.

My chest heaves with each breath I force into my lungs. Each breath is painful and labored, as if the weight of an elephant is sitting on my chest.

It's not the weight of an elephant; it's much worse.

It's heartbreak, pain, and regret. All three combined are threatening to pull me under. Not able to sit here a second longer, I jump to my feet.

"Where do you think you're going?" my mother asks. There is so much malice in her tone, it makes me hate her even more than I do for her making me do this.

"I... need the ladies' room," I manage to speak, but my voice doesn't sound like my own.

"We board soon." She raises her eyebrows. It's a silent warning not to run off or do anything that's not "mother approved." It's the same look I've seen from her my entire life.

I swallow thickly and nod before forcing one foot in front of the other and rushing toward the ladies' room. Once inside, I move to the nearest wall and rest against it, pulling large gulps of air into my lungs. My legs wobble, so I slide to the floor, not giving a damn of what I'm about to sit in.

It doesn't matter.

My life is no longer my own. Not that it ever has been. I'm an adult. I shouldn't have to bend to my mother's will, but then she involved *him*. My hopes and dreams are now mere thoughts in my mind, and my heart is shattered. Millions of tiny pieces that used to be his—that still are his—will never be put back together.

Heartbreak.

Pain.

Regret.

All three emotions revolve around him.

I've run this through my head a million different ways, and I know that this is my only option. I have to do as she says, but the thought of losing *him* is tearing me apart inside. I've never felt this kind of hurt. The kind that wraps you in a cocoon, but it's not comforting. It's a constant reminder of what's lost, and what once was.

Fumbling with my purse, I reach inside for my phone. I pull up his name and swallow back the sob that's threatening to break free. I stare at the last message he sent me, and I can no longer hold the tears at bay. I swipe at my eyes, barely able to see the screen. I hover over the keys, but words fail me.

I'm in an impossible situation. I can't see a way out of this, and I know that leaving him alone is best for him. I know that this is the right choice, the only choice, but it hurts. I fear the ache in my chest will forever be there as a reminder of what I've lost.

Locking the screen of my phone, my hands fall to my lap. It doesn't matter how badly I want to reach out to him; I know I can't. I rest my head against the bathroom wall. I don't think about the germs I'm sure I'm sitting in, because all I can think about is him. All I can feel is love for him and hatred for her.

My mother.

It's because of him that I'll never be the same. I'll never love another the way I love him. And my mother... she's ruined any sliver of a relationship we might have had.

I know what love feels like now. True unconditional love, and he's the one that gave it to me.

The day I met Ryder Kincaid changed my life.

Chapter 1

Ryder

M y phone feels like hot coals in my pocket.

She's back.

The love of my life left town without telling me two years ago, and today of all days, the day my brother Archer marries his girl, Scarlett, she reaches out to me. I read her message, but quickly shoved my phone into my pocket and pasted on a smile for my brother. Archer deserves his day to be drama free. My brothers have picked me up and gotten me drunk more times than I can count since the day Jordyn left.

Today will not be about her.

Today, I get to see another of my brothers marry. I'm gaining another sister, and I couldn't be happier for both of them. It's just me and the twins that remain single, and that's a hard pill to swallow. I assumed Jordyn and I would be married by now, at least engaged. I fell hard and fast for her, but she did too. She told me she loved me, and when I looked into her big brown eyes, I saw that love. I could feel it in her touch.

What was supposed to be eighteen months turned into two years, and I still have yet to receive an explanation as to why she left without saying a word. Her message, the one that's sitting on my phone, haunts me. It's taking everything I have not to call her and demand to see her. However, I hold strong. Today, my family needs me, and if I'm being honest, I need them.

I don't know what it means that she's back in town. No matter how bad I want to, I know we can't just pick up where we left off.

It's not that simple.

I love her just as much today as I did the day she left. When she left, I second-guessed myself. I thought maybe she wasn't my one. That maybe she wasn't the only girl for me, but no matter how hard I tried to forget her, I just couldn't. She walked away without a word, and communication has been minimal since she's been gone, but here I am, still madly in love with her.

I *love* her.

But the hurt is still there.

She broke me.

It doesn't help that my brothers are dropping like flies. Marrying the women that they were meant to spend the rest of their lives with. They're having babies, and our family is growing, but I feel as though I'm standing still. As if I'm the same Ryder from two years ago, who knocked on his girlfriend's door only to be told by her roommate that she's gone. Left for Paris without a goodbye.

Shaking out of my thoughts, I put myself into the moment. Archer shifts his stance as he waits for Scarlett to appear. I push all thoughts of Jordyn as far out of my mind as I can, but let's be honest, she's always there. When you love someone, you can't just forget, but I can pretend for a few hours. I can plaster on a smile and appreciate my family, enjoying the moment of yet another one of my brothers pledging to love his girl for the rest of his life, and hug my new sister.

It pains me to ignore Jordyn, but maybe a dose of her own medicine is what she needs. Besides, her message was simple and to the point. She didn't ask to see me. It was simply a for-your-information kind of text. I hate it, and the way my phone sears against my skin, even through the fabric of my pants—demanding I acknowledge her.

> **Jordyn:** *I'm back home. In Atlanta. I wanted you to hear it from me.*

That's it. Not asking when we could meet up, or that she missed me, just that she was back and wanted me to know. Fuck. My heart starts to race when I think about seeing her again. I feel a hand clamp down on my shoulder, and I turn to see my dad smiling widely. He nods to the back and I see Scarlett appear.

Yeah, Jordyn is just going to have to wait.

"Uncle Ryder, it's your turn."

My niece Blakely rushes toward me. I brace myself to catch her, lifting her into the air. "My turn for what?" I ask, placing a loud smacking kiss on her cheek, which makes her giggle. Blakely turned seven in May, and she's a little fireball. She was the first of my nieces and nephews, the first grandchild for my parents, and she remained that way for a few years. We've spoiled her rotten, and none of us would have it any other way.

"To dance with me. Mommy says it's a dance card, but I don't have a card, just a lot of uncles." She shrugs, looking more like a seventeen-year-old than a seven-year-old.

"It's my turn, you say?"

She bobs her little head up and down. "Yep. Didn't you see me with Uncle Archer? He used his arm porn to lift me high in the air. Way, way high." Her eyes are round with excitement and wonder.

"You mean like this." I move my hands to her hips, and hold her in the air over my head, before bringing her back down. She's a tiny thing at seven, but it's still not as easy to do as it was a few years ago. There's a pang of sadness in my chest. She's growing up so fast. It bothers me so I can only imagine how her dad, my brother Declan, feels about it.

"Good job, Uncle Ryder." She places a kiss on my cheek and hugs her arms around my neck.

She wiggles, trying to get me to put her down. "What are you doing?"

"I have more uncles on my dance card," she tells me.

"We didn't have our dance yet."

She shrugs again. "We kinda did, like that movie Mommy and all my aunts watch." She taps her index finger to her chin. "You know, the one with all the dancing and her name is Baby?" She giggles.

Declan walks up, and I raise my brows at him. "You been letting my niece watch *Dirty Dancing*?" I ask him.

"What?" His face pales.

"Relax." Kennedy joins us, a smile lighting up her face. "The movie, you know, with Patrick Swayze."

"He's dreamy, right, Mommy? And he's gots the arm porn like Uncle Archer."

We don't even try to hide our laughter from this kid anymore. We draw looks from others in the room, but that's nothing new when my niece Blakely is involved. "I'll show you arm porn." I flex and she tilts her head to the side to study my arm.

Is it possible to get a complex from the scrutiny of a seven-year-old?

"Meh," she says, and I tickle her sides. She giggles, reaching out for her dad to save her.

"You did this to yourself, sweetheart." Declan sniggers.

"Mommy!" Blakely squirms as she laughs, and points her arms toward Kennedy, who takes her from me.

"We ladies have to stick together." Kennedy drops a kiss to Blakely's cheek, then her husband's before the two of them saunter off, still smiling.

"Lucky bastard," I say, knocking my elbow into Declan's stomach.

He stares after his wife and daughter with a dopey grin on his face and eventually turns to face me. "Yeah," he agrees. His face sobers. "You good?"

"Yep. Why wouldn't I be?"

He gives me a pointed look, and I don't bother to hide the roll of my eyes. "I swear, eight brothers and you assholes gossip worse than sixteen sisters," I grouse.

He shrugs. "All a part of being a Kincaid."

"Yeah, yeah," I grumble good-naturedly.

"So, Jordyn?"

"Wait!" I look up to see Orrin and Brooks headed our way. They're both wearing shit-eating grins, proud of themselves for butting in to our conversation. Into my life. "Proceed," Brooks continues, bouncing his two-year-old daughter, Remi, on his hip.

I reach out for my niece, and she comes willingly. "Tell your daddy and your uncles to behave," I say, kissing the top of her nose.

"Have." Remi points at her dad, and I grin.

"Daddy loves you," Brooks tells her.

"Wuv you," Remi replies immediately.

"What did we miss?" Orrin asks.

"Nothing," I say.

"Yet," Declan adds.

"Nothing to tell."

"She's back?" Orrin asks. It's not like he doesn't already know. This is just his way of butting in to the conversation.

"That's what her message said," I confirm.

"Did you text her back?" Brooks asks.

"Nope. I was a little busy watching our brother get married."

"And now?" Declan asks. He raises his eyebrows, and he reminds me so much of Dad when we were younger and being grilled on some kind of trouble the nine of us were getting into.

"Family first." A pang of sadness fills my chest because I always thought that Jordyn would be my family. In fact, I still think of her that way, and I'll be damned if that doesn't make me feel pathetic.

Brooks reaches over and places his hands over Remi's ears. "Bullshit." He releases her and she giggles.

"Daddy." She reaches for him, and I release my hold on her. I was using my niece as a buffer from my brothers, and now I feel even more emotionally raw and exposed. Not that Remi could mask any of that. No matter the stair-stepped age difference between all of us, I'm close with all of my brothers.

Orrin is the oldest at thirty-six. At twenty-four, I'm second to youngest, next to the twins, who just turned twenty-two. Every two years, my parents had another boy until they got to the last. The twins, Maverick and Merrick, were double the trouble, and they stopped there. It's a running joke. That's not the reason, but growing up, we teased the twins about it. All in good fun.

"She can wait," I finally say. "It's been two years with minimal communication on her end. She picks today of all days to text me and tell me that she's back? I should have known before her plane touched down. Instead, I get a text that she's back, and that's it. She. Can. Wait."

Alyssa, Sterling's wife, steps next to us. She places her hands on my arm, giving it a gentle squeeze. Alyssa has been in all our lives for as long as I can remember. She and Sterling grew up as best friends. We could all see that they both wanted more. It took them a little longer to confess, but once they did, it was full speed ahead. My brother married her as soon as he could, and now she's our sister.

"You boys look pretty intense. How about I take Rem over to see Mommy?"

"Mommy?" Remi reaches out to Alyssa, who takes her into her arms, settling her on her hip.

"You need one of those." Orrin points toward Remi.

Alyssa's eyes light up. "Yeah, I think you might be right." With a wink, and a bomb dropped, she walks away.

"I'm surprised she's not already," I say, as we watch her walk over to where her husband, our brother Sterling, is sitting at a table. He pushes back, and she doesn't hesitate to take a seat on his lap. Alyssa is tiny compared to Sterling, but somehow they just fit. It's always been them, and I couldn't imagine my brother with anyone else. Good thing since they're married and madly in love.

Just like the rest of my siblings. Six of the nine are married and living their happily ever after, and I couldn't be happier for them. It also reminds me of what I lost.

My family has a motto. Work hard, and love harder. It's something our dad shared with us a lot growing up, and we've all molded our lives around it. I've loved Jordyn as hard as I could for both of us since the moment she left, and I want nothing more for her to be back in my life. A permanent part of my world, but at the same time, I need answers.

She's my one.

I feel it deep in my chest, but sometimes love might not be enough. That's a hard pill I've had to learn to swallow since she's been gone. I decided after a late night of drinking with my brothers that I'd give her time. I'd wait for her internship to end and for her to come home and, then we could make decisions from there. I didn't know then that she would extend her time by six months.

I want her.

I love her.

I just don't know if that's enough.

"I agree," Declan says, pulling me out of my thoughts. "She can wait."

"Tell us where your head is at?" Orrin asks.

"Can we wait to have this conversation when everyone is here? I don't really feel like slicing open my heart more than once if I can prevent it."

"Give me five." Brooks saunters off. He stops and kisses his wife, Palmer, rubbing her pregnant belly, before he makes his rounds, pulling all of my brothers to follow him like the Pied Piper.

"Let's step away," Rushton suggests. He turns and walks away, and we all follow.

I love and hate this all at once. I love my brothers and would lay my life down for them, their wives, and their kids. However, I hate that closeness when I'm the one they're trying to fix. They mean well, and hell, I've done it to each of them at one point or the other. I just hate being the one on the receiving end.

I follow my brothers to the other side of the park. I wait for them to talk, but when I see Brooks look over his shoulder, I follow his gaze and see Deacon making his way toward us. Deacon is married to my cousin Ramsey and he might as well be another brother, because we love Ramsey as if she were our sister.

"Sorry, I had to move Bryn to her momma. She finally conked out for her nap with all the excitement."

"Tell us where your head is at?" Orrin repeats his earlier words.

"I assume you all know about Jordyn texting me?" I ask, even though I know the answer. I get a group of nods, causing me to release a heavy sigh. "I don't know where my head is if I'm being honest. It's all over the fucking place."

"Do you still love her?" Sterling asks.

"Yes." Loving Jordyn was never the issue. "But the hurt, it's still there. It's been two damn years, and I still want her, but I'm so fucking mad at her. I don't know how to deal with either emotion."

"So let's break this down," Maverick says. "You should start by deciding if you want to fight."

"Wow." Archer pats Maverick on the back. "Who are you and where is my little brother?"

"Fuck off." Maverick laughs. "I've watched you assholes all fuck up time and time again with your women. I know what not to do, so thanks for that." He smirks.

"Yeah, we've been watching and learning," Merrick parrots.

"It's a good question," Deacon chimes in.

I think about the question, letting it roll around in my mind. Not that I need to. I know the answer. I just give myself time to wonder if I could give her up, and the answer is no. Not unless I know there is no hope for us at all. Even then, I'm not sure I could ever really let her go.

"Yeah," I tell them. "I want to fight."

"We need a plan," Rushton speaks up.

"I want to fight for her, for us. Fuck, guys, I feel as though that's all I've been doing. The last two years loving her from afar, trying to keep this... whatever this is alive. I want her. I love her. That hasn't changed."

"What has?" Sterling asks.

"The pain. It's deeper, more concrete, and no matter how badly I want to run to her, I know that it's not that easy. I want to fight, but I need her to do the same."

"Ryder, bro, I hear you," Orrin says. "But you have to give her the chance to fight."

"I know."

"That means you need to reply and see where it goes," Brooks adds.

"I know. I just... I'm not ready for her to tell me it's over."

"You gotta stay in the present, man. You can't let all the shit in the past cloud what could be your future," Sterling tells me.

"What do you all think about this?" I ask, making eye contact with each of them. "Tell me what you're thinking."

"We want what you want," Merrick speaks up. "Look, I've watched these assholes—" He grins. "—fall in love, and after all the shit Dad used to preach to us growing up, we're all wise enough to understand, you don't get to choose who you love."

"It's going to take work. It might take even more time, but if it's meant to be, it will be," Archer says.

"Mer's right. We're with you." Orrin nods.

"And hey, we've got alcohol. Legally." Maverick grins. "You need a breather. You know how to find us. We can initiate that phone tree shit or the group chat, and we're all there. We got you, brother."

Who would have thought my little brother, the jokester, was so insightful? "I'm holding you all to that."

They all voice their agreement in some form or another. I hate this, but I fucking love these guys.

"Now," I say, laying a hand on Archer's shoulder. "You have a wife to get back to, and we have to celebrate our new sister and the fact that another one bites the dust."

Laughter surrounds me as we make our way back to the reception.

I don't know what's in my future. I hope that Jordyn and I can figure this out, but I meant what I said. I can't be the only one fighting for us. A year ago, maybe, but so much time has passed that I need to see it. I need to feel it and remember that connection. I need to know it's not just something I created in my mind.

Chapter 2

Jordyn

Alone in my hotel room, I grip my phone, willing it to ring. My parents think I'm flying home on Monday. That flight is still booked.

I won't be on it.

It's risky. Reaching out to him. But it's something I knew I had to do. I've been evasive long enough. He needs to know why I left. I should have told him the truth a long time ago, but I was afraid. I'm still afraid, but now that there's a chance I can run into him, he needs to know that we can't be together. As soon as my flight landed, I texted him. It took some time, but he finally replied. Tapping on the screen, I pull up his message, reading our exchange.

> **Me:** *I'm back home. In Atlanta. I wanted you to hear it from me.*

Four long, torturous hours later, he finally replied. I've paced the floor so many times, I'm surprised the carpet in my room isn't worn.

Ryder:	*Archer got married today.*
Me:	*Oh, I didn't realize.*
Ryder:	*It's not like communication has been flowing between the two of us.*
Ryder:	*I didn't even know you were finally coming home.*
Me:	*I'm sorry. It's complicated.*
Ryder:	*Right. Complicated.*
Me:	*Can we talk?*
Ryder:	*You're ready for that? Because I don't want you to spin me some tale. I want answers.*
Me:	*I want to give them to you.*
Ryder:	*Time and place?*

I replied with my hotel and room number. He wrote back with a promise to call when he got to the hotel. I've been clutching my phone ever since. I don't know where the wedding was held, so I don't know how far away he was. I should have asked, but with the way my hands shook during the exchange, I'm lucky I responded at all.

I've been dreading this day. Telling him why I really left. I know Ryder, the man I love. Yes, love, Ryder Kincaid isn't a man you fall out of love with. I know him, and I know he's going to want to fight against this, but I won't let him.

Finally, my phone rings, causing me to jump. I fumble with the phone before hitting the answer button. "Hi."

"I'm here." His voice is soft and sexy, just as I remember. It's been far too long since I've laid eyes on him, and that's about to change. Two long years, and he's about to be here within reaching distance.

"I'm in my room," I say, flopping down on the bed. The exhaustion of what's about to happen weighs down on me.

"I'm on my way up."

"I'll see you soon."

He ends the call, and I stand from the bed. My knees are wobbly, but I ignore that and stand tall as I glance in the mirror. I've lost weight that I didn't need to lose since I've been gone. I guess that happens when you're forced to give up the love of your life. I've been miserable without him.

Wiping my sweaty palms on my jeans, I close my eyes and say a silent prayer that I make it through this conversation. It's going to be hard to see him and not want to wrap my arms around him and beg him to stay. I have no right to ask that of him. Besides, even if I wanted to, I couldn't. There is too much at stake.

A loud knock sounds at the door, and I jump. My eyes open wide, and there's already a light shimmering of tears. I blink hard once, twice, three times, willing them to stay away, but the effort is useless. A golf-ball-sized lump is wedged in the back of my throat. I've waited long enough.

I make my way toward the door just as another knock sounds. Squaring my shoulders, I suck in a deep breath and slowly exhale as I open the door.

I freeze, seeing Ryder standing before me. It's been two years. Two very long, heartbreaking, painful years. Not just for me, but for him. He's grown a beard since I've seen him last. Not a mountain-man beard, just a nice, trimmed beard, and it makes him even sexier. Older, but I guess two years will do that to you. He's wearing a black button-up with the sleeves rolled up to his elbows, and the tight fit across his chest tells me that those two years have been good to him.

"Ryder." My voice cracks, and just as I suspected, all hope of hiding my emotions is washed away.

"Jordyn." His low, deep voice greets my ears.

"C-Come in." I ease back, giving him space to enter my room. He steps inside, his elbow rubbing against my chest as he does. Tingles race down my spine, but I ignore them. Just like I ignore the rapid beat of my heart telling me we're finally home. This isn't home. *He* isn't home, no matter how badly I want him to be.

I take my time closing the door. Slowly, I turn to face him, but it's his back that I see. He's standing in the middle of my hotel room with his head bent and his shoulders stiff. I can't tell if his eyes are closed, or if he's staring at the patterns on the carpet. Either way, he's not looking at me.

I stand frozen, waiting to see what he'll do next. I know he's angry, and he has every right to be, but I'm angry too. Just not at him. Whatever he does, however he reacts, I'm going to take his wrath, and his pain, because it's my family who caused it.

Finally, he turns and his eyes find mine. I stand as still as a statue, only the rapid rise and fall of each labored breath causing my body to move and show signs of life. I feel as though I'm dead inside. If not for that simple movement, I'd believe I was.

"Jordyn," he croaks. The emotion in his voice slays me. I close my eyes, fighting back the pain and the tears, and that's when I feel it. Feel him. And his arms wrap around me. He holds me in his grip, as if he's afraid this might be the last time.

He'd be right.

This is risky, coming home early in hopes of this very scenario, but I'll take whatever punishment I'm given, as long as it doesn't touch him or his family.

I tell myself to hold strong. To not hug him back, but my arms have a mind of their own as they wrap around him. My hold is much weaker than his, but the sentiment is there. We both exhale as our bodies melt into one another, and I feel as though this is my first real breath in two years.

I don't know how long we stand like this. Could be seconds, could be hours, but when he pulls away, I want to scream for him to never let go.

Ryder steps back, pulls a chair out from the small dining table in the room, and takes a seat. "Start talking, Jordyn." His raspy voice a tell of his emotions.

I nod and move to sit on the edge of the bed, putting some distance between us. "I've thought about this day, this moment, a thousand times. If I'm being honest, I wasn't sure it would ever happen." He doesn't respond, so I keep going. "I'm sorry, Ryder. From the bottom of my heart and the depths of my soul, I'm sorry for leaving the way that I did."

"Why did you?" His voice is gravelly.

"My mother."

He tilts his head to the side, and his brow is furrowed. "Your mother? Come on, Jordyn, you can do better than that. I've been to see your parents since you've been gone. She's been nothing but nice to me, welcoming me into their home." He stands. "If you're not going to be straight with me, then I'm out. You've wasted enough of my time the last two years, don't you think?" Anger eclipses his tone, but the look on his face tells me that the words he's saying hurt him as much as they hurt me. He's standing, but he makes no move toward the door. He doesn't want to leave, and I don't want him to either. Not yet.

Then his words register.

"W-What? You went to see my parents? When?" My heart rate kicks into an accelerated rate at the thought of Ryder being anywhere near my mother and her hatred.

"Does it really matter?"

"Yes." I breathe the words, but I'm not sure he heard me, because I can barely hear myself over the rapid beat of my pulse.

"Why does it matter? You left me, remember?" He stalks across the room, peeling back the curtains, and peeking out the window. It's several long, thunderous heartbeats before he turns to face me again.

"Ryder." I shake my head. "You don't understand."

"Then make me understand, Jordyn." His voice rises. "Tell me how you told me you loved me and that we would figure out a way for you to chase your dream and stay together. Tell me how you can tell me you didn't want to leave me, and you felt as though staying was the better choice. Tell me how you told me you didn't even think that fashion was your dream anymore, and then three fucking days later, you disappear. You jetted off to another fucking country and ghosted me. You. Ghosted. Me." His chest is heaving as he pulls air into his lungs. His eyes are fire and pain all wrapped up into one. Both slice through my heart like a sharp knife.

"I didn't have a choice." My voice is soft, but my anger at my mother boils over. I say it again, only this time I shout it. "I didn't have a choice!" I jump from the bed, unable to sit still.

The room is eerily silent and we're caught in each other's stare. I saw this going so differently in my head. I thought he'd come in, take a seat, and I'd calmly explain how my life got turned upside down. However, the passion that still simmers between us that's now edged with pain is far too intense to have a simple conversation.

"Tell me why, Jordyn? Why didn't you have a choice?" His question is calm, his voice gritty, and when I glance down, his hands are fisted at his sides.

"My mother." I swallow hard.

"What about her?"

"She threatened you and your family. Your brothers."

His head jerks back as if I've slapped him. There's intensity in his eyes, but he doesn't defend her like I'd feared from his earlier declaration that he's been to see my parents. "Explain." He takes his seat in the chair once again and folds his hands in his lap, giving me his full attention.

"I didn't want to do it. I didn't want to leave without saying goodbye. Hell, I didn't want to leave at all." Memories of that day wash over me, but I shake them off. I need to stay present.

"But you did." I see the confusion through the pain all over his features.

"The day I left, my mother requested my presence at her place. I know we talked very little about my family, and there's a reason for that. My mother is a control freak, and my father is a workaholic. Neither one of them wanted me. I was a mistake that they had to maintain to keep up appearances."

"Jordyn," he says softly. "I'm sure that's not true."

I scoff. "Trust me, it's true. Anyway, my mother requested that I come to see her, and when Margaret Astor requests your presence, you go." I pause, taking a breath, and start again. "Apparently, she'd had my cousin, Amanda, spying on me. I don't know how she convinced her to do it, but Amanda was feeding her information. The night after we said 'I love you' for the first time, I went back to my apartment and Gianna was out. I had so much hope and love in my heart that I needed to talk to someone. I called Amanda, and we talked for two hours on the phone."

"I'm listening," he urges when the pause to gather my emotions carries on too long.

"I told her how much I loved you. I told her I'd never felt this way about anyone. I didn't leave a single emotion unvoiced during our conversation. I even told her about Paris and fashion. I enjoy it, but it was no longer my dream. It was my mother's, and I was thinking about changing careers. I no longer wanted the big-city life, jet-setting around the world. Hell, if I'm being honest, I never wanted it. I was forced into it, and it was easier to go along with it to keep my mother happy. That is until I met you."

"What happened when you met me?" Ryder's eyes bore into mine as he hangs on my every word.

"You made me see the world differently. It's not about flashy cars and expensive vacations. It's about the people you love. It's about being there for someone when they need you. It's about love. Unconditional love." I pause as I think about my next words. I already decided I'm not holding anything back. Swallowing hard, I hold his stare as I say what's in my heart. "I've never felt that kind of love, nothing close to it until I met you. You brought me to meet your family, and it was like coming home. I imagine it's what seeing or hearing for the first time after years of silence and darkness feels like. I knew instantly, after one long weekend, that the path I was on wasn't the one I wanted to take. I just didn't know how to turn around or switch lanes."

"Me." He taps his hand over his chest, over his heart. "You tell me, the man who loves you above all else, and we figure it out together."

I nod as a tear slides down my cheek. I make no move to wipe it away. I can already feel more brimming, begging to break free. "I wanted that."

"Then why did you leave?"

"Amanda told my mother everything. How I didn't want to go to Paris, how I wanted a small-town life away from the bright lights of the city. My mother was furious. She did, after all, raise me, pay for my education, and because of that, I needed to do what she said. Being an Astor demands it."

"I don't understand."

"I told her it was all true, and that I wasn't going. I told her I wanted to take my career in a new path, and she blew up. She demanded that I go, and when I told her no, she pulled her trump card." I swallow back the emotions threatening to pull me under and keep going.

"My parents have money and a lot of influence. She threatened to get you fired. She threatened your family's businesses. She vowed to close the doors on Declan, Orrin, Palmer, and even Deacon. She told me I had to end my relationship with you and take the internship in Paris. She promised me that if I never spoke to you again, you and your family would stay untouched."

He opens his mouth as if he's going to speak, but quickly closes it. I can see a kaleidoscopic of emotions wash over him. "She can't do that, baby." His voice is soft. "She can try, but this is a small town. We've lived here our entire lives. People know us, and how my brothers, how my family does business. She might have clout, but she can't hurt us." He pauses. "Her words, her threats, that's what hurt me, hurt my family, because she took you away from me."

He stands, and I freeze as he makes his way toward me. He takes my hands in his and brings them to his lips. He kisses the back of both hands before his eyes bore into mine. "We can't let her do this to us, Jordyn."

"Ryder, you don't understand. She has the money, the connections, and the influence to make things happen. It's too risky. Your family... they're amazing people, and you, I can't let anything bad happen to you." My voice cracks, and my battle with tears is lost as they flood my cheeks.

"We'll figure it out," he assures me.

"No. We can't risk it. I won't risk you or your family. I don't want her hate touching any of you. She doesn't even know I'm here. My parents think that I'm flying home on Monday. I took an earlier flight to sneak and see you. I needed to explain. I know what I did was wrong, but I didn't see another way out of it. Now, being home, I know there is a chance we might run into one another, and I needed you to understand why I can't act like we were even together. I refuse to let her ruin you and your family because of the hate that she has for me. You don't know what she's capable of. I've seen her destroy lives, and I won't let that happen to you or your family."

"We fight her."

"You can't." I choke on the words. "Trust me. I know my mother, and you can't. She wins. She will always win."

"So, what? You expect me to just walk away from you?"

"You have to."

"Is that what you want?" He takes a step back, dropping my hands as he waits for my answer.

"I want you and your family to be happy. I want nothing involving my mother to touch any of you. This is the only way I can make that happen."

"Do you love me, Jordyn?"

Yes. I'm screaming the word in my head, but instead of answering, I keep my eyes trained on the floor. His feet come into view, and his index finger lifts my chin. I can barely make out his features from the tears in my eyes.

"Do. You. Love. Me?"

I nod.

"I need your words, baby."

"Yes. Yes, I love you. I'll never love anyone else, but I don't see how this can work."

He drops his hand and crushes me to his chest. I can feel the rapid beat of his heart, which has me giving in. I grip the back of his shirt in my fist as I hold on for all I'm worth.

I love him so much.

When he finally pulls back, his eyes glisten with his own emotions. "We'll figure this out."

"There is no way out of this. I've had two years to think about it, and I just don't see a way. Short of my family going bankrupt and my mother losing her influence, I don't know how we're going to stop her. She has money and the social influence behind her."

"Who knows you're here?"

"No one. I don't know who I can trust."

"Me, baby. You can trust me." He cradles my cheeks in his hands, and I know what's about to happen. I can practically taste his lips on mine. It's wrong. I shouldn't let this happen. It's only going to make it harder when he walks out that door, but I need this.

I need one more kiss to get me through the next fifty years of living without him.

Chapter 3

Ryder

When my lips touch hers, it's as if everything is finally right in my world. Two long excruciating years without tasting these lips. Never again. I'll never go that long without kissing her again.

Her words swirl in my mind as I try to think of how to fix this. I need to talk to my brothers. I need them to know what's going on, and that their businesses are at stake. I know that when we put our heads together, we can figure this out.

I won't lose her.

Not again.

My hand slides beneath her hair and cups the back of her neck. I angle her just the way I want, as my tongue invades her mouth. She moans, and that sound goes straight to my cock.

Fuck, I've missed her.

I allow myself to get lost in her. To relish the fact that she is finally in my arms, exactly where she belongs. It could be minutes, or it could be hours. All I know is that no one knows we're here. Not a single soul will come knocking on our door. She has until Monday before her family thinks she's coming home. There is nothing I have to do that's more important than being here with her.

Easing out of the kiss, I press my forehead to hers. "I fucking missed you."

"I—I missed you too," she whispers. There is a crackle of emotion in her voice that tears at my heart. "I wish things could be different."

Pulling back, I rest my palms against her cheeks. Her big brown eyes stare back at me. I can see her pain. She didn't want to leave me. I believe her. I trust her. Some might call me crazy, but this is the woman I love. I *know* her. That's why I had such a hard time accepting that she just left without telling me. We made plans. Long distance sucks, but our love was strong enough to withstand it.

This moment proves that.

"She won't win, Jordyn. We'll figure out a way. I'm going to talk to my brothers. I'm going to tell them about her threats, and we're going to form a plan. I'm not losing you."

Tears roll down her cheeks. "I don't see how, but we're here together right now." Her hands slide to the front of my shirt, where she begins fumbling with the buttons.

I stand still, letting her undress me. My cock strains in my dress pants and presses painfully against the zipper. It's been two years with nothing but my hand for relief. That's about to change. My girl is home, and I'm going to show her exactly how much I missed her.

Once the last button is freed, I quickly remove my shirt and toss it to the floor. "Arms up," I tell her. Reaching for the hem of her tank top, I lift it over her head. Her chest is heaving with each breath, making her breasts look edible in the white lace bra.

I take my time running my hands over her shoulders and down her arms. Goose bumps break out across her skin, and I bite back my smile. Trailing an index finger down the column of her neck, over her collarbone, and dipping into the valley between her breasts. Needing her skin against mine, I reach both hands around her and make quick work of removing her bra. I assist her in lowering one strap and then the other, before tossing it onto the growing pile of clothes on the hotel room floor. She's here, in the flesh. My Jordyn yet different. She's clearly lost weight that she didn't need to lose, and the exhaustion she carries is evident in her features. I want to take all of her worries away. Tonight, I want her to stay here with me in the present—nothing between us but the love we share.

With one hand pressed against the small of her back, keeping her close, I use the other to trace her nipple with my thumb. She makes a mewling sound in the back of her throat, and I know that no matter how slowly I want to take this, it's just not going to happen that way. Not this time. It's been too damn long since I've been inside her.

I need her now.

"I need you naked, sweets," I tell her.

She lifts her head, and her brown eyes are sparkling. "It's been a long time since I've heard you call me that." The softness in her gaze is all too familiar. A look I've missed more than I can express.

With a quick kiss on her lips, I drop my hands from her sexy body and take a step back. "You're here now. That's what matters."

"Ryder—" she starts, but I raise my hand to stop her.

"Not right now, Jordyn. Right now, I need you naked. I need to feel you all around me, and I needed it about twenty-four months ago."

She nods and strips out of the rest of her clothes while I do the same.

Moving before she can make out what I'm about to do, I grip her hips, and I toss her gently on the bed. Her laughter, a beautiful sound I've missed like a fucking limb, fills the room. I waste no time crawling over her. My hands are flat on the bed next to her head, and I settle between her thighs when she opens for me. It's as if she's welcoming me home.

Staring down at her, my heart squeezes inside my chest. There have been times over the last two years that I often wondered if I made it all up. Did I really love her as much as I thought I did? Did she love me the way she confessed those days before she left? It's hard not to question those feelings during that long of an absence.

However, staring at her now, those feelings burn like fire inside my veins. Shame washes over me that I, even for a second, doubted this. "I love you." The words are a raspy whisper.

"Ryder." Her voice cracks. She raises one hand and rests it against my heart. "I will always love you."

"This isn't goodbye." There's a growl and a bite in my tone that she doesn't deserve. Leaning down, I press my lips to hers before she has a chance to argue with me. The situation feels as though it's impossible, but we'll figure it out. That's the only option.

Pulling out of the kiss, I lean my weight on one elbow, careful not to crush her, and use the other to run the pad of my thumb over her clit. My fingers begin to explore her pussy, and I hiss out a breath.

"That's all for you. Only for you," she tells me.

"I know I should take my time and savor you." I hoped saying the words would help me slow down, take my time, but this burning need I have for her is too hot, too bright. I can't fight it.

She locks her legs around my waist and pulls me closer. "I don't want that. I just want you. I need you, Ryder. It's been too long."

"We're not leaving this room until I've had my mouth on every inch of your skin. But for now." Leaning back on my knees, I fist my cock as I stare down at her. We lock eyes, and she nods.

"There's been no one since you."

I nod. "Same." My voice cracks. I feel like a pussy, but fuck me, she's here. My girl is home and on this bed, ready for me to take her, and that's some heavy shit. After two long years, I can't help but get choked up at her words.

It was only her for me.

It was only me for her.

Us.

Leaning back over her, I place one hand on the bed, while the other guides my cock to her entrance. I push inside her and still. Closing my eyes, I focus on breathing. Her legs wrap around my back, locking her feet at her ankles, and she uses her position to pull me closer.

Dropping both elbows to the bed, I open my eyes. "Hi, sweets." I kiss her lips. It's a soft peck, a gentle swipe of my tongue across her lips.

"You feel like home."

"That's because that's what we are for each other." I want to say more, but I kiss the tip of her nose, and lift myself up. "Hold on."

She looks confused until I pull back and rock my hips into hers. "Oh," she moans.

"Headboard, sweets." Doing as she's told, she reaches her hands over her head and grips the gold metal bar of the hotel bed. "You good?" I ask.

She nods, licks her lips, and I let loose.

I'm relentless in my pursuit of our pleasure. Her tits bounce with every thrust, and when she moans my name, I know I'm not going to last long. "Touch yourself for me, sweets. I need you to come."

"I'm close," she pants. She makes no move to release the headboard that she's tightly gripping with both hands.

"Jordyn," I growl, and it's as if me saying her name flips a switch. Her pussy squeezes my cock like a vise. She arches her back and cries out for me.

Me.

My girl is crying out for me.

I don't bother trying to hold off as my release barrels through me. I still as I release inside her for the first time in two very long years. My body finally relaxes, and I lean down, pressing my lips to hers. Lazily, I stroke into her mouth, tasting her. I'm stalling because I'm not ready to lose this connection between us. Not when we just got it back.

Eventually, I pull out of her heat, despite how badly I want to stay rooted where I am, and move from the bed. Making my way into the bathroom, I wet a washcloth with warm water and clean up, before doing the same to another, taking it back to the bed. I stop to take Jordyn in. Her long brown hair is spread out over the pillow. Her eyes are closed, her chest is rapidly rising with each breath, and her naked body is on full display for me. I realize I'm creeping on her, so I move to the bed and settle on the edge.

Her eyes pop open. "Hey." A blush sneaks up her neck, coating her cheeks. It's been so long. She's shy in front of me. She doesn't need to be. Every inch of her is perfection.

"Let me take care of you." Her face is still flushed, but she gives me a tiny nod and opens for me. I clean her up quickly, before tossing the washcloth through the bathroom door, where I hear it land on the tile floor with a splat. "Move over, sweets, I'm coming in."

She giggles but moves over, and I wrangle the cover so we can slide beneath to ward off the chill of the air conditioning.

"Can we stay here, just like this until I have to meet my family at the airport on Monday?"

"Yes." I already plan to call my foreman and tell him I need to use a vacation day for Monday. I hardly ever miss work, and over the last two years, I've picked up more hours than everyone else. He won't have a problem with it. "I planned on taking off work Monday so I can be there when you greet them."

"No. No." She turns to face me, and her face has gone ghostly white. "No."

"Hey, it's all going to be okay. I promise you."

"No." She sits up in bed, pulling the sheet around her breasts, and stares down at me. "My mother... she's not someone you mess with, Ryder."

There's something she's not telling me. "Explain."

"I can't. I just—we can't push her. Promise me."

"I can't make that promise, Jordyn. Not when it means that you're not a part of my life. What am I missing? What has you so scared?"

A tear slides down her cheek, and I pull her into my arms. I hate that this is hurting her, but she told me she loved me. She's home and in my arms where she belongs. No way am I just walking away because her mother wants to toss out some threats.

No way.

I move us so that we're lying face-to-face on the bed. My arms are still wrapped around her tightly, letting her know I'm here. I'm here and I'm not going anywhere. I wipe at her cheeks, and she opens her eyes. The pain I see twists like a knife in my chest.

"I had a brother." Her confession is soft.

The hesitancy in her voice has me on edge. She had told me she was an only child. Why would she have lied to me?

"I know. I'm sorry I didn't tell you," she says, reading my expression. "Jeremy. His name was Jeremy, and he was twelve years older than me. I was an 'oops' baby."

"You could never be an 'oops' anything," I assure her.

"Thank you, but it's true. They never wanted me. They needed a son to carry on the legacy my father and my grandfather built. Someone to pass the law firm down to. They got that with Jeremy. They didn't need me."

The tone of her voice tells me she's just accepted this as her truth. What has happened in her life to make her think she wasn't wanted?

"Sweets, I'm sure that's not true." I've met her parents, her father just once, but her mother a few times, and I'm having trouble picturing her as a mother who made her daughter feel as though she was an accident. Not that I don't believe her, I do, but that's not the woman I've met.

"It is. Anyway, I was ten when it happened. Jeremy graduated college and told my parents he wouldn't be going to law school. He was in love with a girl; her name was Holly. She was really pretty, and she was always nice to me. Anyway, Holly's family owned a small accounting firm, and Jeremy wanted to go work for them. He was always good with numbers. He used to help me with my math homework," she says, a sad smile tugging at her lips. "He told my parents that he was going to ask Holly to marry him, and that they needed to get on board with his plans or consider him no longer their son." She pauses to collect her thoughts.

"At the time, I didn't understand why he would say that. They were our parents, and I was his sister. We were family. How could he threaten to leave us like that? I was scared and confused, but I didn't dare say anything. Instead, I stayed at the top of the stairs, listening to them argue. It was my thing. I was supposed to stay in my room, but I was a part of the family too. I was also nosy and wanted to know what they were saying. They always treated me as an afterthought, and even though I was only ten, I wanted to be in the know. I thought it was a genius plan, but it turned out that there is a reason you shouldn't eavesdrop. You might hear things you're not supposed to. Things you can't unhear."

Lifting my hand that's been resting on her hip, I brush her hair out of her eyes. "What did you hear, baby?" I keep calm and try not to show my unease on my face, but there's something deep inside my soul that's telling me her next words are going to knock me on my ass.

She's worried.

No, that's not the right word.

She's scared, and whatever she heard that night upset her.

"Not that night."

"But you heard something?"

"Yeah. Jeremy, he, uh, he was in a car accident a week later. He didn't make it."

"Oh, sweets." I pull her into my chest and press my lips to the top of her head. "I'm sorry."

She eases back and wipes at her cheeks. "I was sent to my room a lot after the accident. My mother's words were, 'I don't have time to deal with you. Go to your room.' I did as I was told, but I also snuck out to sit at the top of the steps."

"You heard something that spooked you?"

"My parents were talking. I remember thinking it was weird that they were calm. No crying or yelling when all I wanted to do was cry and scream for my big brother. Anyway, I heard my mother say that it wasn't supposed to be him."

Oh, fuck. I think I know where this is going.

"As I listened, I learned she hired a guy to scare Holly. To make her leave Jeremy. However, it wasn't Holly driving her car that day. It was my brother. The windows were tinted, and the guy Mom hired either couldn't tell or wasn't smart enough to see it was my six-foot-two brother, not his petite girlfriend behind the wheel."

She sucks in a ragged breath and slowly exhales. "Jeremy caught on that someone was following him and tried to lose them. The guy Mother hired sped up, and when Jeremy lost control, he couldn't stop in time, and when Jeremy's car turned, the guy hit the driver's side door, ultimately taking both of their lives."

"Son of a bitch," I mutter under my breath.

Jordyn holds my stare. "She killed him, Ryder. My brother. Her son. Her flesh and blood. She wasn't even upset about it. She's evil. They're both evil, detached, and capable of ending lives."

My head is spinning as I try to make sense of what she's just told me. "We'll figure it out."

"We can't. My mom informed me before I left for Paris that when I got back, they'd have a respectable man for me to marry, who they can leave the law firm to. Not me. To the man they choose for me to marry to bring into the family so Dad can pass the torch."

"Fuck that. They can't make you do that."

"They can," she says sadly. "I'd do it a thousand times over if it protects you and your family."

"No. No. Jordyn, we will figure this out. You—" My voice cracks. "This is where you belong." I hold her as tightly as humanly possible. She probably can't breathe, but I need her in my arms right now.

"We have this weekend. I have to be at the airport at eleven on Monday. My flight is set to land at noon, so I want to be sure to be there when the car arrives to pick me up."

"The car?"

"My parents do not pick me up from the airport. That's beneath them. They have staff for that. There's a chance they're going to find out that I came back early to see you, and well, she's going to be pissed. We have this weekend, Ryder," she says again.

How is it that life kicks you when you're down? I'm having a difficult time wrapping my head around everything that she's told me. It's not that I don't believe her. It's that the people she described tonight are nothing like the ones I've met.

Over the last two years, I stopped by her parents' place a handful of times. Her mother was always polite and gracious, the perfect Southern Belle, if you will. She pretended to sympathize with me and how much I missed and loved her daughter. She played me. She knew why Jordyn left me and that she was behind it. I fell for her fake act hook, line, and sinker.

Fuck, I feel like such a fool.

She's home, she's here with me, where she was always meant to be, where she wants to be, but we have this huge fucking obstacle in our way. I need to talk to my brothers, but I'm not leaving this room until I have to. I don't know when I'll get to see her again.

I will see her again.

Chapter 4

Jordyn

I'm exhausted. My eyes burn from lack of sleep, but I refuse to close my eyes. Ryder slumbers peacefully next to me, but all I can do is stare at the shadows dancing across the ceiling of this hotel room. Oh, and the clock. The red numbers are like a beacon of light during a tropical storm. As time passes, the heaviness in my chest grows.

I've turned the situation around and around in my head. I've considered different ideas, but I get the same answer every single time. My mother has no heart, and I will never let her hate touch Ryder and his family.

A family who welcomed me with open arms. The Kincaids showed me what it means to be a part of a family. To know without a shadow of a doubt that those people have your back always. It's a gift that's priceless to me. I'll do whatever I have to do, marry whoever they chose to protect that. To protect them.

I'll never love another the way I love Ryder Kincaid. The last couple of days have been a dream come true. I missed him more than I can express, and the red glaring numbers on the clock remind me that in a few short hours, I have to walk away from him again. I have to leave the man I love, the one who owns me heart and soul.

I have to save them from her.

This time, however, when I walk away, I'm not hiding the reason why. I know my Ryder, and he not only deserved the truth, but he wouldn't stop trying to get through to me. He would fight for us, just as he has the past two years. He never wavered.

He loves me.

I feel that love in every fiber of my being.

Tears fill my eyes, and not for the first time since he knocked on my door on Saturday evening. My chest is tight, and the pain of knowing this is it for us grips my heart like a vise. A sob breaks free, and I cover my mouth, trying to hold it in.

"Jordyn?"

I swallow the pain presenting as a lump in the back of my throat. "Go back to sleep," I whisper, but there's no hiding the crack in my voice.

"Come here, sweets." He rolls me toward him and pulls me into his chest. He doesn't try to tell me it's going to be okay, because he can't promise that. I know he wants to, but we've talked enough since my confession that he understands my mother is not who she presents to the world.

My father, well, he lets her do her thing. My parents are criminals. How they got away with what happened to my brother is beyond me. I'd love nothing more than for justice to be served for his death, but I have no proof. I was a little girl listening in on a conversation. Unless we find something concrete, it's my word against theirs.

My father is even more detached than my mother is. I don't ever remember getting a hug from either of them, and the last person to tell me that they loved me was my big brother a few days before we lost him.

Until Ryder.

Suddenly, it's important to me for him to understand that love will never fade. "There will never be anyone else for me, Ryder. I might m-marry because they demand it, but I'll never love him. My heart will forever be yours."

"I don't know how, but we will figure this out. I need to talk to my brothers. We'll figure out a way. Even if you and I have to leave. If that's what it comes to, then so be it."

"No. I won't let you leave your family. They need you."

"I need you in my life, Jordyn. You're a part of me." He kisses the palm of my hand and presses it against his chest, over his heart.

"I hate her." My voice breaks with my tears. "I hate them both."

"I need you to stay strong for me. We will figure out a way."

"I don't see how."

"It will work out."

He sounds so confident. "Promise me you will remember that I'll only ever love you."

"I love you too, baby."

"I'll never forget this time with you. I'm so sorry for leaving the way that I did. I never wanted to hurt you, but I was scared, and I didn't know what to do. I know that I put you through hell. From the deepest part of my soul, I'll never forgive myself for putting you through that."

"I need you to stay present, baby. You were in an impossible situation. I understand."

"How can you be so forgiving?" I don't deserve him. This just further solidifies that. My family should never touch the goodness that is Ryder Kincaid and his family.

"I can see your pain, Jordyn. I can feel it rolling off you in waves. I see it in your eyes. The woman I love is here in my arms. She didn't walk away to hurt me. You were protecting me, and I love you even more knowing what you're willing to sacrifice for me and my family, but, sweets, I'm not going to let you. We will figure this out. I won't live without you."

We won't agree on this. I know that, and from the look in his eyes, so does he. This is going to be torture for both of us. We're at an impasse. I won't let this touch him or his family, and Ryder, well, he thinks it will all work out. For a few more hours, I can let him believe that.

Hours.

I have mere hours to savor the feel of his arms wrapped around me. To drown in his kisses and to memorize what it feels like for him to be inside me. No more talking. It's time to make memories that will have to last me a lifetime.

Pushing him to his back, I straddle his hips. He immediately sits up, draping the blanket over my shoulders before wrapping his arms around my waist. No words are said. I can't see him from the darkness in the room, but that's okay. I think it's better this way. I will never forget his eyes or the intense way he watches me. I don't think my heart could take that when I'm already thinking about how this is our last time.

My arms are locked around his neck, and he runs his hands up and down my spine. They're rough and calloused from his work as a lineman. I've missed the feeling, and it's one I know I'll forever crave.

He moves to cup the back of my neck, bringing my lips to his. He nips at my bottom lip, and I open for him, exactly as I'm sure he was hoping I would. His tongue slides against mine in a slow tangle. He's making love to my mouth. I feel every stroke of his tongue in my core. His cock is hard between us, pressing against my belly, but neither one of us rushes to break this connection.

My hands roam over his shoulders, and settle on his chest. Ryder pulls out of the kiss and moves to rest his forehead against my shoulder. His breathing is ragged. The reality of the moment is weighing just as heavily on him as it is on me.

"This is not goodbye, Jordyn."

"Can we just... be in the moment? Stay present?" I ask, repeating his earlier words. We can say this isn't goodbye all we want, but we both know it's true. My mother has my future set. There is no way out of it, but she can't take this from me. She can't take this night, this moment with him. It's all mine, and I plan to enjoy every single second until we have to part ways.

"I'm right here," he whispers huskily.

"I need you here." I reach between us, gripping his cock as I rise up on my knees.

"Here?" he asks, running his fingers through my pussy. "You're ready for me." He kisses my neck as he slides one long digit inside of me.

"Always," I breathe.

He pumps his finger lazily in and out, driving me crazy with need for him. I groan in frustration as my grip on his cock grows tighter. "Tell me what you want, sweets."

"You. Inside me."

"Put me in." His words are barely past his lips when his hand is gone, giving me the green light to guide him to where I want him, where we both need him to be.

I sink down over him. He grips my hips, giving me time to adjust to him. "You okay, sweets?" he asks.

"I'm perfect."

"Yeah," he agrees. "You are." He kisses me, his hands touching what feels like every inch of my skin. I feel him everywhere. I remain seated, his length buried deep inside me, while his hands map my bare skin. I push thoughts of leaving out of my mind and feel. Slowly, I lift, rising back up on my knees. His cock slides out, just to the tip, before I slide back down just as slowly.

"You making love to me, baby?"

"I'm savoring you. Savoring this moment."

He cups my breasts as if he's testing their weight in the palm of his hands. Bending his head, he sucks a pert nipple into his mouth, and I toss my head back in ecstasy.

The things this man can do with his mouth.

His lips trail from one breast to the other, and back again. My body is on sensation overload. His hands, his mouth, and his cock. I'm surrounded by all things Ryder, and it's a heady feeling. Tears prick my eyes, but I fight back against their onslaught.

When he reaches my ear, he nips at my lobe before whispering, "Mine." One single word, in a hushed whisper, has a ripple of desire racing down my spine.

"Ryder." His name is a plea on my lips.

"Tell me what you need, sweets. Name it, and it's yours." His hands find their way to my hips. This time, it's him who is lifting me and guiding me back down over his cock. "So fucking tight," he breathes, as he repeats the process at a slow but steady pace over and over again.

"This. I need this. I need you."

"I'm right here, and I'm yours. You have me, Jordyn. You hear me, beautiful? You have me."

"So close." I can feel my orgasm building. It's as if I'm ready to high dive off a cliff. The anticipation of the fall is there, growing stronger with each thrust.

Ryder moves closer. We're now chest to chest as he holds me tightly. One arm wraps around my waist while the other slides between us. His thumb begins to make small circles on my clit, causing my eyes to roll back in my head from the pleasure it brings. I rest my hands on his shoulders and grind against him. The response is immediate, and I detonate like a bomb of desire.

I call out his name. He grunts mine as he, too, finds his release. I slump against him, wrapping my arms around his neck and holding on with everything I have inside me. He does the same. With his strong arms holding me so tightly, I can't be sure where he ends and I begin.

Neither of us is willing to break the embrace as time creeps up on us. Finally, it's Ryder, who relaxes and leans back. He cradles my cheeks in the palms of his hands and kisses me tenderly.

"Shower with me?"

"Yeah," I agree easily, because we need to get cleaned up so I can pack. It's almost time to go. With my heart in my throat, I slowly rise, feeling the evidence of our lovemaking coat my thighs, and climb out of bed.

Ryder is right behind me with his hand on the small of my back, guiding me into the bathroom.

Ryder insisted on driving me to the airport. He also insisted on walking me inside. It's risky, but I couldn't say no. Not when I know that, when he turns and walks away, that's it for us. I was lucky enough to find the love of a lifetime, and because of the hatred that lives inside of my mother, I have to set him free.

"One more hug," I tell him. "Then you really need to go."

"What if they forget to send someone to get you? I'm not leaving until I know you have a ride."

"Ryder, if whoever she sends sees you, they'll report back to her, and I don't need that on top of knowing this is it for us."

"No." His voice is hard. He grips my shoulders and bends his knees so we are eye to eye. "This is not it for us. This. Is. Not. It. I'll find a way, and if we have to sneak around until then, that's what we'll do."

"It's too risky."

"Trust me, sweets. I'd never let anything happen to you. We can be discreet. I'll call you."

"No. You can't. I don't know when she'll be around, and I'm sure she's watching my phone."

"Then she already knows you're home early."

I nod. "Probably. I'll tell her you were still bothering Gianna, and I needed to end things with you once and for all."

He pulls his phone out of his pocket and skims over our messages. "That should be believable."

"Yes.'"

"Okay. Stay right here. Give me five minutes." He takes off, jogging across the airport to the gift shop. I watch as he grabs something, takes it to the counter, and makes a purchase. It's longer than five minutes, more like ten, but when he reaches me, he's smiling as he holds his hand out.

"What's that?"

"A prepaid cell phone. One your mother won't know about. You can call and text me anytime day or night. I already put the number in my phone. Just hide it from her. This is our connection, so we can see one another under the radar until I find a solution."

I want to tell him we're just delaying the inevitable, but the thought of being able to talk to him and maybe see him again, to consider that maybe this isn't goodbye gives me enough hope in my heart to keep my mouth shut.

"We'll get through this, Jordyn. This will make the last two years look like a cakewalk."

I smile up at him. "I want to believe everything will work out in the end, but it's hard."

"The last two years didn't break us, and this won't either." He pulls me into a kiss that has my knees going weak. "I'm going to walk away now. I love you. I am yours, and you are mine, and we're going to make this work. I'm going to stand off to the side and make sure you have a ride before I leave. Call or text me when you get settled."

"I love you." Tears well in my eyes.

"No more tears, sweets. You're home. I'm going to call my brothers and rally the troops. We're going to talk about this and try to form a plan."

"There isn't a plan, Ryder."

"Then we'll talk about what needs to be done for us to leave town."

"I won't let you do that."

"I won't let you marry some other man because your mother is a monster. You gave me your heart, Jordyn Astor, and I intend to keep it."

"It's only ever been yours."

He nods, kisses me quickly, and steps back. "You and me, baby." He gives me a smile that doesn't quite reach his eyes, and he turns and walks away. I watch as he pulls a ball cap from his back pocket, tugs it low on his head, and takes a seat by a pole. He looks like any of the other travelers here in the airport, but I know better.

He isn't just anyone.

He's the man I love.

The man I made a vow to protect from my family.

No matter how optimistic he is, I know what my mother is capable of. I've lived with her evil my entire life. I've endured her dictating my life. When I found Ryder, I thought I was done. I was going to break away, just as Jeremy wanted to, and live my life for me.

My mother ruins everything, and I'll be damned if I'm going to let her touch Ryder and his family. Turning the new phone on vibrate, I shove it into the bottom of my purse on the off chance my parents, either one or both of them, decide to grow a heart and pick me up. Taking a calming breath, I wait for my ride.

Not five minutes later, I see a man in a dark suit, holding a sign with my name on it. I want to look at Ryder, but I know that's asking for trouble. I have no doubt my mother has already had this man, whoever he is, be on the lookout.

"Hi, I'm Jordyn." I wave, pulling my luggage behind me. The man nods, grabs my bags without a word, and I trail behind him to the black SUV sitting at the curb. He loads my luggage while I climb into the back, and just as we're pulling away, I catch a glimpse of Ryder standing just outside the door, watching as we drive away.

I pray to anyone who's listening that this isn't the last time we see one another.

Chapter 5

Ryder

W atching her drive away was almost harder than living without her these past two years.

Almost.

I watch until I can no longer see her taillights, and reach for my phone in my pocket. I type out a quick text to the group. Not just the group with my brothers, but the one that includes my sisters-in-law, and my cousin Ramsey and her husband, Deacon, too. This is an all-hands-on-deck situation. It could potentially affect all of them, so it's only fair that they are clued in.

> **Me:**   *My place tonight.*

I don't bother with a time. They'll all head over after work. They know I'll wait until everyone is there to fill them in.

> **Orrin:**   *Missed you at Sunday dinner. You good?*
>
> **Me:**   *I'm good.*
>
> **Brooks:** *How's Jordyn?*

Me:	*Perfect.*
Palmer:	*Aw... But we need answers for how she treated you.*
Me:	*We have them.*
Me:	*I need your help.*
Declan:	*Whatever you need, brother. We'll be there.*

My phone continues to vibrate, but I shove it back into my pocket and stalk off toward my truck. My sisters-in-law will want more details, and my brothers will sit back and let them do the asking, knowing damn good and well that if their wives were not the ones firing off questions, they would be.

I barely remember the drive home as my mind replays my time with Jordyn. The pain etched in her features, the way she's lost weight from the worry and the stress. Hearing her story blew my mind. Her mother was always super sweet, but that's what she wanted me to think. I hate myself for falling for her trap, but I didn't know.

As soon as I get home, I take a long, hot shower to try to clear my head. It doesn't work. Not that I really expected it to. I don't know how to do this. I don't know how to go up against her mother with the kind of money and influence that she has, but I know one thing. I will not give Jordyn up. I meant what I told her. Even if we have to go away, that's what we'll do. I love my family, and I'd miss them, but Jordyn, she's deep in my bones. I'm going to love her harder because everyone before me failed to do so. I'm going to do it because there is no other way. I gave my heart to her a long time ago, and even with time apart, my love for her never wavered.

So, yeah, if it comes down to leaving, we'll figure it out. We'll devise a plan where I can see my family on the down low, and... fuck! I hate this.

Running my fingers through my still-wet hair, I plop down on the couch and text her.

Me: *Hey, sweets. Did you make it home okay?*

I don't expect a reply because she has to hide the phone, and I'm sure her mother is badgering her with questions. Shit, what if she found out that Jordyn came home early? Is she safe there? My heart rate kicks up, and I will myself to calm down. I hope my brothers and their wives have a solution because I can't live without her.

"Where's Jordyn?" Alyssa asks. "I thought she'd be here."

"That's why you're all here," I tell them. My living room is packed with my brothers and their wives on their laps, and my cousin Ramsey and her husband, Deacon, are sitting the same way. We brought the chairs in from the kitchen, because my house is not big enough to hold all of us now that we're growing. However, from the looks on my brothers' faces, they're not the least bit upset to have their wives on their laps.

"What's going on, Ry?" Orrin, my oldest brother, asks, as he wraps his arms around his wife, Jade, and pulls her back to his chest.

Envy washes over me. My girl should be here. "Jordyn's back."

"And you spent the rest of the weekend with her," Archer fills in. He and his new wife leave for their honeymoon in the morning. I hate that I'm dropping this on them before they leave, but they need to hear this too. I need all the help I can get.

"I did." Leaning forward, I drop my elbows to my knees and run my fingers through my hair. "I don't even know where to start," I say, keeping my eyes locked on my sock feet.

"The beginning," Ramsey says softly. "We're here. None of us are in a hurry to leave. Just start talking, Ry, and we'll figure out whatever it is that's eating away at you."

"I love her." It feels important that I start with those three words. It's not new information. They all know I've been holding on to us and what we had until she came home to me.

"We know, brother," Sterling says gently.

"Why did she leave?" Palmer asks.

"It's a fucked-up story." That's the only warning I give them before launching into everything I learned about Jordyn and her family from the moment I stepped foot into her hotel room late on Saturday night.

"Damn," Maverick mutters.

"What does this have to do with why she left?" Merrick asks.

"She wasn't going to leave. She was going to turn down the internship. She didn't want it anymore." I go on to tell them how she made the decision and spilled to her cousin, who reported back to her mother.

"Fuck," Archer comments.

"That's not the worst of it. Her mother threatened her. She threatened us, your businesses." I make eye contact with everyone in the room. "Jordyn was protecting us. Protecting me and our family. That's why she left. Her mother was monitoring her phone."

"That's another level of crazy," Brooks says.

"Yeah, I bought her a burner phone at the airport. I texted her earlier but haven't heard from her. She's sure her mom will have seen the text she sent me Saturday, telling me she was back in town, and I don't know what to do. Is she okay? They won't hurt her, right? I mean, they didn't set out for their son to get killed. It just happened, but fuck me, I'm scared for her."

"Our family is well-known," Orrin says. His tone tells me he's taking this threat seriously. Not that I expected anything less from him, or any of them.

"She can try to ruin us," Declan chimes in.

"She can. You didn't see the fear in Jordyn's eyes. She was trembling with it. I've been trying to think of a solution. Something to take her down, but all I can think of is Jordyn and I packing up and leaving."

"No" comes from Brooks. "That's not the answer, brother," he says.

"There is no answer!" I shout. "Help me," I plead with the room. "I have to get her away from them and leaving her is not an option."

"We don't expect you to walk away from her, Ry," Sterling says calmly. "Not a single one of us sitting in this room wants that for you."

"We were mad at her," Alyssa speaks up. "We hated to see you hurting, but I think I can speak for everyone when I say that her willingness to not only protect you but our family gives her a free pass."

They all murmur their agreement, and the pressure in my chest eases just slightly. I open my mouth to say what, I'm not sure, because my phone beeps, alerting me to a message. Everything in my mind drifts away, and all I can think about is Jordyn. Is this her? I stand and dig my phone out of my pocket and sigh when I see her name on the screen. "It's her," I tell them, knowing they're all wondering.

My hands shake as I open her message.

> **Jordyn:** I'm home. She knew I came in early. I covered telling her I wanted to inform you I was going to be married and that nothing could be between us, even though I was back in town. She bought it.

"Shit."

"What?" Kennedy asks.

"I forgot to mention the part where her mom and dad are expecting her to marry a man of their choosing. One they can pass the law firm down to."

"Fuck that," Merrick says vehemently. "She can't marry someone who's not you."

"She thinks she has to go through with it to protect us. I told her to hold off as long as she could to stall to see if we can think of something."

"We need dirt on the parents."

"That they had their son killed isn't enough?" Rushton spits. His wife Crosby places her hand on his and his shoulders relax.

"Like hire a private investigator?" Scarlett asks.

"My wife is a genius," Archer says, kissing her shoulder.

"I don't have that kind of money. I could sell the house, and move back in with Mom and Dad," I say absentmindedly as ideas of how to get more cash float through my mind.

"No," Ramsey speaks up. "I can't let you do that. Find someone, and send me the bill."

"Rams—" I start, but she holds her hand up to stop me.

"Listen to me, Ryder Kincaid. *You* are my family. Your parents took me in when I had no other options. All nine of you welcomed me, not as your cousin, but treated me like a sister. I have the money."

"That's your trust fund. I can't let you do that."

Deacon, her husband, laughs. "Um, Ryder, man, she can afford it."

"Thanks, baby." Ramsey turns and places a kiss on Deacon's cheek.

I hate to take a handout, but I have to get Jordyn out of there. This is the answer. We need to get dirt on her mother, and blackmail her, or fuck, turn her ass in, and Jordyn will be free from her controlling, vindictive ways.

"I'll pay you back." My voice is low and cracks with the emotion threatening to pull me under.

"You'll do no such thing. This is a family matter. Deacon and I have our practice, Orrin and Declan have their shops, and Palmer has her studio. Brooks has his nursing license, and the list goes on and on. It's all at risk, everything we've all worked for. This is a family matter, and there is nothing better I can think of to spend some of this money on. Trust me, there's plenty. I won't even notice it's gone." She smirks, and I can't help but grin.

"Show off," Orrin mutters, making us all laugh, and effectively breaking up the tension in the room.

Ramsey sticks her tongue out at him, and he chuckles. "Right, so how do we find a good private investigator?"

"I have a client who hired one from Atlanta," Deacon speaks up.

"Perfect. Can you get his info and send that on to Ryder?" she asks.

"I think one of us should call," Rushton suggests. "I think Ry is too close to this."

"I'll do it." Orrin raises his hand. "I'm the oldest, and I have a business she's trying to ruin. It makes sense, should any of this get back to Jordyn's family before we're ready for it to."

"We're not breaking the law," Deacon, the lawyer, chimes in.

"I know, but I'll still do it," Orrin tells him.

"That's putting a larger target on your back, Orrin. I can do it," I tell him.

"No. You stay calm. Keep your phone handy. Check in on your girl. Sneak to see her if you can, and let us take the lead on this."

"I—" My words get stuck in my throat. "I love you. All of you. I knew you could help me. Help us. I told her that I just needed to speak with all of you and we could figure it out." I pause. "Ramsey, I promise I'll pay back every dime. It may take me a lifetime, but I will."

"Nope. I don't want your money, Ryder. I just want you to be happy."

"Wait," Deacon speaks up. "How about some babysitting?" He grins and wags his eyebrows at his wife.

"Done. Anytime. I'm your guy." The words are barely past my lips when my phone rings. Looking down, I see Jordyn's name and smile. "It's Jordyn."

"We'll get out of your hair," Alyssa says and stands from Sterling's lap, and the others follow suit.

"Hey, sweets," I answer.

"Hi." Her voice is soft.

"Hi, Jordyn!" Maverick calls out, and the rest of my family follow suit. I put the phone on speaker so they can all call out to her.

Jordyn expels a heavy breath. It's almost as if she's in disbelief that they're being so welcoming.

"H-Hi," she stammers, her voice soft and uncertain.

I take the phone off speaker and place it to my ear. My girl is worried about my family being upset with her. I explained what happened, and they're willing to do whatever they can to help us, but that's not something I can prove to her over the phone. It's going to take time, and probably a visit, much like we had tonight, for everyone to lay their feelings out on the table and move on. "Do I have time to say goodbye to them?" I ask Jordyn.

"Yeah, I'm at the park. Taking a walk."

I pull my phone down and open my arms. One by one, my brothers and their wives all return my hug. Orrin and Deacon make plans to connect tomorrow as everyone filters out of the house to head back to their own.

"Hey," I say, with one last wave before closing the door and turning the lock.

"Hi."

"You're at the park?" I ask. "Do I have time to come and see you?"

"No. It's near to my house. I just needed to get some fresh air."

"She believed you?"

"She did. She was pissed, but I told her I needed to tell you in person so that you would accept it."

"I'll never accept it."

"Ryder, I love you, but we've been over this. There isn't a way out. My mother has too much power."

"I had my brothers and Ramsey over with their wives and Deacon tonight."

"That's who I heard?" I can hear the smile in her voice.

"We might have a plan. Well, we do have a plan."

"You do?" The shock in her voice is clear.

"Yeah, we're going to hire a private investigator. Deacon is an attorney who knows of a PI that one of his clients used. We're going to reach out to him and get some dirt on your mom, or even your dad." I should feel bad that I'm talking about her parents like this, but I don't. Not after everything they've done and put her through.

"Ryder, that's expensive. Besides, they've gotten away with this for years. If there was something out there to pin on them, it would have surfaced by now. You don't have my family's level of wealth and not have enemies. I can't imagine that a PI will be able to find anything."

"I know, but Ramsey, she's taking care of it, and I told her I'd pay her back. It will be a fight, so I'll more than likely end up being their full-time sitter anytime they need one."

"Aw. Uncle Ryder," she coos.

"I'm all the kids' favorite. Just ask them."

She laughs, just like I knew she would, and the sound fills my soul with light.

"I'm pretty sure all of your brothers, and even Deacon, have said that same exact thing at one point or another."

"I'm sure they have, but it's only true with me."

She giggles, and my smile widens. I close my eyes and rest my head back against the couch.

"I've missed you," she whispers.

"I've missed you too, sweets. It's going to take some time, but we're going to figure this out. We're going to be together, just— don't marry some asshole before we can get what we need to make your mother back down."

"She didn't bring it up, so I'm hopeful that she and my father have yet to find who they deem a suitable candidate. Ryder, I'll do whatever I have to do to protect you and your family."

"It won't come to that." Conviction fills my tone that can't be missed.

She's quiet, and I'm ready to ask her if she's okay, when she speaks softly, "It's what I dream about."

"What do you dream about, baby?"

"You. Me. Us. I want nothing more than to build a life with you in Willow River."

"That's the goal, but if we have to leave, we will."

"We can't do that. Your family."

"My family knows what it's like to find the other half of your soul." She sniffs, and I inwardly curse for upsetting her. "How was the rest of your day?" I ask her instead.

"After my lecture from my mother, and once I managed to convince her it was to tell you to back off, I spent the rest of the day unpacking and hiding away in my room like a damn teenager."

"Maybe you can sneak me into your room."

"Too dangerous," she's quick to say, and I can picture her shaking her head.

"Well, one day soon, your room will be my room."

"Ryder, it's best we don't get our hopes up."

"Hope, sweets. Hope, and wish, and pray, or whatever it is you want to do. That's a dream that we both have that will damn sure come true. I'll make sure of it."

"Tell me about your family. How are they?"

I launch into telling her about the recent additions to the family, the wives, and the babies. I fill her in on everything she's missed since she's been gone. All the things I didn't get to tell her because we spent the weekend wrapped in each other's arms. I talk so long it's now dark outside.

"Did you drive to the park?" I ask her.

"I did. I should get going. It's dark, and I'm sitting here under the lamplight on a park bench, staring at my car. I don't want to go home."

I want more than anything to tell her to come here, but I know we can't do that. Not yet. "Stay on the phone with me until you get home."

"I'll be fine."

"I know you will be. I'm just not ready to let you go yet. I don't know when I'll get to talk to you again."

"I'll sneak away as much as I can."

"Temporarily. Soon, we'll be together again, and nothing will come between us."

"How are you so forgiving? I hurt you, Ryder. My mother is evil and threatening your family. I don't know how you're able to move past that?"

"Stay present with me, baby. That's all in the past. Well, not your mother, but we're working on that. Keep thinking of all the things we're going to do once this nightmare is over. Make a list, and we'll make it happen. I don't care how big or small."

"I like that idea."

"Me too, sweets. Me too."

"I'm getting ready to pull into my driveway."

"Damn, you were close to home. Okay, well, sleep well and I'll talk to you soon. I'll hopefully have more for you in a day or so about the PI."

"I love you, Ryder Kincaid."

"I love you too, Jordyn Astor." I end the call and drop my phone on the couch next to me. My girl is home, and I'll be damned if I'm going to let someone keep me away from her.

Chapter 6

Jordyn

It's been three weeks since I've seen Ryder, and that streak will be broken in a few short hours. I haven't told him yet about my plans for this weekend, but I know from our chats that he has no plans. I hope it's a pleasant surprise.

My best friend and former roommate, Gianna, is going to visit her grandmother in Birmingham, Alabama. She didn't want to make the trip on her own and asked for me to ride with her. That's the story. It's not all untrue.

Gianna is going to Birmingham to see her grandma, but her cousin Talia is going with her. They did also invite me, but another idea popped into my head. After some brainstorming with my bestie, we devised a plan.

Gianna will take my cell phone with her. My mother can track where I am like we know she will. Gianna rented a car for me. My car will stay parked at her apartment all weekend. I don't have to worry about my mother calling to check on me. She never does. At the most, I get a snarky text message here or there. I was in Paris for two years and talked to her a handful of times at best.

This is ridiculous. I'm sneaking around like a damn teenager, but with a mother like mine, knowing what she's capable of, we have to do it this way until we can find something to stop her.

What's even more ridiculous is that my mother is still refusing to let me get a job. Why bother paying for my education and allowing me to go to Paris—no, insisting I go—if I'm not allowed to utilize my education?

Oh, that's right, it's for bragging rights to all her socialite friends.

That's okay, though. I worked while I was living in Paris and saved up every penny. My parents paid for everything. I was forced to go when I wanted to stay in the States with Ryder. So I lived frugally and saved money from my allowance as well. My father is still giving me a stipend, and that, too, gets pulled into a separate account.

I may have to run, and I need money to do that.

Shaking out of my thoughts, I focus on the here and now. On the present, and that is Ryder. We have a plan. We'll leave together in the first rental, and drive to the mall for me to slip into the second, and I can hightail it out of town.

Toward Willow River.

Toward Ryder.

It's the perfect chance to spend the entire weekend with him. Gianna will respond to any messages. She's even going to take a picture so I can tell her how to reply. It's perfect, and it's been hard for me to hide my excitement.

"Are you packed?" My mother appears in the doorway of my bedroom at my parents' place.

"Not yet." Lies. I've been packed since we finalized the plans, but she can't know that I'm excited.

"I swear, Jordyn. You are so last minute. You can't have Gianna waiting on you."

"We're not leaving for a few hours." *Trust me, Mother, I've been counting down the seconds.*

"Still. You should pack so you can go over everything and make sure you didn't miss anything."

"We're just going to her grandma's."

"Always be prepared, Jordyn. I taught you better than that."

"I know. I'll pack now." I was prepared for this conversation. You don't grow up with a control freak like my mother and not learn her quirks. I disappear into my closet and pull out my suitcase and begin to pack.

"Make sure you pack options. You are representing the Astor name every time you step outside of this house."

Ugh. I wish I could move back in with Gianna, but after I left, she downsized to a one-bedroom. My mother paid for her to break her lease because heaven forbid anyone have anything bad to say about an Astor.

"Always, Mother." There is sugar in my tone, because placating my mother is something I learned at a very young age.

"You're coming home Sunday?" she asks.

"Yes. We plan to leave Birmingham after lunch on Sunday. We're going to take her grandma to church."

"That's sweet of you girls." She nods as I begin to carefully fold my clothes and place them in the suitcase. "I'll be gone when you leave. I'll see you on Sunday." With that, she turns and walks away.

No "let me know you get there safely," or "have fun." No hugs, and never an "I love you." None of those things did I grow up with.

Ryder and his family showed me an all-new way of life. Of showing those you care about what they mean to you, and spending quality time with them, even if that's just sitting around a fire and talking about nothing and everything all at once.

I pack the clothes I know my mother expects for me to take. I wouldn't put it past her to have an inventory of my wardrobe. My small satchel is already packed with shorts and tank tops, and a pair of flip-flops. My mother hates them and complains every time I wear them. The sad part is that I feel more at ease in flip-flops than I ever did in heels. I was born into this life, and it's not what I want.

My mother wants me to be her clone. A socialite. But that's not who I am. I want to be a good friend, a wife, and a mother. I want a simple life where I'm not always feeling like I'm competing to have the best of the best. I want to love and be loved, and I have that with Ryder.

I've been given tremendous opportunities, and I've never had to want for a single material thing. However, that's not what's important. It's the hugs, the "I love yous," the "be safes," and the "let me know when you get theres" that I crave. Money can't buy any of that.

Money can't buy love or trust.

Once I'm packed, I carry my bags down to my car. My mother is already gone, so I head out early. I can't stand to be in this house, this lonely, cold, enormous house. I'd rather wait around at Gianna's tiny one-bedroom apartment.

The drive is about twenty minutes, and when I pull in, I scan the lot, looking for someone who might be following me. I never had to worry about that before, but after what my mother did to my brother, and knowing she wants me to stay away from Ryder, I'm extra vigilant. I've never given her a reason to worry that I was disobeying until now. Hopefully, she's still in the dark. The extra phone was a genius idea, and I've told Ryder that several times. Gianna and I even use it. I don't know that my mom can read messages, but I know she can track my location, and that's enough for me to be extra cautious.

Locking my car, I make my way to the door, and my hand is poised to knock when Gianna pulls it open.

"Hey, you." She smiles and hauls me into a tight embrace.

This. *This* is what life is about. The connections you make.

"Hi. I needed out of that house," I tell her, stepping into her apartment.

"I bet. How are things?"

"Same. She's dictating my life. No talk of marriage, so I'm counting that as a win. I know it's coming, though."

She gives me a sympathetic smile. "I'm sorry, Jordyn."

"It's not you. You're doing me a huge solid by letting me use you as my cover this weekend."

"He was devastated. Ryder, I mean. That day when he showed up here. It was so sad to watch. He really loves you."

Hot tears prick my eyes. "I love him, too." It's not that I didn't believe her. Gianna is my best friend, and I trust her, but while I was away, it was easier to pretend as if her words weren't true. I was hurting and missing Ryder so much, and I knew, or at least I thought I knew, there was no way around doing what my mother asked. If only I would have gone to him, we could have started this search into her sooner.

Maybe we could have already been living out our happily ever after.

"I hope this gets resolved. You two deserve to be together after everything that you've been through."

"It's a long shot, but until I'm forced into marriage, we'll continue to sneak phone calls and visits when we can, and—" I shrug, because I don't want to say the words out loud.

And when the time comes, I'll have to walk away.

It will break both of our hearts all over again. I stare up at the stars every night and wish for a miracle, one I'm not sure we're going to get.

"It's all going to work out."

"I love your optimism, friend."

"Love always finds a way." Gianna gives me a cheesy grin, and I can't help but return it.

"When is Talia getting here?"

"She's not. She's picking up one of the cars, and her boyfriend is getting the other. They're going to meet us at the mall parking lot. He's going to drive my car back to his place and park it in his garage."

"Really?" Emotion clogs my throat. They don't know the true threat, but they're helping me anyway. It's better this way. I'm already risking Gianna and the entire Kincaid family. I don't need more worry on my shoulders.

Gianna pulls me into another hug. "We got you, Jordyn. What your mother is doing is wrong, and we're all team Jordyn and Ryder. Well, Talia and I are. Jeff is team Talia, so his vote is default." She chuckles.

"Thank you. I don't know how I can ever repay you for this."

"Ryder has single brothers, right?" She wags her eyebrows.

"Only two that are single. The twins. They're younger than us."

"I'm pretty sure any woman would take any Kincaid brother at any age." She winks. "I'm just teasing. I've kind of been seeing someone."

"What? And you didn't tell me?"

"I didn't want to gush about him when you're fighting for your relationship with Ryder."

"No. I want to hear about your life. I want to be there for you. I need that distraction. Come on, we have some time. Tell me all the things."

Gianna grins and grabs my hand, pulling me to the couch. "His name is Calvin, and we met at the coffee shop just down from my office. He's a real estate agent."

"Have you gone out on a date yet?"

She nods. "Yeah, a few times. He's sweet, and so damn sexy." Her face blushes and I smile.

"You're smitten."

She nods. "I'm not even going to deny it. I've been dying to talk to you about him."

"I'm so happy for you, G." I reach over and place my hand on top of hers. "Don't hold back on me. I want to hear that you're happy. I want that for you." Gianna deserves happiness, and just because my life is a cluster of epic proportions doesn't mean I don't want to hear about all the good and wonderful things in her life. She was there for me in my darkest times, and I plan to repay that over and over throughout our lives.

"I just know your love life is crazy right now, and I don't want to feel braggy."

"Brag. Please, woman, brag!" I laugh. "I love hearing about you and your life. I missed so much while I was gone, and my love life is a mess. But Ryder, he forgave me. Why, I'm not so sure, but he did, and he's got a plan. I don't know if it's going to work, but I'd do anything. Give up anything to be with him, so I'm holding on to the hope that he breathes into me every time we talk."

"Are you excited to get to see him?"

"Yes. I'm second-guessing not telling him, but it was better this way. The thought of disappointing him if plans fell through made my heart ache. I've hurt him so much because of all of this nonsense with my mother."

"I'm glad you finally broke down and told him everything."

"I've only ever told you, and now Ryder. How sad is that? My brother deserves to be remembered. To be talked about. I miss him every day, but it's as if he was erased from our lives." I trust Gianna. I hate that this now lies on her shoulders, too, but I needed my best friend. I needed to talk to someone other than Ryder about all this, and as my best friend, she deserves to know.

No more secrets.

"I'm proud of you, Jordyn. I know it's difficult breaking away from your controlling family. You're fighting for what you want, and there are so many who would be too afraid or scared of losing everything."

"I just want Ryder. The rest—" I shrug. I don't care about the rest. The fancy car or name-brand clothes and designer handbags. None of it makes sense if I'm lonely. I'll take love and affection, a genuine connection over those things any day. I know that makes me sound like a spoiled, pretentious bitch, but that's how I was raised. I am not that person, no matter how much my mother wishes for me to be. One day, maybe we'll find what we need and justice can be served for my big brother.

I miss him every day.

"Come on. Let's load up and head out. You have a man to surprise, and I have road trip snacks to consume." She grins.

I stand and pull her into a hug. My hold on her is fierce, because I can't find the words to tell her what this means to me. "I love you, Gianna. Thank you for this. I'll never forget it."

She eases away, her eyes shimmering with tears. "I love you, too. You're the sister I never had, and I'd do anything for you." She wipes at her eyes. "I was going to say I'd do anything for love, but that's too much of a Meatloaf moment."

"Stop." I laugh, swatting at her arm. We move to gather her bags and load them into her car before grabbing mine as well. I lock my car and settle into the passenger seat. I bite down on my cheek to hide my smile, but then I remember where I am and who I'm with. I don't have to hide my excitement.

We pull into the mall at the same time as Talia and her boyfriend, Jeff. I thank both of them for their help, and they wave off my praise. There are so many good people in the world, it's a shame the bad overshadow that. I make a mental note to do something nice for the two of them. Gianna, too. I owe them all so much for helping me make this weekend happen.

I quickly transfer my bags, as do the others. Jeff kisses Talia and speeds away in Talia's car.

"Call me if there are any issues." I hand her my cell phone.

"I've got you. We better go. We don't want her to see that we stopped here for too long."

"I already have a plan. You ordered a gift for your gram, and we had to stop and pick it up." Not that I expect my mother to be watching every second, but I want to be prepared.

Gianna grins. "We're really good at this undercover business."

She pulls me into a hug and when she releases me, I hold my arms open for Talia. With one final wave, we quickly gather in our cars and head in the opposite direction of one another.

Glancing in the rearview mirror, my smile is blinding.

I'm ready to see my man.

Gripping the wheel of the rental, I pass the Welcome to Willow River sign. I navigate the town as if I've lived here my entire life. I guess that's the advantage of small-town living, and I, for one, am here for it. I love the closeness and how you can walk down the street and someone calls out your name. Everyone knows everyone. It's a completely different world, and I love it.

My hands tremble when I get to Ryder's. I pull into the driveway. His truck is there, as well as another. I'm sure it's one of his brothers, but I don't know which one.

I hate that. I should know these kinds of things. I can only hope that one day we'll be in a place where that information is something that comes freely to me.

Pulling behind Ryder's truck, I put the car in Park and take a deep breath. I don't know why I'm nervous. He tells me daily, even when I don't get to reply every day, that he misses me and that he loves me. He's going to be happy to see me. I need to let the negativity of my mother go and just be me. The me who is madly in love with the man who owns this house. The man who stole my heart and stood by my side through two hellish years.

The man who never once gave up on me.

That thought pulls me out of my head and has me grabbing my keys, my burner phone in case Gianna needs me, and making my way to the front door. Squaring my shoulders, I knock on the door. I hear shouting inside, and then the door opens. A smiling Maverick—I think—greets me.

I can see the moment it registers who's standing before him, because his mouth falls open in disbelief. I grip my phone and keys tighter and will myself not to squirm under his gaze.

"Hi," I whisper. Ryder has assured me his family isn't upset with me for hurting him, for trying to protect all of them, but this is my first run-in with any of them since I've been back. I hate that it's one of the twins and I can't tell them apart. I'm pretty sure it's Maverick, but I'm not certain.

A slow, sexy grin pulls at this twin's lips. He winks and turns over his shoulder. "Hey, Ry, there's some hot chick at your door!" he yells. He turns back to me and points at his chest. "I'm Maverick."

I nod, grateful for the help. "I should be able to tell you two apart."

"It's been a while." He shrugs, as if my time away was no big deal.

"Fuck off!" I hear Ryder call back.

"Bro, you're going to want to come and deal with this." Maverick turns back to me and winks.

I feel myself relax a little.

"I'm not interested!" Ryder calls back.

"You sure? You might regret it. I plan to take her back to my place and make her mine."

"What the fuck are you going on about?" Ryder steps up behind him and peers around Maverick. Shock is written all over his face. "Jordyn? Baby, are you all right? What are you doing here? What happened? Are you hurt?" He rattles off questions as he runs his calloused hands down my arms, his eyes raking over every inch of me.

"I'm fine." I smile up at him. "I found a way to come see you. I'm free until Sunday afternoon, but if you have plans—" I point over my shoulder, and he immediately shakes his head and pulls me into his arms. He exhales loudly when I wrap my arms around his waist and rest my weight against him.

"Let's get you inside." His voice is low and gravelly as he keeps an arm around my waist and leads me into the house.

"Whoa." Merrick stops in his tracks. "Long time no see." He smiles.

"Hi, Merrick."

"So, we're gonna go," Merrick says.

"No. Please don't go on my account. Ryder didn't know I was coming. I can go to a hotel or something."

"That's not happening, sweets. Guys, you can stay, but so is she."

"Enjoy your time together. I'll let the group chat know you're not available until Sunday afternoon." Maverick wags his eyebrows.

"No. I don't want to take you from your family."

"You're not," Ryder assures me, pressing his lips to my temple.

"We were just keeping our big bro busy, since he was missing you," Maverick tells me.

My heart skips a beat as his words register. Not only that, but Maverick seems to accept that I'm back in Ryder's life. Just as he said his entire family would.

"It's good to see you," the twins say at the same time.

"You, too." I wave awkwardly as they turn and head for the door. I hate that they're leaving. Guilt sets in. I should have told Ryder I was stopping by.

"Stop. I can hear you thinking, and you don't need to worry. I see my brothers every day. I haven't seen you in far too long."

"I missed you." I relax into his embrace, feeling not only loved but safe and content.

"I missed you, too, sweets." He kisses me, and just like always, it feels like coming home.

Chapter 7

Ryder

I can't believe she's here. I should be used to us being apart, but it feels worse knowing she's just an hour's drive from me, and I can't go to her anytime that I want.

"Not that I'm complaining, but how are you here?"

She tries to move off my lap, but I hold her tightly. I'm not willing to let her go, not yet.

Not ever.

"Gianna's going to Birmingham for the weekend to see her grandma. She invited me to go along with her and her cousin Talia. Instead, they took my phone with them. That way, when my mother tracks me, like we know she will, that's where I'll be."

"What if she calls to check up on you?"

"She won't. She thinks tracking me is enough. She might text, but if she does, Gianna is going to send me a screenshot from her phone to the burner so I can tell her how to reply."

"Wow. That's actually genius."

"Right? I owe Gianna so much for doing this for me."

"For us. Tell me what I can do for her."

"She just wants to see me happy."

"Me, too," I say, pressing a kiss to her shoulder. "So, how long do I get you for? Until Sunday, right?"

"Yeah, Mother is expecting me back home later in the day, on Sunday. I'll have to meet Gianna and Talia at the mall again to swap out the rentals. Talia and her boyfriend helped with that too. I parked my car at Gianna's. She drove her car, and I have the rental, which is in Gianna's name."

"Damn, sweets, that's some spy, shit." I laugh.

"Hey, a girl has got to do what a girl has got to do." She kisses me quickly, and it takes everything in me to stop from tossing her over my shoulder and stalking off toward my room. I have half a mind to keep her naked in my bed all weekend, but I know we can't do that. This is more than just good sex for me.

"So, nothing from the private investigator yet," I tell her.

She nods, a solemn look crossing her face. "I don't expect for him to find anything. My mother is not only vindictive, she's smart."

"Well, it's a start. If nothing comes up, we'll have to move on to Plan B."

"What exactly is Plan B?"

"Right now, it doesn't exist." I keep my voice calm and in control, even though I'm nervous that we don't have a Plan B.

"Ryder. We have to face the fact that this might not end how we hoped."

"It ends with us being together. That's how this ends. There is no other outcome. That may look different from how we hoped, but it's still the same result."

"I love you." She turns to straddle my lap and places her soft hands against my cheeks. I wrap my arms around her waist, still hardly believing she's here. "You're my favorite person on the entire planet, but I won't let you give up your life. I won't let you give up your family, who loves you, for me. I love you too much."

"I love you too much to lose you again. If the last two years have proven anything, it's that our love is stronger than ever. I know I can't and don't want to live without you. We'll figure out a way to still see my family. It won't be as often as if we were living in Willow River, and more than likely not all of them at once, but we will find a way." My tone is full of conviction.

"Ryder, listen to yourself. You can't leave Willow River. I would have given anything to have a family like yours. Siblings who stand beside you no matter what. Two parents that love you, and show you affection. I won't let you do it."

There is a determination in her voice that scares me. I hold her a little tighter because I can see it in her eyes too. I don't even want to think about what she might be planning in that beautiful head of hers.

"We're staying present, right? Presently, I'm holding my girl in my arms, and she's mine for the entire weekend. What do you want to do?"

"This." She hugs me, wrapping her arms around my neck.

I run my hands beneath her shirt, tracing her spine. "Are you hungry?" I ask as her stomach growls.

She lifts her head and shrugs. "I was too excited to eat."

"Well, we need to fix that." Standing with her in my arms, she squeals in delight, locking her legs around my waist and her arms around my neck. I carry her to the kitchen and place her on the island. I kiss her swiftly before pulling away.

"What are we having?"

"Tacos." My eyes find hers. "That okay with you?"

"Yep."

"That's what I was planning on making when the twins showed up."

"What were you all planning to do tonight?"

"No plans. They're the only two left who aren't either married or in a relationship. Actually, I'm the only one in a relationship that isn't married." I hold her gaze. "We need to fix that." I wink when her cheeks blush. "Anyway, they decided to come and keep me company. They knew I'd be holding down the couch."

"Oh, you should call them and invite them over. I can go to a hotel for the night. I dropped by unannounced. I don't mind. We can see each other tomorrow." She gives me a huge, reassuring smile, and I know she's speaking from a good place. She's always thinking of everyone else.

"Like hell." I step back between her legs, and on instinct, she wraps them around my waist. Resting my palms against her cheeks, I make sure I have her full attention. "You're here until you have to leave on Sunday. You're not leaving my sight, sweets." I kiss the tip of her nose. "I love my brothers, but I've missed my girl, and they know that. They're not mad that you showed up, and I sure as fuck am not mad about it."

"They didn't have to leave, but I understand why they did. I know I'm probably not their favorite person."

"Hey, that's not true. They know what happened. My family doesn't hate you."

"I put you through so much."

I understand her guilt, but it's misplaced. As far as I'm concerned, she has nothing to feel guilty for.

Do I wish she'd come to me earlier, before she left?

Absolutely.

But I'm not playing lip service when I tell her we have to stop living in the past.

"Jordyn, you did what you thought you had to do to protect us. Stay right here with me. Stay present, baby. That's all in the past. We're going to find a way to take care of your mother's threats, and all of this will be behind us."

She slides her arms around my neck. "No matter what happens, know that I love you, Ryder Kincaid. I'll never love anyone the way I love you."

"Good. Because we're end game, sweets." I kiss her. I take my time tasting her while exploring her mouth. "Now," I say, forcing myself to step back. "I need to feed my girl."

"What can I do to help?" She drops her legs, allowing me to step away from her.

"You need to sit your ass right there and look beautiful while I make you dinner. So, just be you." I wink, and a blush coats her cheeks.

"I've missed you."

"Me too, baby."

I get to work making our dinner. We talk about what's been going on in our lives since we last saw one another. It's not new information. Jordyn has started taking daily walks to the park near her parents' place so we can talk every day, but there is just something about having her here, hearing about her days in person while I make us dinner. It's normal and domestic, and it's something we've not been able to do since she left for Paris.

I want this with her, and I'll fight to get it.

"What are we watching?" I ask Jordyn after dinner.

She sits next to me on the couch, and I pull her into my side, keeping my arm wrapped tightly around her shoulders. "You pick."

"It doesn't matter to me because I won't be paying attention anyway," I confess.

She turns and peers up at me. "Why won't you be paying attention?" Her brows furrow as if she can't imagine a single reason why I wouldn't be watching whatever plays on the eighty-inch flat screen hanging on my living room wall.

"Because you're here, sweets. You get all of me and all of my attention all weekend long."

"Then I say we don't watch TV."

"What do you want to do?" I sweep her hair out of her eyes.

"I'm content to just be in your arms, Ryder."

"Where you belong." I press a kiss to her temple, and her body sinks into me as she relaxes even further.

"I used to lie in bed at night and wrap myself up in a blanket and pretend that it was you." She raises her hands to cover her face. "I can't believe I just admitted that."

"I would have given anything to be there to hold you. I didn't know where you were in Paris. I couldn't get anyone to tell me. Not even your mother, which makes sense to me now. I would have visited you as much as I could."

"I want to believe that this is going to work, Ry. I really do. I'm scared something is going to happen to you or your family. That she's going to ruin the businesses and livelihoods of your brothers and sisters-in-law, and you—I couldn't live with myself if something happened to you."

"I'm right here, sweets. Nothing is going to happen, and we'll figure it out."

"Can we pretend? This weekend, can we pretend my mother isn't the devil and trying to rule my life while threatening everything I love? I want to be with you. Like we used to be before my life imploded."

"Done." I shift and lift her onto my lap before standing and walking toward my bedroom. I gently toss her on the bed. She bounces, and her laughter fills the room, my house, and my fucking soul. I point an index finger at her. "Don't move."

I turn and stalk out of the room. I make sure the house is locked up and all the lights are off. It's just after seven, far too early to be going to bed, but we won't be sleeping.

When I get back to my room, my girl is lying on the bed where I left her, but she's now completely naked and the bedside lamp is on, casting a glow over her gorgeous body. "Jordyn." My voice cracks, and my heart squeezes in my chest. Saying that I missed her isn't enough. For two years, a piece of me was thousands of miles away. Now, she's back, but still too far away.

"You take my breath away."

"You're wearing too many clothes, Kincaid."

"Yeah?" I take a step closer.

"Mm-hmm," she hums.

"Tell me what you want, sweets?"

"You. Naked."

"What else?" I tear off my T-shirt and toss it on the bedroom floor. My jeans and boxer briefs are next to join the pile.

"I want—" She hesitates.

"Tell me, Jordyn." My voice is gruff and laced with my need for her.

"I want to feel you all around me, inside me." She holds my stare, and her whispered reply might as well be a shout from her pouty lips the way it wraps around me like a warm embrace.

I grip my cock and stroke myself to ease some of the ache of wanting her. We've got all fucking weekend, and I'm not rushing this. "Tonight, this is your show, baby. I'll give you anything and everything you want, but you have to ask for it."

That wasn't the plan, but her telling me she wants me inside of her sealed the deal. It might be selfish of me, but I need her words. I spent two years not knowing where she stood. I understand why she left like she did. I understand the distance she put between us emotionally and physically, but my heart still hurts, and I need this.

Tonight.

Her words.

Her heated gaze.

Her commands.

I need it all.

"Where do you want me to start?" My eyes never leave her as I watch her trail her hand over her naked breasts, over her stomach and the final landing spot. Her perfect pink pussy. "Here," she says, running her fingers through her folds.

I move, climbing on the bed at lightning speed, and kneel between her legs, which she readily opens for me. "Here?" My fingers follow the trail of hers. "Is all this for me, sweets?" I ask, as her desire coats my fingers.

"Only you."

"Is this what you wanted?" I slip a finger inside her.

"More," she breathes.

"More what? Tell me, Jordyn."

"Your mouth."

I move to my stomach, my feet hanging off the bed, and do exactly as she asks. I suck gently on her clit, and her back arches off the bed. I get lost in her. In the way she tastes, the way she grips my hair, holding me where she wants me. I'm consumed by this woman, and I wouldn't have it any other way.

Settling in, I lift her legs over my shoulders, and feast on her like the starved man that I am.

"R—" she starts, but ends up moaning instead.

I lift my head, licking my lips, holding her gaze. "Tell me."

Her eyes are burning with desire, but her features soften. "I want you to make love to me, Ry." Her bottom lip quivers, and her eyes well with tears.

I'm on the move, and lying next to her. We're face-to-face and she's in my arms. "Why the tears?"

"I don't want to lose you. I'm so afraid that each time I'm with you, it will be the last. If this is it, if tonight is all we have, I want you to make love to me." A single tear slides down her cheek, and I catch it with my thumb.

"This isn't all we have, Jordyn." I know she's scared. She's been holding this threat that her mother has been hanging over her head for two years, and it's settled in her mind that there is no way out of this mess.

She's wrong.

I don't know how. I hope that the PI we hired finds something, but this won't be the last time we're together.

This is not how we end. There is no ending. Not with us.

"Stay present, baby. You're in this moment with me. We're pretending, remember?"

"I'm not pretending. My heart is so full of love for you, and happiness to be here, and then there's the fear of this being it. I'm sorry, Ryder. I don't know how you've forgiven me so easily. I hate what I did to us, what I did to you. I can't—I can't stop thinking about how I hurt you."

"You did hurt me," I admit, hating the pain and devastation in her gaze. "However, I understand why you did what you did. We're past that. We're moving forward."

"There is so much that's unknown."

"I know I love you. I know you did everything in your power to protect me and my family. I know I spent two years loving you from afar when I wasn't sure you'd ever really be mine again. I know that we're looking toward the future, and mine has you in it. I see you right beside me, taking my last name, having my babies, and living happily ever after."

I smile, and she gives me a watery one in return.

"That's what you want?"

"All of that and more. The pain is still there, the hurt from you leaving, but I've forgiven you. You had good reason, and I thank you for sacrificing so much to protect us, but, baby, we're one. You and me. You're not fighting this on your own anymore."

She grabs my hand and places it over her heart. "Saying I love you doesn't seem like enough, but I don't have the words to explain it any other way."

"Yeah," I agree. "I can't find the words, either, but I can show you."

She gives me a watery smile as I press my lips to hers.

Rolling to my back, I pull her on top of me, never breaking our kiss. My hands trace down her spine. She reaches back and pulls the cover around us, then sits up. She rises on her knees, and guides me home, because let's face it, this woman, she is my home.

"Nice and slow, sweets," I say, as she settles on my cock. She leans forward, her lips finding mine, and it's Jordyn who's making love to me. It's the hottest and slowest, most sensual sex of my life.

This moment is everything.

She is everything.

I grip her hips and assist her with rocking back and forth. Her hips spread wider, bringing us close together. I get lost in her kiss while she rocks back and forth on my cock. Her body clenches around me, and I know she's close. Sliding my hand behind her neck, I hold her to me while I deepen the kiss. She moans, the sound coming from deep in the back of her throat, and then she's tearing her mouth from mine. Her head tilts back, and she cries out for me.

I don't even try to hold back, releasing inside her. Part of me hopes that her birth control fails. I'm ready to start my life with her. Sure, a baby right now would complicate things even further, but maybe her mother would disown her, too, and we could ride off into the sunset. We could settle here in Willow River and live happily ever after.

Jordyn rests her head on my shoulder, her body slumped against mine. My cock is still buried inside her. "I cherish every moment with you, Ryder Kincaid."

I wrap my arms around her and hold her as tightly as I can without hurting her. "Me too, sweets. Me, too."

Chapter 8

Jordyn

I wake up to the feel of Ryder's lips on my bare shoulder. "Morning, sweets."

"Morning," I croak.

"You grab the first shower while I make us breakfast."

I glance at him over my shoulder, mindful of my morning breath. "You're not going to shower with me?"

"Oh, I want to, but I'm not going to. We'll never leave this house today if we start out with your naked, wet, soapy body beneath my fingertips." He grins and kisses my shoulder once more. He smacks my ass gently and rolls out of his side of the bed.

"Why do we have to leave the house?"

"Because as much as I want to keep you in bed, I know we can't. I want to spend time with you being us. The us we were before you left."

"We can't risk being seen."

"Trust me."

I nod. "I'll get in the shower."

"That's my girl." He bends over me, bracing his hands on the bed, and presses his lips to my forehead. When he stands to his full height and pulls on a pair of gym shorts, I watch his every move, just soaking in this time with him. "Get moving, sweets. We're burning daylight." With that, he walks out of the room.

Clutching my bag, I grab my toiletries and make my way into his bathroom. Pulling open the shower curtain, I freeze when I see all of my shower stuff inside. The same shampoo and conditioner, and body wash. There's even my pink body scrubber. I don't understand what I'm seeing.

Stepping out of the bathroom, I snatch up Ryder's discarded shirt from last night and slip it on before padding down the hall to the kitchen. I stop and watch him as he whisks eggs in a bowl. He looks up and smiles.

"What's up?" he asks, placing the bowl on the island.

"I was about to get into the shower."

"Is something wrong? Are you feeling okay?" He makes his way toward me and places his hands on my shoulders.

"I'm okay."

"What's bothering you?"

"I pulled back the shower curtain, and all my stuff's there. Well, not my stuff, but the stuff that I use." I know I'm rambling, but I'm rushing to get the words out while I still try to understand why. Are they mine? Do they belong to someone else? Ryder wouldn't do that, right? Maybe one of his sisters-in-law? My mind is racing, trying to understand.

"They're yours, sweets."

"You bought them?"

"No. They're yours."

"Mine?"

"They were yours when you would stay over."

"You kept them?"

He shrugs. "You still have a drawer in my dresser too."

"Ryder."

"I'll throw them away, the shower stuff, I mean. Now that you're back. I mean, I know you can't use them. I'm sure they're expired."

"Why did you keep them, Ry?"

"I wasn't willing to toss anything that reminded me of you. But you're here now, and we can replace them with new ones."

"You kept them." I know I'm repeating his words, but I'm trying to wrap my head around this.

He grips my hips and lifts me. On instinct, I wrap my legs around his waist as he carries me to the island and sets me down. "Tossing them felt final, Jordyn. I couldn't do that. In here"—he places his hand over his heart—"I knew you would come back to me. Until then, I needed every piece of you I still had surrounding me."

Tears fall from my eyes. I blink hard, trying to stop them, but it's no use. "I'm so sorry," I sob, and he wraps me in a hug.

"Don't cry, baby. It's all in the past. We're moving forward."

"I-I'm trying to move past it, but every single time I see you here hurting from my actions, and those of my family, my heart aches. You kept my things, Ryder." The guilt I'm feeling weighs heavily on my heart. This man, this incredible man—I don't deserve him.

"I don't deserve you."

"You do deserve me, Jordyn. Did you want to leave me?"

"No."

"Did you want to pretend I didn't exist?" His voice cracks.

"No."

"You were protecting me. Protecting my family. You were so fucking selfless, Jordyn. You did what you had to do, and, baby, I love you for it. Were the last two years pure hell without you? Yes, but you're here and we're going to figure this out. I promise you, Jordyn."

"You can't make that promise."

He doesn't say anything; instead, he wipes the tears from my cheeks with his thumbs. "Come on, let's throw out the old and replace it with new." He lifts me into his arms.

"I can walk," I say through my tears.

"Yeah, but I can carry you. Humor your man."

"My man."

"Only yours." He kisses me softly while still walking toward his room.

"You better watch where you're going."

"I won't do anything to hurt you, Jordyn."

"I know. But you can't see."

"I've walked this hall thousands of times. I've got you, sweets. No matter what, it's me and you."

I ignore that statement because I know what he's thinking. He's willing to run from his incredible family to be with me, and I refuse to let that happen, which he knows. We're at an impasse, and I don't want to argue over it. I know if it comes to that, I'll have to do something drastic to keep Ryder with his family, and I'm prepared to make that sacrifice.

I did it once; I can do it again.

When we make it to the bathroom, he sets me on my feet and reaches into the shower to grab the bottles. He tosses them in the trash before turning to look at me with a smile on his face. "Add a stop to replace those to today's agenda." He winks.

"What else is on today's agenda?"

"You and me, sweets. That's all that matters, is you and me." He leans in as if he's going to kiss me, and I lift my chin, ready to accept his lips on mine. "Shower," he says huskily. He stands to his full height and walks backward toward the door. "Keep the shirt, baby. You look sexy as fuck." With that, he shuts the door, and leaves me standing in the middle of his bathroom feeling like I've been through a tornado and have somehow made it to the other side.

"I love you, Ryder Kincaid." I whisper the words because they need to be said. As I reach into the shower and start the water before pulling everything I need out of my bag, I peel out of his shirt and fold it neatly.

He said it's mine and I intend to keep it.

"Fishing?"

"Yep."

"I've never been."

"So I get to be your first?" He wags his eyebrows, making me laugh.

We've had a great day. After I showered, we ate scrambled eggs and toast, and I cleaned up while Ryder showered. Our very first stop was the store to get my shower stuff for his place. He insisted I get feminine products as well so we'd have them if I needed them. I didn't bother arguing with him. I could see it in his eyes that this was important to him.

Next, we headed to the grocery store. Ryder needed everything to pack his lunch for next week, and the week's groceries. I know it sounds crazy, but it was nice getting to do normal everyday things with him.

Before my mother stepped in, this is the life I envisioned for us. Living in this sleepy little town of Willow River, raising a family here along with his siblings. If I'm being honest, I still thought about it every single day while I was away. I knew it was a dream, a wish that would never come true, but thinking about Ryder and the life I hoped I could have built with him got me through many lonely, sleepless nights.

And now, apparently, we're going fishing.

"Yeah, you're my first fishing experience." I laugh. "Do I have to touch the fish?"

"Not if you don't want to. I'll do it for you."

"I'll try, but I hold veto power."

"Fair enough, sweets." He parks his truck in his driveway and turns his mega-watt smile on me. "Let me get this unloaded, and I'll grab everything we need."

Climbing out of the truck, I gather a few bags and help him carry everything inside. "How long is this fishing expedition we're taking?"

"Just a few hours."

"Do you need snacks?"

He stops to look at me. "I thought we'd hit the diner in town for lunch. Do you need snacks?"

"No, but I don't know a damn thing about fishing, Ry. This is all new to me."

"We do sometimes take snacks, but I don't think we're going to need them this time."

"Okay, well, I'll put these away, you go do"—I wave my hand in the air—"manly fishing stuff."

He tosses his head back in laughter. "You're cute." He kisses my cheek and disappears into the garage.

I unpack everything. Most of it goes in the pantry. For everything else, I just guess. He'll find it, eventually. I smile when I think about him calling me and asking where something is. That's a normal relationship, and that's what I want. I've never seen my parents go to the store, let alone unpack groceries. They have staff for that.

Once everything is put away, I head to the bedroom to grab a hair tie. It's hot as hell outside, and if we're going to be outside fishing, I'm definitely going to need to put my hair up. I grab all the bathroom essentials on my way and place them in the bathroom. My heart squeezes. I don't know what I did in my prior life to deserve a man like Ryder Kincaid. He's the greatest person I've ever known, and I'll do everything I can to protect him and his family. I won't allow my mother to treat them as she did my brother and his fiancée.

"You ready, sweets?" I hear Ryder call out for me.

Shaking out of my thoughts, I finish putting everything away in the bathroom closet, grab a hair tie out of my toiletries bag, and turn off the light. Ryder is stepping into the bedroom from the hallway.

"Hey, you okay?"

"Yeah, I was putting everything away and grabbing this." I hold up the hair tie. "I assume this is going to be a lot of sitting and waiting. That's what fishing is, right?"

"Yeah." He chuckles. "There is a lot of sitting and waiting."

Slipping the tie on my wrist, I smile and link my arm with his. "Let's do this. We need to catch all the fish."

"Such enthusiasm, baby."

"Ryder, we could be watching paint dry, and I'd be thrilled to be here with you. In your home, spending time with you. I don't care what we do. I'm going to be excited about it."

"My girl's got sweet words today."

"Just calling a spade a spade." I shrug.

"Come on. I'm starving and the fish are waiting." He leads me out to the truck, locking the door behind us, and we're off to a late lunch and an afternoon of fishing. I'm not gonna lie. I'm nervous. I'm a big-city girl, at least that's how I was raised. The first night I ever stayed with Ryder in Willow River, I fell in love with the peaceful town.

"You want me to do what?" I ask incredulously.

Ryder grins. "You have to bait your hook."

"You want me to put that hook through the worm?"

"Like this." He takes the hook and spears it through the poor worm, hooking it through its squirming body. "See?"

"That's just cruel."

"They can't feel it. The curling is a reflex."

"Do you know that for sure?" I plant my hands on my hips.

He smiles. "No, sweets, I don't know for sure."

"I don't think I like fishing."

"I'll do yours." He grabs the second pole and baits my hook. "Now come here and I'll show you how to cast."

Not wanting to be a buzzkill, I drop my hands and accept the pole. Ryder steps in behind me and kisses my bare neck. We weren't out in the heat a full minute before I was pulling my hair up in a messy knot on top of my head. Ryder continues to explain what I'm supposed to be doing, but he's close. Too close for me to concentrate.

"Now you try."

Shaking out of my thoughts, I try to remember what he said and cast the pole. I end up tossing it into the river. Although it doesn't make it far, landing on the bank, only half immersed in the water.

"I think I'll observe." I laugh.

"You want to go?"

"No, but I think I need to watch so I can learn."

"Fair enough."

I watch as he expertly casts both poles and sets them up in holders on the bank. The next thing I know, he's taking my hand and pulling me from my chair. He takes my seat and I'm about to complain until he pulls me onto his lap.

"Why did you bring two chairs if we were only going to use one?" I ask the question, but if I'm being honest, I don't really care what the answer is. I'd rather be sitting with him, anyway.

"Hell if I know. I like you better on my lap."

I settle against him as he kisses my bare shoulder. "It's peaceful out here."

"Yeah, most people go to the other side of the river. My brothers and I have been coming to this side forever."

"I love how close you all are."

"Yeah, it's a blessing and a curse," he replies.

"How so?"

"I have eight brothers, and now six new sisters, and they love me, and I would do anything for them. I love them dearly, but they're all up in my business."

"Like you're not all up in theirs?"

"Fine." He laughs. "It's what we do." He's quiet for several minutes. "I called my brothers. Well, one of them actually when I found out you left, and within the hour, they were all sitting in my living room. They were there for me."

"I'm sure they hate me. Told you to let me go."

"They didn't. They asked me what they could do and asked what I wanted. They held me together while I waited for you to come home to me."

"You feel like home to me, Ryder."

"I am your home, sweets. Just like you're mine."

"Do you really think that the PI will find something?" I hate to even bring it up, but it's weighing on me, on both of us.

"I'm sure of it."

Neither one of us says anything else. There is nothing we can say that we haven't already. I need to snoop around, listen in on some phone calls. After I heard my parents talking about my brother and his death, I stopped trying to listen. I was too afraid of what I might hear next. I'm kicking my ten-year-old self in the ass for that decision. I need dirt on her. I know I should feel guilty for wanting to blackmail my mother, but I can't seem to find an ounce of guilt where she's concerned.

"We got a bite." Ryder taps my thigh, and I jump from his lap. He grabs the pole and reels it in. "A bass." He grins.

"How do you know it's a bass?"

He shrugs. "Years of fishing. You want to help me take it off the hook?"

"Nope." I cross my arms over my chest, and he laughs. "Is it hurt?"

"Nah, just hooked his lip."

I watch as he works the hook out of the fish's mouth and holds it up for me once it's freed. "Throw him back."

"I will. You want to touch him?"

"Not even a little bit." He holds the fish out toward me, and I squeal, stepping back, almost tripping over the lawn chair that's not being used.

"I'll toss him back." He bends down, releases the fish into the water, and wipes his hands on his shorts.

"Now I know why you brought two chairs." I nod toward his shorts.

"I have some hand wipes in the truck."

"That doesn't help your shorts." I wrinkle my nose.

"You saying you're not going to let me touch you until I change?"

"Yep."

"Jordyn?"

"Yeah?"

"Run." He lunges for me, and I turn on my heel and take off running through the field that's surrounding this side of the river.

I don't know why I'm even attempting to outrun him. His legs are longer than mine, and he's faster. I feel his hands on my waist, and he lifts me into the air. I laugh as he spins us around. When he finally places me on my feet, I turn in his arms, and he smiles down at me.

"Never dreamed I'd fall in love with a city girl."

"Yeah, well, this city girl never imagined she'd give her heart to a country boy."

"Baby?"

I smile up at him, raising my brows.

"My fish covered shorts are pressing up against you."

I slap at his chest, and he snickers. The next thing I know, he's lifting me over his shoulder and carrying me back to the truck. He sets me on the tailgate. "Let me pack up and we'll head home to shower."

"Now we both need a shower."

He winks. "I was counting on it."

Ryder is more than I ever could have dreamed of. I'm going to find something incriminating on my mother. I'll be damned if I give this man up again. I'll fight until the end. A love like ours is worth fighting for.

Chapter 9

Ryder

I can't close my eyes. Jordyn is sleeping peacefully with her head resting on my chest. When we came home, we showered together, which is a memory that will be in the forefront of my mind for years to come. We made dinner together—spaghetti, nothing fancy—and curled up on the couch to watch a movie. She fell asleep, so I carried her to bed, and we've been in this same position ever since. I can't stop thinking that she's leaving me in a few hours.

A few hours.

Glancing at the clock, I see it's just after 6:00 a.m. I've been lying here all night long, holding her and letting my mind race. I don't want her to go. I know she has to, but I hate it. I want her here with me. In my bed. In my arms. In my house. My town. My life. I want it all.

I hate that I don't know the next time I'll get to see her like this. How long will it be before I get to wrap my arms around her? There's also the fact that the PI has yet to find anything on her mother. I don't have a plan B. Trust me, I've tried and failed to come up with something. Short of us leaving the country, I don't know what else to do if this fails. Even then, there's a chance she will destroy my family's name and businesses.

I fucking hate being in limbo. I'm ready to start my life with her.

This weekend has been incredible. She touched base with Gianna a few times, and there was nothing from her mother. She said she didn't expect there to be, but I could still see the relief in her eyes. I hate that she's afraid of the woman that gave her life. It eats at me every fucking day that I can't be with her. She should be here with me and my family so we can love her the way she deserves to be loved.

We're Kincaids; we love harder after all.

Jordyn stirs in my arms, and I hold her a little tighter.

"Hey," she croaks. "Why are you awake?"

"Memorizing the moment."

Her reply is to kiss my bare chest and snuggle deeper under the covers. "I have to leave today."

"I know."

"I don't want to go."

There's a part of me that wants to tell her to stay and to tell her mother to fuck off. I know Jordyn never would. She would never risk me or my family, and I love her even more for it.

"When can I see you again?"

"I've been thinking about that." She moves so that she's on her side facing me. The early morning sun is shining through the blinds, and she looks like a beautiful, sleepy angel.

"Let's hear it, sweets."

"Atlanta is a big city. Maybe we can meet up. I was thinking about the movies. It's dark and we can arrive and leave separately."

"You think we can pull that off without being seen?"

"I do. I can have Gianna go, too, and sit with us, or go to a different movie?"

"She can sit with us."

"I'm kind of selfish where you're concerned. Especially if our time together is so sporadic."

"I'm all in, sweets. If you think it's safe, I'm there. You tell me when and where and I'll make it happen."

"It won't be like this. It won't be—intimate, but it's time together."

"This is more than sex, Jordyn. Tell me you know that."

"I do." She smiles. "But I like the sex part."

I pull her naked body closer. "We're really good at the sex part."

"You think? We should probably practice just to make sure."

I swoop in for a kiss, my tongue exploring her mouth with lazy strokes. My hand cups her ass just as a phone ringing interrupts us.

"That's mine." She scrambles out of bed, almost tripping over the covers that pull off to the side, and she scrambles to grab her phone from the nightstand. "Hello?" Her voice cracks, and the fear I hear pisses me off.

We have to find a solution to this.

"Oh, yeah, um, okay. I can do that. No, it's fine. I promise. This weekend was more than I could have hoped for. Okay. I'll see you soon." She ends the call and places her phone back on the nightstand.

"Everything okay?"

"That was Gianna. Her cousin Talia got called into work, and they're leaving now. I have to meet them at the mall parking lot to hand off the rental in two hours."

"Right. Well, you get showered, and I'll make you some breakfast. I can't let my girl leave hungry." I climb out of bed and pretend that her leaving isn't tearing my heart to shreds. I walk to where she's standing and kiss the corner of her mouth. "Love you." My words are soft to hide the emotions rolling through me like a tidal wave.

I'm at the door, almost free to let my mask fall when she calls my name.

"Ryder."

I stop, school my features, and turn to face her.

"You're my everything. I need you to know that."

Turning on my heel, I stalk back to where she's standing and lift her into my arms. I hug her so tightly, she probably can't breathe, but I can't seem to lessen my hold on her. This woman, she's a fighter. My girl, she's sacrificed her own happiness for so many, and it's important to her for me to know that I'm her everything.

"You are my life, Jordyn," I whisper huskily. "I need you. I love you. You own me. You, too, are my everything. We're going to get through this, and then we'll live happily ever after."

"You big on fairy tales?" she teases to lighten the mood, but I can still hear the pain in her voice.

"Blakely and I have watched many, and the others too," I say, speaking of my many nieces and nephews.

"So when our daughter wants to play dress up with Daddy?"

"I'm in," I tell her. "I'm in on practicing for this daughter. I'm in for being her daddy and letting her dress me however the fuck she wants to." I can see it all clearly in my mind. Jordyn and I sitting on the back porch, watching our kids play with their cousins. It takes everything I have not to beg her to start trying for a baby right now.

She laughs. "One day, Ryder Kincaid."

"Forever, sweets." I release her and wink, before turning back around and leaving the room.

When I reach the kitchen, I brace my hands on the island and bow my head. I hate this. I don't know that I've really hated anything. I dislike avocado. I dislike bare feet on a cold floor in the winter months. But I truly hate the distance between us.

Grabbing my phone, I call Deacon.

"Hey, Ry," he answers. "You good?"

"Sorry to call so early." I wince.

"It's fine. We were up. Brynlee thought it was time to party at five this morning and the little bugger is still going strong." I can hear the love he has for his daughter in his tone.

"Bring her over. I'll watch her while you all catch up on sleep."

"I might take you up on that, but we won't be sleeping. Well, not the whole time." He laughs.

"Dude, she's my sister."

"She's your cousin," he counters. "And she's my wife."

"Fair enough, but she's more like a sister than a cousin."

"Still not apologizing for wanting... adult time with my wife."

I think about Jordyn and smile. "Yeah, don't expect you to. I was giving you shit. Anyway, have we heard anything from the PI?"

"Nothing, man. These things take time. He'll find something, or she'll slip up and we'll get something on her. Trust me, it can take months."

"I don't have months," I mutter.

"Why? Did something happen? Is Jordyn unsafe?"

"I don't have months to start my life with her, Deacon. I've spent two years loving her from thousands of miles away. I'm ready for this shit to be over, and for her to be home. Here with me."

"I know, brother," he says. "We're working on it. I talk to him every few days. Just hang in there."

"Easier said than done. She slipped away for the weekend. Her parents think she's in Birmingham, but she's getting ready to leave, and I fucking hate that I don't know when I'm going to see her again."

"What can I do, Ry?"

"Nothing, man. Nothing you're not already doing. Thanks for listening, and if you hear anything, please call me right away."

"You know it, man."

"Give that baby girl of yours a hug from her uncle Ry."

"Will do."

I end the call, laying my phone on the island, and get to work scrambling some eggs and popping some bread into the toaster. This is my last breakfast with my girl, for I don't know how long, and no matter how much I hate this, I can't let her see that. She's beating herself up enough about leaving how she did. The guilt still sits heavily on her shoulders. I need her to stay present so that we can both survive this bump in the road.

That's all it is. A bump, one that we're going to get past and starting forever together soon enough.

"Text me when you make it to the mall, and again when you get home. If you can," I add, because I know she might not be able to do it as soon as she gets home.

"I will." Jordyn wraps her arms around my waist and holds me tightly.

I do the same, resting my chin on top of her head. "You tell me when and where, baby. I'll be there."

"I'll get something worked out and let you know during our calls."

"The weather is supposed to be shitty this week," I say, inwardly cursing mother nature. "Your walks in the park might not be an everyday thing like we're used to."

"I'll figure something out. I know I'll need to hear your voice, even if it's just a quick hello."

"I love you." My words are soft as I try to mask the pain of letting her go.

"I love you too. I'll see you soon." She pulls away, and I have no choice but to let her. I live for the day that she's no longer so close yet so far away from me.

I stand still as she climbs into the car and slowly backs out of my garage. She waves before pulling out onto the street and driving away. I smack at the button on the wall and the garage door whines as it closes. Stalking back into the house, I plop down on the couch and close my eyes. I'm exhausted, but the sleepless night was worth it. Time with her is worth everything.

Checking to make sure that the ringer is turned on and on the loudest setting on my phone, I clutch it against my chest, and let sleep claim me.

My phone rings and I jump, almost dropping it. I rush to swipe the screen. "Hello."

"Bro, were you sleeping?" Rushton asks.

"Yep."

"It's like two in the afternoon."

"And your point?"

"Long night?"

"Something like that." I don't have the energy to explain that I was too afraid to miss a second with her.

"You coming to Mom and Dad's for Sunday dinner?"

"Not sure. I didn't sleep at all last night."

"Come on, it's free food. Besides, Caden misses his uncle Ry."

"Does he?" I ask, chuckling. "You all hide behind your kids."

"It works, brother," he says smugly. "Just wait until you have one of your own. You're going to do the same thing."

"So, what's this really about?"

"We're worried about you. The twins sent a message to the group text that Jordyn was at your place Friday night and staying until today. Is she still there?"

"Nah, she had to head back."

"Then you need to come. You need to be around family."

"I need sleep."

"You can sleep tonight. Besides, if you sleep all day, you'll sleep like shit again tonight, and the workday tomorrow will suck."

"You sound like Mom."

"Thank you."

I laugh. "Fine, I'll be there."

"Good. Mav and Mer are on their way to your place to pick you up."

"An ambush."

"Nope, just loving our little brother a little harder today."

"I'm their big brother," I fire back.

"You know what I mean. They'll be there in ten." The call ends, and I laugh, shaking my head.

I love my brothers. No doubt Rushton was the one who was chosen to call and convince me to come to our parents' for Sunday dinner. The twins, being my chauffeurs, isn't necessary, but I'm tired as hell, so I'm going to let them without complaint. Well, I might complain a little, but it's not going to keep me from climbing into whoever's truck they're driving and nap all the way there. The entire fifteen-minute drive.

With a groan, I stand from the couch and stretch. I slept for a couple of hours, but I could have used about eight more. I check my phone, certain I didn't miss anything from Jordyn, but want to double check. Just as I'm sliding my phone into my pocket, it chirps with a message.

> **Jordyn:** I'm home. Sorry, we were rushing to switch cars when I got to the mall. It's just me home right now.
>
> **Me:** Glad you made it home safe. Use the time to plan our next visit.
>
> **Jordyn:** Good idea.
>
> **Me:** I'm headed to my parents' for Sunday dinner. Rush called and guilt-tripped me, saying Caden missed his uncle Ry.
>
> **Jordyn:** So many recent additions to the family. I'm going to have to learn their kids' names. I hear you talk about them, but I don't think I have the order and parents in order in my mind just yet.
>
> **Me:** LOL. There are a lot of us. That's fine. They'll love their aunt Jordyn no matter what.

Jordyn:	I never thought I'd get to be an aunt.
Me:	I got you covered, sweets.

My heart constricts when I think about her losing her brother and the tragic way it happened. I want to give her the life she deserves, full of so much love and more family than she can keep straight.

Jordyn:	Maybe dreams really do come true.
Me:	I'll do everything in my power to make all of yours.
Jordyn:	You're my dream, Ryder.
Me:	Back at you, baby.

There's a knock at my door.

Me:	The twins are here to pick me up. We can keep chatting, but if I'm delayed in responding, that's why.
Jordyn:	My mother is on her way home from the country club, so I should go anyway. Enjoy family time.
Me:	Wish you were here.
Me:	Love you.
Jordyn:	Love you too.

The front door pushes open just as I'm sliding my phone into my pocket.

"Are you avoiding us?"

"No, I was texting Jordyn, and she's my priority."

They both nod. "You ready?" Merrick asks.

"Yeah, who drove?"

"Mav." Merrick points to his twin.

"I'm sleeping on the way there."

"It's like fifteen minutes." Maverick laughs.

"Didn't sleep last night."

"Oh, did Jordyn keep you up?" Maverick wags his eyebrows.

"She did, but not for the reason you're thinking. She was sleeping peacefully in my arms where she belongs."

"Ah." Maverick nods like he gets it.

"Come on, man, dinner with the family is what you need." Merrick slaps my shoulder and walks out the door with Maverick on his heels. Grabbing my keys, I follow after them, locking the door behind me.

Sitting in the back of Maverick's truck, I close my eyes. But I should have known these two jokers weren't going to let me sleep.

"How was it?" Merrick asks. He turns in his seat as much as the seat belt will allow to look at me.

"How was what?" I play dumb. If he won't let me sleep, he's going to have to work for the information he wants. The same information I'm going to have to repeat for the rest of my brothers as soon as we settle in at my parents' place.

"This weekend."

"Too short."

"Come on, bro," Maverick says. "You have to give us something."

"The woman I love had to hide to see me. She was supposed to be here a little longer, but her cover got called into work early. I laid awake all night, not willing to miss a single second of time with her, even though she was sleeping soundly. The weekend was way too fucking short, and incredible all at the same time."

"We thought you could use a drink." This comes from Merrick. "That's why we offered to come and get you. That and we wanted to make sure you came with us."

"I have to work tomorrow."

"I said a drink, not get sloshed, old man," he jokes.

"I'm two years older than you, assholes," I fire back.

They both crack up laughing, and my mouth twitches with a grin. I fucking love my brothers.

Chapter 10

Jordyn

I've been avoiding my mother. I've barely seen her this week, thanks to some charity she's working on, and it's been glorious. My father practically lives at his office. So much so that he stays at the apartment on the top floor of the Astor building that houses his law firm that was handed down to him from my grandfather.

Last weekend, when I snuck away to stay with Ryder, it opened my eyes to a lot of things. So, while my mother has been preoccupied, it's given me some time to think. I've let her control me my entire life. I'm an adult, and I can make my own choices. Sure, the threat against Ryder and his family is still very much there, and I can't push her where he's concerned, but I can push back. I made the decision, lying in Ryder's arms, that I'm going to fight for us.

To do that, I need to start fighting for me.

I need to start standing up to my mother. In her eyes, she'll see it as defiance, but in mine, it's going to be living my life the way I want. Maybe if I'm lucky, she'll give up on me and set me free from her clutches.

If only.

The fight for me starts today. That's why I'm sitting at the dining room table with my phone scrolling through social media while eating a bowl of Lucky Charms.

"What on earth are you eating? Put your phone away at the table."

"Lucky Charms. Want some?" I smile up at my mother.

She wrinkles her nose in disgust. "That junk will go straight to your thighs, Jordyn. You know better. You should have some fruit."

"I didn't want fruit." My heart pounds as I talk back to her. It's not something I've ever done. I've been afraid of being me in my own home for years. Speaking of my own home, it's time for me to look for a place and a job. I'm going crazy sitting around this empty mansion all day long.

My mother takes her seat at the table, and I cross my legs in the chair, knowing it will drive her insane.

"Jordyn," she scolds. "Sit like a lady and what on earth are you wearing?"

I look down at the T-shirt I have on and grin. It's the one I took from Ryder. It's old and faded. It's plain black, but it's so faded it's gray. "A T-shirt."

"It's ratty. Where on earth did you get such a thing?" Her nose literally points toward the air with all of her stuck-up presence.

"It's Ryder's." The truth falls from my lips and it's freeing.

Out of the corner of my eye, I watch her stiffen. "Jordyn." Her voice is low and holds all kinds of warning. "You remember what we talked about?"

"It's a shirt, Mother." I roll my eyes because I know she hates it.

"What has gotten into you?"

I shrug. "I was sitting here eating my breakfast minding my own business. You're the one who started in on me."

"You won't talk to me like that," she seethes. "I am your mother. You will speak to me with respect."

"Respect is earned, Mother." I take a big bite of my cereal, slurping the milk off the spoon, knowing the sound is the equivalent to nails on a chalkboard for her.

"Watch yourself, Jordyn."

She's pissed, which is what I was hoping for.

"You know. I heard that they lost a patient in the emergency room over at Willow River General. Wouldn't it be terrible if it were somehow that Kincaid's fault? You know, the male nurse." She says "nurse" as if it isn't a noble profession. Nurses bust their asses day in and day out to save lives. My mother could only dream of being that noble.

"I hadn't heard," I reply, trying to be aloof and keep my heart rate steady at the mention of Brooks Kincaid.

"Shame," she utters, but thankfully, she doesn't say more.

I have to stop letting her walk all over me. It's going to be hell living with her like this, but I'll do anything to be with Ryder. If she cuts me off like she threatened to do with my brother, I'm in the clear and so are all the Kincaids, at least I hope so anyway. I'm out of ideas, but I know I can't sit back and let this happen. I can't continue to let her treat me as if I'm a show pony. However, her not-so-subtle reminder hangs in the air like a thick, heavy smoke of a forest fire between us.

I shrug as if her threat doesn't have my insides shaking. I finish my breakfast under the watchful and hateful eye of my mother. I can feel her glare, but I continue to ignore it and pretend as if the hatred rolling off her in waves doesn't affect me.

Once I've finished my cereal, I pick up my bowl along with my phone and walk it to the kitchen sink.

"I need you today."

"Can't. I have plans." I do have plans, but not until later. I'm meeting Ryder at the movies. Gianna and her new man are going as well. It's a double date kind of thing, in the dark theater, but whatever. I'll take whatever time I can get with my man. I'm nervous we're going to get caught, but he's going to wear a hat and glasses, and Gianna's man is meeting us there as well, so it looks like it's just her and I as we enter the theater. This is over the top, but I don't trust my mother.

"Jordyn, you live here rent free. We provide for you. I need your help at the club. We're trying to pick out place settings for the Christmas ball, and we can't seem to decide."

"Mother, you've never had an indecisive day in your entire life. You don't need me there. Whatever setup you're trying to orchestrate, I don't want any part of it. As for me living here, you requested I come back home, and I listened. However, I'm happy to start looking for a place if that's more convenient for you."

She scoffs. "And how do you plan to pay for this new place of yours? You can't expect your father and I to pay for it. We dealt with your defiance in college, but it's time to start acting like the twenty-four-year-old adult that you are and plan your future."

"I'd love to plan my future. In fact, I was doing that until you threatened him and his family." I'm fuming, but so is she. I know bringing Ryder and his family up isn't a good idea, but I can't just sit back and listen to this bullshit anymore. She wants me to live the life she's planning for me, and not one that will bring me happiness and love.

So much love.

"You are an Astor." The malice in her tone is clear.

"Really? I wasn't aware," I sass.

Her neck gets red, and the color spreads across her cheeks. If it were possible, I'm sure there would be steam coming out of her ears. I've pissed her off.

"You can be a disrespectful little snit all you want. Your future husband will have a field day breaking you of that particular habit," she sneers.

I bite back my fear. "He can try." What I don't say is that unless the man's name is Ryder Kincaid, I won't be marrying him. I'll disappear first. I won't do anything else to hurt the man I love. My mother has caused him enough pain, and me by association, and fear.

No more. That stops now.

"I'm going to Gianna's. I'm staying at her place tonight." Before today, I would have asked for permission, and let her tell me no. That's the old Jordyn. The new Jordyn knows how it feels to have a man fight for her. To hold on to their love even when he wasn't sure that love would be returned.

"I told you I need you at the country club."

"And I told you that I have plans." With more courage than I feel, I stalk out of the room and up the stairs, slamming my bedroom door for good measure. I'm acting like a mouthy teenager, but I guess I skipped those years, so it's only fair I give dear old Mom a dose now.

I know I need to be careful. I'm walking on thin ice with her, but as long as I don't let on that I'm still with Ryder, it will be fine. She'll be pissed, and that's what I want. It's the opposite of what I strived to achieve growing up. I never wanted to upset her or make her unhappy, but that ship has long since sailed.

Disown me, Mother.

Please.

I smile as I strip out of Ryder's T-shirt and hide it because I wouldn't put it past my mother to have it tossed out, and head to the shower.

I'm vibrating with excitement as we enter the theater. Ryder texted me fifteen minutes ago to let me know he was here. He's sitting in the back row and saved us some seats.

"You want snacks?" I ask Gianna.

"Is that a real question? Yes, to all the snacks. The butter needs to be seeping out of that bag of popcorn, my friend."

I laugh as she links her arm through mine, and we hit up the concession stand. I grab a bottle of water and a large soda, a large popcorn, and a box of Junior Mints. Ryder loves them.

Once we're loaded down with the goods, we make our way to screen number seven. Inside, we make our way to the very back row, and just as promised, Ryder is there with a hat pulled down low on his head, and one seat over from him is Calvin. I met him earlier this week, and he seems to be just as smitten with my best friend as she is with him.

I take a seat next to Ryder, and he takes the drink and popcorn from my hands. "Hey, Ry," I whisper. The theater is dark, and when he leans in and presses his lips to mine, I don't shy away.

"Hi, sweets. What's all this?" He nods at the large drink and popcorn I'm holding.

"Oh, there's more." I reach into my purse and pull out the bottle of water and the Junior Mints.

"Missed you," he says, kissing me again.

Gianna leans over. "Hey, Ryder. Nice to see you."

"You too, Gianna. Thanks for helping me see my girl."

"Thanks for keeping my guy company." Calvin leans forward and holds his fist out for Ryder, who also leans in so they can bump knuckles.

"Anytime, my man," Ryder says, settling back in his seat. He lifts the armrest and pulls me close.

"Don't you dare get us kicked out of here, Ryder." I playfully swat at his chest.

"Never, baby. I just need you closer, that's all." He sets our drinks in the cupholders in front of us. I hold the popcorn with one hand, while eating with the other. Ryder takes a handful as well. We're just a regular couple on a movie date with friends. It's how we used to be before my mother ruined it all.

I push her out of my mind and focus on the here and now.

Stay present.

That's what Ryder keeps telling me to do, and tonight, the present is all I'm worried about. He's here, I'm in his arms, and there isn't much more I can ask for at the moment.

When the final credits roll, I swallow back my tears. The night is over, and I'd give anything to be going home with him. I'm slow to stand, and so is he.

"Hey, how about we all head back to my place?" Calvin suggests. He nods at Ryder. "Leave your truck here, and I'll bring you back."

"Really?" I ask hopefully, unable to hide the crack in my voice.

Ryder pulls me into him and holds me close. "That would be great, man, thanks," he says, holding his fist out for Calvin. They bump knuckles, and my eyes find Gianna's. She's smiling with tears in her eyes. She knows what this means to me, and her man just made it happen.

Ryder places a kiss on my cheek. "I'll see you soon, sweets. Be safe." The words are barely out of his mouth before he and Calvin leave the theater.

"Did that just happen?" I ask Gianna.

She nods. "You get to spend more time with Ryder." Her smile is huge.

"Calvin." I shake my head. "He's a keeper." My best friend tosses her head back in laughter.

"I really like him, Jordyn."

"I really like him, too. Not just because he read the room and made it happen, but because of the way he is with you and the way you light up when you talk about him. Hell, as soon as you laid eyes on him, there was a twinkle there"—I point to her face—"that I've never seen before."

She plops back down in her chair, and I do the same. We need to give the guys a head start, anyway. "He makes me feel things I've never felt before."

I nod. "I know exactly how you feel."

"I get it, you know. The reason you left like you did. I was mad at you for the longest time. Ryder was... devastated. He kept stopping by and calling and I couldn't understand how you could leave someone like that behind. Four months later and a call in the middle of the night to you crying and I still didn't fully understand. When you told me your story, I could see how what your mom was doing was terrible, but I also saw how much he loved you."

She pauses to collect her thoughts, and I don't interrupt her. Whatever it is that's on her mind, she needs to say it. Ryder isn't the only one I left.

"I would do it too. For Calvin, I mean. If the roles were reversed, with the way I feel about him, I would have made the same choice."

I can't stop my tears. "I'm sorry, G. I'm so damn sorry."

Reaching over, she tugs me into a hug. Luckily for us, the theater has cleared out, so no one is here to witness our emotional breakdown. "It's all in the past," she says, as she hugs me tightly. When she pulls back, we're both wiping at our eyes.

"I'm glad you found it. Found him. A man who showers you with love so pure you feel like you're a part of him."

"Oh, we haven't said I love you."

"You love him, right?"

She nods slowly. "I do. It's so soon. We've only been dating for a little while, a handful of months, but he's—unlike anyone before him."

"My best advice is to be open and honest. I ran from Ryder. I was scared out of my mind about what my mother might do to him and his family, and I took the coward's way out. I'll live forever with the regrets of my choices. I let her manipulate me, and I could have lost him, G. I could have lost the man who loves me above all else. Two years." I shake my head, emotion clogging my throat. "I was gone for two years, with very limited communication, and he was still willing to listen. He accepted my apology and welcomed me back into his life, and into his heart with open arms. I honestly don't know how I'll ever live without Ryder being a part of my life."

"That's not going to happen."

"If we can't find any dirt on my mother, it will. I won't let him give up his family, or the life he has in Willow River, to chase me across the country to hide from my mother. Besides, who's to say she won't figure it out and still go after them out of spite? It's a risk I'm not willing to take."

"Just take it all one day at a time. It will all work out."

"Yeah, I'm sure my brother thought that, too, and look how that turned out." My stomach hollows out at the thought.

"I'm so sorry, Jordyn. For what she's putting you through, and all that you've been through. You don't deserve this."

"One day at a time." I offer a smile I don't feel.

"Come on, you. The guys are probably at Calvin's by now. Our men are waiting."

We stand and make our way out of the theater.

"Thank you for making tonight happen. And Calvin, please thank him for me, too, if I don't get the chance."

"Oh, don't you worry. I'll take care of Calvin." She wags her eyebrows and the heaviness of the moment passes. We're both laughing and enjoying life and I plan to hold on to that, onto this moment, and this feeling for as long as I can.

I don't know what I did in this life to deserve a best friend like Gianna, but I will be forever grateful for her friendship. She could have kicked my ass to the curb, just as Ryder could have, but here we are and they're still by my side. I'll take genuine connections, genuine friendship and love over money and power all day long.

Chapter 11

Ryder

I t's the last week of August and balls hot outside. It was also the only weekend that my brothers, Deacon, my dad, and I were all available to do our annual camping trip. It's a rarity with the kids, wives, and day jobs that we're all available at the same time.

Life is rapidly changing for the better.

I'm going to miss sneaking away to see my girl this weekend, but I'm also pumped for this time with my brothers and dad. And yeah, Deacon isn't my brother by blood, but he's married to Ramsey, my cousin, who is more like a sister, so he counts. He's in for life.

My phone rings as I'm going over all the items I have by the front door, ready to take out to my truck. Pulling my phone out of my pocket, I smile when I see Jordyn's name. "Hey, sweets."

"Hi. Are you all packed up and ready to go?"

"I think so. I'm going over my mental checklist to make sure I didn't forget anything. What are you up to? I didn't expect to hear from you this soon."

"I'm home alone, which is typical. I'm hiding away in my bathroom. Why, I'm not sure. I guess I just feel safer the more doors that are potentially between me and my mother."

"I hate that you have to do that so that you can talk to me."

"Small price to pay. Besides, my bathroom is huge. Nothing but the best for the Astor offspring. At least that's what my mother would like for people to believe."

"Are you still going to Gianna's this weekend?"

"I am. I need a break from this house."

"You know you're welcome to come to mine. Park in the garage and hide away. Wait, if that's going to happen, I'm not going camping."

She laughs, and the sound brightens my day. Scratch that— my life.

"You can't skip out on this trip. Besides, I can't be there if you're not there."

"Yes, you can. Hell, if I had my way, you'd live there with me, or we can buy something different."

"You want me to live with you?"

"Yes."

"You're something else, Ryder."

"Yours. I'm yours. Honestly, if you need to get away, you know the code to get into the garage. The door to the house from the garage is unlocked. Make yourself at home."

"I might snoop."

"I have nothing to hide." I'm an open book, especially where she's concerned. You can't share your life with someone without giving them an all-access pass to your life. Jordyn has that.

"I would be too lonely there without you."

"I'll stay home." If I get to see my girl, my brothers and my dad will understand.

"No. It's important for you to go. This is a Kincaid thing. I'm never going to stand in the way of that."

"You wouldn't be standing in the way. They all know what we're going through. They would understand."

"It's only been a week since we've seen each other."

"A lifetime," I counter, making her giggle.

"Go. Have fun. Is it okay if I still call or text while you're gone?"

"Hell, yes. We even made sure that where we're going, we have good cell service. Brooks is freaking out because Palmer is pregnant, and the rest of my brothers want to make sure their wives—and Dad, too, with Mom—can get ahold of them if needed."

"So, I won't be cramping your style?"

Her tone is teasing, and something happens inside my chest. I've missed her so fucking much. She's the other half of me, and now that she's back, everything feels right again. It sounds cheesy as fuck, and I'm sure my brothers would have a field day if they could read my mind, but I feel complete.

"Never, sweets."

"Good. Text me when you get there."

"I will. If you change your mind, you know what to do."

"I won't, but thank you. I love you. Be safe. Have fun."

"I love you too. I'll see you soon."

"See you soon," she agrees, and the line goes dead.

I slide my phone back into my pocket and get my head back into the trip and off the love of my life. I mentally run down what

I'll need and if I've packed it. We all pitched in on food like always—now that we're adults—and that includes the beer. Orrin and Dad were taking care of all of that. Deciding I have everything, I start loading up the truck. Once I'm finished, I make sure the house is secured and head out to pick up the twins.

The sun is setting, and even though it's hotter than Satan's ball sack, we're sitting around a fire. We all have a beer in our hand. Well, all of us except for Brooks. He's clutching his phone, ready to head home should he get a call from his wife. Palmer is only halfway through her pregnancy, and she's been perfectly healthy, she and the baby, but Brooks is on edge, being over an hour away from her and their firstborn, Remi.

He's missing his girls, and I get it. I think we all do. Well, maybe not Maverick and Merrick, but they've seen us all fall, so I'm sure they have an idea.

"I love my sisters," Maverick speaks up. "I love all of my nieces and nephews, but y'all are old and boring." He snickers.

We all know he's just kidding, but there is also some truth to his words. "This is what we always do. Sit around the fire, drink a few beers, and shoot the shit," I counter.

"Yeah, but we used to go swimming at night, and do more than just sip a few beers," Merrick points out.

"Things change, little brother." Orrin holds up the beer he's been nursing.

"When I find my woman, I'm not going to change," Maverick tells us.

"We're still us," Sterling speaks up. "Just better now."

"Better?" Merrick asks.

"They make us better," Declan adds.

"That's the love of a good woman," Dad chimes in. "I'm still me," he continues. "I'm a better me. It's not just me, because she's a part of me." He taps his chest over his heart. "When I make a decision, even something as simple as what to bring home for dinner, I consider your mother. Every single choice I make in life is with her and you boys in mind. You're all grown, and most of you have your own families, and I know you understand." He looks at me, and then at the twins.

"Ryder, I know you get it, son. You've endured a path with your Jordyn that none of us have had to travel. You're still fighting for your forever, and, son, that's all you can do. Fight for her. Fight for your love. It will be the hardest yet most rewarding fight of your life." He pauses, taking a sip of his beer before turning his gaze toward the twins.

"The babies of the family." Dad smirks, and the twins scoff, making us all laugh. "Double the trouble, but you've had the advantage of watching your older brothers on their path to their futures. Sitting around this fire, you have a wealth of knowledge and support. When the time comes, when you get to the 'love harder' part of the family motto, remember that. Remember that you have this big, loving family to support you, and we've all been there."

"He's right," Brooks speaks up. "Outside of Orrin, who'd already found Jade, I was flying solo when Palmer and I got together. Nothing against Dad, but sometimes it's nice to have someone who's closer to you in age—" Brooks coughs the last word, and we all laugh, including Dad. He knows we're just giving him shit. "—to talk to."

"I'd like to think after watching all of you, we're all set," Maverick tells us.

"Yeah, we've got this." Merrick holds his fist out to Maverick and they bump knuckles.

"It seems that way." Rushton nods. "Until you're living it."

"When you hear people say it's complicated, that shit is fact," Archer agrees.

"Try being a single dad and finding someone who will love your daughter like you do," Declan speaks up.

"Pfft, Kennedy fell for Blakely first," I say teasingly.

Declan nods. "Right? The hard part was convincing her I was worth the effort."

"Come on, fellas." Maverick leans forward in his lawn chair, resting his elbows on his knees. "You expect me to believe it was that hard?"

"Not every moment," Sterling tells him. "But, yeah, it was tough."

"Because you were blind," Merrick quips.

"Possibly." Sterling bobs his head. "I didn't want to lose her, and I was the dumb ass who pushed it all down. I was so caught up in losing Alyssa as a part of my life, I missed the signs. I wasted so much damn time."

"See." Dad points toward the twins. "You two can learn a lot from your brothers."

"Things that you think are obstacles aren't," Deacon speaks up. "I was stuck on the fact that Ramsey is ten years younger than me, but at the end of the day, no one else could love her the way I do."

I smile at Deacon. He's never been one to shy away from being real, and one thing he will shout from the rooftops is how much he loves Ramsey. Hell, none of us are shy about it. Maybe we have Deacon to thank for that. He and Ramsey were together before any of the rest of us. He fell in love with our little cousin, and he had zero apologies for loving her.

That's loving harder.

Like we've always said, his last name might not be Kincaid, but he might as well be. He works hard and loves harder, just like we do, and I couldn't think of anyone better suited for my cousin.

"Come on." Orrin stands and tosses his beer can in the bucket we're using to collect trash. "Let's go for a swim."

Everyone stands except for me, Brooks, and Dad. "You not coming?" Declan asks.

"Nah, I'm going to stay where I know I get reception." Brooks holds up his phone. "Just in case."

"There's reception," Rushton assures him. "I made sure of it. We all want them to be able to reach us, bro. Come on."

Brooks nods and stands, following along behind our brothers. "Ry?" Declan asks.

"Nah, man. Jordyn is supposed to call, and I don't know when she can get away. I'll come down once I talk to her."

"Pops?"

"I'll keep this one company." Dad points his bottle of beer toward me.

"All right, you know where we'll be if you change your mind." Declan grabs a beer from the cooler and jogs off to catch up with the others.

"How are you doing, son?" Dad asks.

I blow out a breath and tilt my head back, staring up at the star-filled sky. "I'm doing."

"Any news from the PI?"

"Nothing. So far, both of Jordyn's parents are squeaky clean. He tells me that these things take time, and that secrets can be buried deep. I want to stay hopeful, but it's hard when I miss the hell out of her."

"Ryder, you're in a position that none of us have ever been in. Your path is different from ours, so you're going to have to speak up when you need help. You know we like to meddle." He laughs. "But if it's more than that, you're going to have to tell us what you need."

"I just need her," I tell him honestly. "She's struggling. She's still stressed about how she left, and she's worried about everyone hating her for it."

"We don't hate her."

"I know that. How do I convince her?"

"Actions. Our actions will speak louder than your words or even ours. We'll show her."

"And until then? Hell, I barely see her."

"Until then, you stay present in her life, even from a distance. Show her that this fight is one she's not fighting alone. When it's time for us to step up, we will."

I can't help it, I chuckle. "I pretty much told her the same thing. That I needed her to stay present and let the past go. It was out of her control, and she thought she was protecting us."

"She was protecting us."

There's conviction in his voice, and I swallow the lump that suddenly appears in the back of my throat. My family, they always have my back, and it's something you get used to, but at times like this, it means the world to me.

"We've got you, Ry. You and Jordyn. When it's time, we'll all rally and love her harder. She's the love of your life, so it will be easy. If you're happy, we're happy. It's that simple."

"Love you, old man," I say, not bothering to hide the quiver in my voice.

"Love you too, Ry," he says as my phone rings. "I'll give you some space." He grabs another beer and heads toward the trail that leads to the lake where my brothers are.

"Hey, sweets," I answer.

"Hi, handsome. Am I interrupting?"

"Never, Jordyn."

"Everything okay?"

"Everything is perfect. I was just having a little one-on-one chat with my dad."

"Oh, I can let you go."

"Nah, he went down to the lake with the others. It's just me here sitting around the fire."

"It's too hot for a fire," she remarks.

"Agreed, but you can't camp without it. It's part of the experience."

"I'll take your word for it. I've never camped before."

"Never?"

"Nope. I was invited once, but I wasn't allowed to go. It was a friend in elementary school. It was right after we lost Jeremy, and my mother wouldn't budge."

"I'll take you. In fact, we've been saying for a while now that we need to make a family trip, not just a guys' trip. Everyone but the twins has a wife, and most of them have kids now. It's time to start bringing the families."

"You're not married."

"I'm married in my heart. That's what matters."

"Ryder—sometimes it's hard to believe you're real. The way you speak from your heart and love without restraint, it's something I've missed, and it's one of the reasons I fell so madly in love with you."

"I wish you were here, sweets."

"Me too, but I'll see you soon. Maybe we can figure something out for next weekend?"

"Yeah, tell me the plan, and I'll be there. How's your night?"

"Good. I just left Gianna's. I'm on my way back to my parents' place."

I notice she's no longer calling her parents' place home. "Are they home?"

"I don't think so. They had some kind of work dinner for my father. I honestly don't really listen. I let it go in one ear and out the other. I just nod where I think it's appropriate."

"I hate you going back to that house all alone."

"The staff will be there."

"You know what I mean, Jordyn."

"I know, but, Ryder, this is my life. I don't know anything different. I would spend the night with friends when I was allowed, and my parents would send a car for me. They wouldn't even bother to ride along. It sounds unusual to you, but it's all that I know."

"Life with me will be different."

"I'm banking on it, Kincaid. Ryder, when I think about my future, now and in the past two years, it was always you and me, living in Willow River surrounded by family. When I have kids, I want that for them."

"We. When *we* have kids."

"When we have kids," she amends. "I want that for them. For us. I was born into this lifestyle. I'm forced to continue to live it, but that's not what I want. I want you. I want a normal house, and I can drive myself. I want to be a soccer mom and drive a minivan and bake cookies for the bake sale. I know it sounds crazy and old-fashioned, but I feel as though I haven't been living. Just going through the motions, following orders and expectations. I just want to be me."

"You keep thinking about what our life is going to look like, baby. Write it down if you have to, and we'll make every single dream come true." I hate her family and how they've treated her. I hate even more that she kept it locked away for so long. She's been deprived of love and affection, but that's okay. She's about to be a Kincaid, and if there is one thing we know, it's love and affection. She's going to be surrounded with it.

"Life with you is my dream, Ry."

"You know how to get a guy all up in his feels."

She laughs. "Sorry. I'm home, so I'll let you go. Be safe and have fun. I'll call tomorrow when I can."

"You better. I love you, sweets."

"Love you too, Ry."

I end the call and shove my phone into my pocket. Grabbing a bottle of water from the cooler, I start down the trail that's sure to lead me to chaos. Sure enough, when I get there, the twins and Rushton are in line to use the rope swing that will toss them into the dark, murky waters of the lake.

"Everything good?" Brooks asks.

"Yeah, she's good. You know, we've talked about this for years, but it's time we do a trip with the entire family. Keep this one, because it's always going to be our tradition, but maybe we should start one with the rest of the family too."

"Ry, that's the smartest thing I've ever heard you say." Brooks grins.

"I like it," Dad agrees. "It was never my intention to exclude them. This started as a way to give your momma a break."

"Yeah, but I like the idea of taking care of the wives. We grill all weekend, teach the kids how to skip rocks, fish, and roast marshmallows," Declan says.

"And we plan it all," Sterling adds. "Alyssa takes care of so much. I like the idea of bringing her here and spoiling her. Maybe working on adding to the Kincaid brood." He wags his eyebrows.

We all laugh.

I chance a look at our dad, and he's nodding with a smile tugging at his lips. I know he and Mom are down for more grandkids. I mean, they had nine sons. They had to know what that would mean when we all got older. If I didn't know better, I'd think they did it on purpose. They love us, and never went a day without telling us, but they go crazy over their grandkids.

"Brooks, your weekends are the hardest. Send me some dates, and we'll plan something."

"What about Jordyn?"

"We'll make it happen. Hopefully, she's living in Willow River full-time before we get this planned."

Where she belongs.

Maverick calls out, "Cannonball," and the conversation shifts. We spend the next hour laughing, cutting up, and taking turns on the rope swing. It's a great night and I realize I've missed this. Missed my brothers, and our time, but I'm just as excited for the ladies and kids to join us.

Chapter 12

Jordyn

As I sit here at the kitchen table, trying to force myself to eat, my heart is heavy. It's been two weeks since I've seen Ryder. He was camping with his brothers and dad last weekend, and I miss him. We had plans to get together tonight, meeting at the movie theater again, but a big storm rolled through last night and knocked out the power. We, of course, have a home generator system, so it hasn't affected us, but half of Atlanta is still without power, which means Ryder is going to be working well into the night. As a lineman, he can work crazy hours when storms wreak havoc.

So, yeah, I'm missing him, but I understand. I'm proud of him and the hard labor that he does. Ryder has busted his ass for everything he has, and he loves his job. It's dangerous, and I worry constantly, especially on nights like last night when he was out in the mess of a storm. I slept with my phone, and he kept me updated, which made knowing he was out there in the thick of things easier to swallow.

What's worse is that I had to leave my phone, the extra one, upstairs because I couldn't risk my mother finding out about it. Speaking of my mother, she strolls into the kitchen and curls her lip at me.

"Really, Jordyn? I thought I told the staff to clear out all of that junk?"

The staff... does she even know their names? Probably not. Something like that is beneath her.

I shrug. "I went to the store yesterday." Luckily, I was able to get there and back before the worst of the storm hit.

"That stuff is going to go straight to your hips. Can you at least hold off until I get you married off to a decent man at your father's firm?"

"Nope," I say, picking up my bowl and slurping the milk to piss her off. I don't normally do that, to be honest, I'm not a huge fan of milk unless it's chocolate, but I can eat it with my cereal. Drinking it from the bowl after finishing my cereal is not my jam, but from the horrified look on my mother's face... totally worth it.

"What on earth has gotten into you?"

"This is me." I shrug. I'm not going to pretend to be her perfect clone for one more day. I've been looking for jobs close to Willow River. Not that I can actually start, but I want to know what's out there that might interest me. Fashion design is not it. I love clothes, but I know that I don't want to be involved in designing them. Before I left for Paris, I thought I'd like to open my own boutique. Maybe, if this all works out, if I get to stay in Willow River with Ryder, I can do that. A small shop that I'd be able to bring my kids to work with me. I have to bite down on the inside of my cheek to keep from smiling at the idea.

"This is not the daughter I raised."

"No, it's the person I am on my own. Can you really say you raised me? I spent more time with my nanny and then holed up in my room than with you or Father."

"That's enough." She raises her voice, and her face turns as red as a tomato. "I will not let you talk to me like that. You're on thin ice, little girl."

I ignore her. I can take her threats and hateful stares as long as they are only trained on me. I finish slurping my milk and decide to go for gold by wiping my mouth on the back of my arm.

"Use a damn napkin." She tosses a cloth napkin at me.

"I'm all set. Thanks." I smile at her. I can practically see the smoke coming out of her ears.

"I'm going out of town for the weekend. What will you be doing?"

I shrug. "I'll probably call Gianna and see if she wants to hang out."

"Fine." Mother nods. She's not Gianna's biggest fan, but she doesn't see her as a threat, either. "I'll be home Sunday night."

"Father?"

"I'm not his keeper, Jordyn. Your father is a busy man."

Translation in Margaret Astor language: I don't give a fuck where your father will be. I'm only worried about myself.

Without another word, she nods to one of the staff who stands next to her holding her bags, and they disappear. I quickly rinse my bowl and place it in the dishwasher. We have a housekeeper for that, but I'm perfectly capable of doing it on my own. I move toward the hallway and watch as my mother slides into the back seat of the SUV.

I wait until I can no longer see it before making my way up to my room. I close and lock my bedroom door just in case, then rush to my nightstand and dig around for my phone and see I have a message from Ryder.

Ryder:	*Just checking in, sweets. It's going to be a long one. Missing you. I'm sorry I had to bail on our plans.*
Me:	*You've said that already, and you have nothing to be sorry for. This is your job, Ryder. This is who are you, and I love you for all that you are. I miss you too.*
Ryder:	*I'll make it up to you.*
Me:	*All I want is for you to stay safe.*
Ryder:	*Always, sweets.*

It's just after nine in the morning and I'm already bored out of my mind. Phone in hand, I make my way into my en suite bathroom and start a bath. I might as well spend some time practicing self-care. It's been a while since I indulged in a long, hot bath. Going back to my nightstand, I grab my Kindle, thankful that it's waterproof, and take it back to the bathroom with me.

I'll get lost in the spicy rom-com I'm reading from Rebel Shaw while I'll soak in the tub and wait for my next update from Ryder.

The sun is setting by the time I pull into the lot of Gianna's condo. She doesn't know I'm coming over. I probably should have called first, but I know my bestie, and she's not going to be upset that I just dropped by unannounced. Well, I mean, she could be in a compromising position with Calvin. Shit, I should have thought about that. Oh, well, I'm here now. Grabbing both phones, my purse, and keys, I climb out of the car and make my way to her front door.

I knock and wait for her to come to the door. When it opens, I see the surprise on her face. "Jordyn. Hey. Is everything okay?"

"Yes." I nod as well because, for some reason, I'm nervous. "I came to ask for a favor."

"Anything. Come on in." She steps back, and I head inside, leaving enough room for her to shut the door. "We just ordered pizza. Are you hungry?"

Starving, but that's not why I'm here. "I'm good. Thank you."

"What's going on, Jordyn?"

Reaching into my purse, I pull out my phone, the one I know my mother tracks. "I was hoping you could keep this for me for tonight, maybe the rest of the weekend. I don't think she'll message since she's out of town for the weekend, but I—" I glance at Calvin and he gives me a kind smile and a wave. "I'm embarrassed to admit this, but Ryder is out in storm for his job, and we were supposed to meet at the movies, and it's been two weeks since I've seen him. I miss him. He's not home, but he told me I can go to his place anytime, and I just—I want to be close to him without being close to him, if that makes any sense. I'm rambling. This was a stupid idea." I drop my phone back into my bag.

"It's not a stupid idea," Gianna says soothingly. "You miss him. I get it."

Calvin stands and walks toward me. When he gets close, he pulls me into a hug. "I know I'm not Ryder, but I thought you could use a hug."

Tears prick my eyes. "Thank you," I say, hugging him back. I feel another set of arms around us, and I laugh as Gianna joins us.

"You two can't leave me out," she says, and I hear the emotion in her voice. She's finally found her a good one. A man like Ryder, who is supportive of rambling best friends who show up asking for ridiculous help to deceive her mother just to be able to sneak off and be next to her boyfriend's things while he's working.

"I needed that," I say, pulling out of their embrace and wiping at my eyes.

"Come sit." Gianna takes me by the hand and leads me to the couch. "Now, tell me what's going on."

"Ryder and I were supposed to get together at the movie theater tonight. The storm knocked out the power, as you know, and he's working, getting everyone back on the grid. By the way, how do you have power?" I tilt my head to the side.

"The building has a generator. It's one of the reasons I signed the lease." She smiles. "And thankfully the east side of town is also up and running. Should we thank Ryder for that?" she jokes.

"Nice, and probably." I chuckle. "Anyway, Ryder keeps telling me that if I miss him or need to get away to go to his place. I know the code to the garage, and well, I miss him, so I thought maybe I'd go to his place. Maybe clean, do some laundry, and just—be around his space. It's stupid."

"It's not," Calvin speaks up. "From a man's perspective, if my girl"—he flashes his eyes to Gianna—"missed me, and did that, not for the cleaning and laundry, but just to be close to me?" He nods, tapping his hand over his chest. "That shit hits you here, J." He smiles. "If Ryder told you it was okay, then he means it. If that's what you need to get through this night without him, then go." He reaches over and pulls Gianna onto his lap. "We'd love to have you, but I think your heart is telling you something else."

"Thanks, Calvin. I needed to hear that."

"Jordyn, you have to stop second-guessing. He forgave you. We all did. You were in an impossible situation. Ryder loves you. Go with your gut."

I nod, then reach into my purse and pull out my phone. "She's out of town, but I'm sure she's still going to track me like the control freak that she is. Can I leave this here?"

"You know it." Gianna takes the phone from my hand. "I hate that you have to do this, but I'm always down to help my bestie. You still have the other phone?"

"I do. You can call or text if she messages, which I don't expect her to. As long as she thinks that she knows where I am, she won't bother."

"Either way, I got you. We have no plans this weekend."

"Staying in," Calvin says, sliding his hand around her waist. "We have plans to stay in."

"Which is perfect." I smile at him. "My car won't be here, but I don't think she's having me followed." Honestly, I'm sick and tired of worrying about it. I don't want her to know where I am for fear of what she would do to Ryder and his family, but sneaking around like a damn teenager... I'm over it.

"Take my Jeep," Calvin offers.

"What?" My mouth hangs open as I try to process what he just suggested.

"Take my Jeep. We're in for the weekend and if we do go out, we'll take G's car." He reaches over to the side table and grabs his keys, tossing them to me. Thankfully, I snap out of my stupor and catch them.

"I doubt she's following me. She didn't find out about the last trip."

"Take my Jeep," Calvin says again.

"That's too much. It's bad enough you have to hold on to my phone, keep it charged, and watch for messages from the she-devil."

"It's fine. We have no plans."

"Jordyn." Gianna waits until I look up at her. "You have a shit family. Let the one who chose you, help you. Cal wouldn't have offered if he wasn't okay with it. Stop punishing yourself and let yourself be happy. Take the wins where you can get them. Today's win is the keys in your hand. Go to Willow River, even with Ryder not there. I know that's where your heart is."

I nod. "I love you."

"Hey, now, don't be hitting on my girl," Calvin teases.

"I love you both." I stand, hug them, and thank Calvin several more times before I make it out of the door. I transfer my overnight bag into the Jeep, lock my car, the keys already on the coffee table in Gianna's apartment.

I point the Jeep toward Willow River and with each passing mile, I feel the stress, the worry, and the ache from missing Ryder slip away.

I feel like I'm heading home.

Thanks to the internet, I found a recipe for roast, potatoes, and carrots in the Crock-Pot. I thought it would be something that Ryder could eat for a few days. I might have to put it in the freezer if he doesn't make it home before I leave on Sunday, but that's okay. I'll know he's being fed.

Last night, I stopped at the store, stocked up on his favorites, got everything I needed for the recipe online, some brownies, and everything else I would need to stay hunkered down for the weekend. Part of me thinks I should tell someone I'm here. I was planning to tell Ryder, but he only texted last night. He said they were in the thick of things and he'd call me today.

That call never came. Instead, it was a text message that said they worked until late in the night, then took a small break for food, and a few hours' sleep, and got back up early to hit it again today. Apparently, his crew, and I'm sure the others, are eager to get everyone back on the grid so they can head home. That's all a part of being a lineman. When the power goes down, these men and women work around the clock to get everyone back up and on the grid.

It's now after eight Saturday night, and the house smells divine. I've scrubbed every room from top to bottom and done all of his laundry. I even cleaned the fridge. I miss him, but being here in his space helps. I haven't talked to Ryder today—well, not more than a few text messages—but that's okay. He's busy, and I didn't tell him I was here because I don't want him to feel guilty that I needed him, needed to be near him and he's not home.

I know he won't be mad, but he will be disappointed. I never want to disappoint Ryder again, not as long as I live. I have so much making up to do. Once this is all worked out, and we can be together without sneaking around like kids, I'm going to make it my life's mission to make up for all the pain I've caused him. His family too. I know the Kincaid family well enough to understand that if one of them hurts, they all hurt.

I packed up the roast and placed it in single-serve containers that I bought at the store, so that Ryder can just grab a meal and heat it up. It probably sounds odd, but I've enjoyed being here. I've enjoyed doing these things for him. He works so hard, and although it's small, it's something I'm able to do for him. It's a start to show him what he means to me, and start chipping away at that "I owe you" list.

Not that I need to do either. He knows that I love him. He also says he's forgiven me for leaving the way I did, but it's my heart that needs to do this. In a way it's healing for me. I know it sounds crazy, but I feel as though I need to do more than explain and say I'm sorry. I guess I'm doing it more for me than I am for Ryder.

There isn't a single doubt in my mind that he loves me. When I really think about it, I guess it's to show him with actions that he's the love of my life and we're in this together. For two years Ryder fought for us. He never gave up, and now it's my turn to do that as well.

It's us against the world.

I'm in his bed watching TV. All the lights are off in the house because I don't want his family to drive by and see someone here. I'm certain they know he's out in the storm right now, so yeah, that would be bad. I'm actually shocked none of them have stopped by to check on things. Maybe Ryder has assured them it's not necessary. Either way, luck is in my favor. I'm not ready to face his family. Sure, I saw the twins, but they left after a quick hello. I need to have my apology ready, and if I'm being honest, I've been rehearsing it for weeks. I also need to thank them for being there for Ryder when I couldn't be.

Ryder is my life.

I need their acceptance. Even more so, I want it. I want to be a part of their world. I got a small taste of it before I left, and I want more. I want to pave my own way in life, and I want to do that here in Willow River with Ryder. My heart races at the thought of forever here in this sleepy little town with the man I love.

A girl can dream.

My belly is full, and I made brownies earlier. I have one on a small plate next to the bed, with a bottle of water. I have yet to eat it. I'm too damn comfortable to move. Ryder's bed is made of clouds. Then again, maybe it's just because his scent surrounds me. Either way, I feel myself drifting off to sleep, and I don't fight it.

Not here, surrounded by him.

I let sleep claim me.

Chapter 13

Ryder

I'm fucking exhausted. It's after two when I pull into my driveway. I hate that I didn't get to talk to Jordyn today, and that I missed our time together this weekend, but that's the job of a lineman.

I'm not the only man who missed out on family time to do my job. I don't bother pulling my truck in the garage. I have all my clothes to take inside tomorrow and wash, on top of the huge mountain of laundry sitting in the bottom of the closet in my bedroom and bathroom. I'll deal with all of it tomorrow. Right now, I need a shower and sleep.

I'm tempted to text Jordyn so she'll see it first thing, but I don't want to risk waking her up. I'm certain she's already asleep.

As soon as I push open the front door, a delicious smell hits me. I smile, thinking that either my mother or one of my sisters-in-law brought over food. It's weird because it smells like it was made here. Hell, maybe it was. My family has full access to my house at any time. I have the same with theirs.

Making my way into the kitchen, I pull open the fridge and see a stack of containers that I'm pretty damn sure are not mine. I grab one and pull off the lid. My mouth waters when I see roast, potatoes, and carrots. I thought all I wanted was a shower and sleep, but this home-cooked meal is calling to me.

In the dark, with only the moonlight lighting my way, I pop it into the microwave and pull it out before it beeps. I'll eat it half cold at this point. I just want some food in my belly, that hot shower I've been dreaming about, and my bed.

I scarf down the food, then place the dirty container in the sink where I can deal with it tomorrow. Shuffling down the hall, I push open my bedroom door and immediately freeze. I blink hard once, twice, three times, making sure my mind's not playing tricks on me.

The moonlight shines in through the blinds, and lying in my bed, with her hair splayed out on the pillow, is Jordyn. She's sound asleep, clutching my pillow to her chest. I'm not gonna lie. My throat swells with emotion. I've fucking missed her so much, and I hated canceling on her last night.

But my girl, she's here. She's where she belongs—safe in our bed. I told her if she needed me to come here anytime. I don't know how she got away, but she's here, and all I want to do is curl my body around hers and sleep for a week.

Okay, maybe I want to do more than that, but I need a solid eight hours to recharge before I can even think about ravishing her like she deserves to be ravished. And a shower. My rank ass can't slide into bed next to her, smelling like sweat.

Slipping back out of the room, I make my way down the hall to the second bathroom. It's a guest bathroom, but it still has everything I'll need since my brothers use it when they stay over. They don't do that as often now that all but the twins and me are married, but I'll forever keep it stocked for them.

That's what brothers do.

As quietly as I can, I close the door and rush through a shower. It's probably the quickest of my life. I have a bed and my girl as motivation. Right now I want them both in equal measure. That's saying something for how exhausted I am. I never imagined I'd ever want anything as much as I want Jordyn.

Shutting off the light, I walk my naked ass back to my bedroom. I'm light on my feet, careful not to wake her. However, as I reach my side of the bed and slide beneath the covers next to her, she bolts up in bed and clutches her hand to her chest.

"Ry?"

"Yeah, sweets, it's me." I pull her back down and into my arms. "I'm sorry I woke you."

"I would have been mad if you didn't."

"I was trying to be quiet."

She turns over so that we're lying face-to-face. She runs her fingers through my wet hair. "I'm sure you're drained."

"I was until I saw this beauty in my bed. I thought I was imagining you. I had to blink a few times to make sure my eyes weren't playing tricks on me."

She giggles softly, and my heart squeezes in my chest. I want to live the rest of my life making this woman happy.

"Are you hungry? I made a roast."

"That was you? I smelled it as soon as I walked into the house. I ate some already. It was delicious." I lean in for a kiss. "Thank you. You didn't have to do that."

"I wanted to do something nice for you." She runs her hands over my bare chest. "Is it okay that I'm here?"

"Yes. Always. Think of this as your home, Jordyn."

"I cleaned and did some laundry and bought some groceries. Just trying to stay busy while missing you."

"You're spoiling me, sweets."

"Good. I have a lot of time to make up for."

"No." My voice is firm, more than it needs to be, but I need her to understand. "Stop with that. Please," I say, softening my tone. "You had good intentions, and that's all in the past."

"We're still dealing with it."

"In the present." I lean in and kiss her again, sliding my hand behind her neck and guiding her lips to mine. I kiss her like I've been dying to do since the last time I laid eyes on her.

When I have to come up for air, I let my hands roam over her body. She's wearing one of my T-shirts, and fuck me, my cock turns hard as steel.

"The guilt is a heavy burden that rests on my chest. Maybe it's because we're still battling my mother, even though she doesn't know. I'm being pulled in two different directions, and it's hard to let everything stay in the past when I'm living it."

My hand rests on the small of her back, and I pull her closer. "You can't let the guilt eat at you. Think about this, what if our roles were reversed? How would you feel if I kept apologizing when you've already forgiven me?"

She nods. "I know. I'll do better." There's just enough moonlight for me to see her bite down on her bottom lip. "I've been being me more."

"Explain that, sweets."

"With my mother. I've been eating food she tells the staff to throw out. I just buy more, like cereal and cookies. I'm not letting her walk all over me anymore."

"I'm proud of you, baby, but I need you to be careful." Panic wells in my chest when I think about her mother hurting her, more than she already has. "I need you to do what you have to do to keep the peace until this is over."

"I'm hoping she'll disown me like she threatened to do with Jeremy. Then, I can do whatever I want. I can live for me, and for my big brother who never got the chance to break free."

"I don't want you to hurt," I whisper. Even saying the words guts me. I hate thinking about her being so far away for two long years, constantly worrying about me and my family. There was no one there to offer her comfort or support. My girl did what she felt she had to do. I love her for what she did. Do I wish she would have talked to me? Absolutely, but we can't change our past, yet we can mold our future.

My future is with her.

"I hurt every day I'm not with you, Ryder. I've lived through thinking I'd never be with you again. Now, here we are, and I'm fighting for that. For me. For us. I'll fight until I can't anymore."

Her words reach inside my chest and wrap around my heart like a fist.

Rolling to my back, I pull her so she's lying on top of me. My cock is thick and demanding where it's nestled between her thighs. Just like that, my exhaustion slips away. I'm still tired, but I'll never be too tired for her. I know she's going to have to go home tomorrow. I don't know what time, and I don't want to ask. I want this moment with her without that knowledge hanging over my head.

Speaking of her thighs, I run my fingers over her silky-smooth skin. My fingers find their way beneath her panties, and she's ready for me. "Always so wet for me," I rasp.

"Only you."

"Are we attached to these?" I ask, pulling at the waistband of her panties.

"My panties? Uh, no, why?"

I rip one side, then the other. She gasps, but I ignore it and tap her on the ass. "Lift for me, sweets." Like my good girl, she rises on her knees and allows me to toss the now-ruined panties to the floor. "Shirt off, baby."

She immediately complies, lifting the shirt over her head, and tossing it to the side.

"I liked that one. I slept in it last night too."

"You can have it. You already have all of me, Jordyn. What's mine is yours." None of it means anything without her.

"This too?" She grips my cock.

"All of me."

Lifting on her knees, she guides me to her entrance. She takes her time slowly sinking down on my cock. She's hot, wet, and so fucking tight. I have to stiffen my body to fight off the urge to thrust inside of her.

"Let me take care of you for a change," she whispers, leaning over and pressing her lips to mine.

"You always take care of me." I sound like a sappy tool, but fuck me, I'm exhausted, and my girl is here after I haven't seen her for two long weeks. And after a never-ending shift at work, I've earned the right to be a little sappy.

"I'm so full," she murmurs, tilting her head back.

Her long hair hangs down her back, and I can't help but bury my fist in it, giving it a little tug. She moans, so I do it again, and her pussy pulses around my cock.

"I feel you, sweets." I lift my hips as she widens her legs, and I'm buried inside her as far as I can go. "Fuck, that feels good."

"Mm-hmm," she agrees. She rocks her hips, and I grip her waist, needing something to hold on to. Something to ground me because I'm seconds away from flipping us over and taking control.

"Ryder."

"Tell me what you need, baby."

"More. Harder, faster—just more."

Fuck yes.

I move with lightning speed I didn't know I was capable of considering how tired I am, flipping Jordyn on her back. Her legs are locked tight around my waist, and her hands are clasped behind my neck.

"I need you to hold on tight. Move your arms under mine and grip my back. I want to feel your nails biting into my skin."

"I don't want to hurt you."

"Sweets, it will hurt if you don't. I need to fuck you, Jordyn. I need it hard and rough, and I want you to hold on. I don't care what that looks like. Mark me with your nails, bite, scream. Whatever you need, this is going to be fast and dirty."

Her pussy squeezes me, and I kiss the tip of her nose.

"I'm going to fuck you, but I'm still making love to you. It will never be anything but love between us."

"I'm here, Ryder. I'm yours, and I want this. I want you. I want you to lose control and give me everything. You have all of me." She moves her hands to rest on my cheeks. "Fuck me, Ry."

"Yes, ma'am." Pulling out, I thrust back in and allow myself to get lost in her. Her nails dig into my back as my thrusts grow harder and faster.

"Yes. Yes. Yes," she repeats over and over.

"Touch yourself." My voice is gravelly and winded as I continue to thrust my hips. The words are barely out of my mouth when her pussy grips my cock like a vise, and she screams out my name.

Fuck me, it feels incredible. I should tell her so, but right now, it's taking all of my brain power to focus on chasing my release.

That familiar tingle starts at the base of my spine. With one more thrust of my hips, I still as I come inside her.

Not for the first time, the thought of her growing round with our baby hits me like a load of bricks to the chest.

Leaning down, I capture her lips with mine, and she tangles her hands in my hair. I hold my weight off her as long as I can, but I'm physically drained. Easing the kiss, I force myself to pull away from her and climb off the bed.

"I'll be right back."

I feel her behind me when I enter the bathroom. "Ry, you're exhausted. Let me help you."

I turn to face her, leaning back against one side of the double vanity. My eyes trace her every movement as she reaches into the closet, pulls out a washcloth, and waits for the water to warm. With shaking hands, she runs the cloth under the water, wrings out the excess, and steps in front of me. She drops to her knees and gets to work cleaning me up.

"The cleanup was going to be for you, sweets." My cock stirs, and fuck me, I don't know how since I'm spent. That's the effect Jordyn has on me.

Ignoring me, she takes her time, and when she stands, I pull her into a kiss.

"Go lie down. I'm going to cleanup and be right there."

"Let me," I offer.

"Not this time, Ry. Go. I'll be right there." She kisses my cheek, and I'm so damn tired, I listen to her. I take a mental note to make it up to her next time.

A few minutes later, she's climbing into bed and snuggling up next to me. I hold her close and breathe her in. She smells like her, like me, and sex. The perfect combination.

I close my eyes and feel my body start to relax. However, there's still one question I have to ask. "What time do you have to leave tomorrow?"

"Probably early. I don't know what time my mom is going to be back, and I need to get Calvin's Jeep back to him."

"Calvin's Jeep?"

"Yeah." She goes on to tell me of how she ended up here, and why she's driving Calvin's Jeep.

"Remind me to thank him."

"Right? Babysitting for life when the time comes."

"Yeah, we can do that. Our kids can play together."

She's quiet, and I settle back in. I'm almost asleep when I hear her whisper, "I love you so much, Ryder. I want nothing more than to live this life with you."

I don't know if I reply. I want to, but I'm so damn exhausted. I don't think I do. Just something else I'll make up for tomorrow. I'll get a few hours of sleep, wake up, make love to her, then cook her breakfast in bed before she has to go back to Atlanta.

I'm really looking forward to the day when she never has to leave.

Jordyn

I'm lying in bed texting Ryder when my bedroom door bursts open. I rush to slide my arms under the covers as I stare at my mother.

"Knock much?" I ask, leaving the phone beside me beneath the covers, and sit up.

"Seriously, Jordyn. Can you not find something better to do with your time than lie around in bed like a lazy bum?"

"Well, you've instructed me not to look for employment. You're in charge, Mother. I'm just being the dutiful daughter, waiting for your next instruction." I don't bother to hide the annoyance in my tone. She walked in on me looking online for jobs a couple of weeks ago and threw a fit, well, as much of a fit she can manage in her snooty way that only she can pull off.

I know why she doesn't want me working. Her excuse was, I just got home after being abroad for two years. I needed time to acclimate to society. It's complete and utter bullshit. She wants to marry me off, and she thinks me wanting an escape from her, from this house, will make me more amendable.

She's wrong.

Unless Ryder is the one standing at the end of the aisle waiting on me, I won't be walking. Not in this lifetime, and I'd like to believe not in the next either. Our love is that powerful. We've battled so much to be together, and no way will I tarnish that by marrying another man to appease my mother.

I'll disappear first.

I know I need to step up my game. I know that being snarky and eating junk food isn't enough to push her over the edge. The thing is, I want to stand up to her, but I'm also scared as hell of what she's capable of.

She ignores me and pushes forward with the reason she barged into my room. I take a mental note to be sure to lock my door at all times moving forward.

"We're having dinner tonight. A family dinner."

"Right." I laugh humorlessly.

"Your father works extremely hard for this family. He's coming home and we will sit together and share a meal. End of discussion."

"Fine." I fight the urge to roll my eyes. My father is the man who lets my mother do whatever the hell she pleases. He didn't fight her on her choices that killed my brother and for that, he will always be in the villain column, just like my mother. He was never around growing up, and he's still not. He's strictly my sperm donor, at this point. I feel no love or connection to either of them. They burned that bridge years ago.

"I expect you to be dinner appropriate," she sneers, eyeing the T-shirt I'm wearing.

"Yes, Mother," I say sarcastically.

"And, Jordyn, leave your attitude in here." She glares at me before turning on her heel and walking out of the room, not bothering to shut the door behind her.

I'm fuming because Ryder and I were supposed to meet up at the movie theater tonight. Another failed attempt at seeing each other. This is getting old. I'm an adult, and my mother is ruling my life.

Standing, I stalk toward my bedroom door and slam it hard. The sound rattles the walls. Turning the lock, I rush back to my bed, dig under the covers for my secret phone, and text Ryder.

Me: *My mom's demanding a family dinner.*

Ryder: *When?*

Me: *Tonight.*

Ryder: *Can we meet after?*

Me: *I don't know. Apparently, my father is going to be there, and my presence is required.*

Ryder: *I can sense the sarcasm, sweets. Keep me posted, and I'll do whatever. I'll come to Atlanta anyway and be close in case you need me.*

Me: *That might be a wasted trip. I hate for you to do that.*

Ryder: *Not a wasted trip if there's a chance I get to see my girl.*

Me: *Anything from the PI?*

Ryder: *No. Nothing. If your mother did anything shady, she's covered her tracks, and your father is squeaky clean as well.*

> **Ryder:**   *These things take time.*
>
> **Me:**   *I don't know how much longer I can live like this. Let her control me.*
>
> **Ryder:**   *Are you safe, baby?*
>
> **Me:**   *I'm safe and annoyed.*
>
> **Ryder:**   *Can I call you?*
>
> **Me:**   *Give me a minute.*

Jumping from the bed, I race to the bathroom and turn on the shower before hitting his name.

"Hey, sweets."

"Hi." Just the sound of his voice eases some of the turmoil that's raging inside me.

"You're safe?"

"I am. She's not hurting me, just being a raging bitch."

"That hurts too, sweets." His tone is gentle, and if I thought it were possible, I'd say I just fell a little more in love with him for his concern and understanding.

"If that changes, we get you out."

"She's irritated with me. I've been talking back and refusing to be her puppet. As long as I don't step too far out of line, I'll be fine." Though I do seriously dream of her being frustrated enough that she'll kick me out.

"We know what she's capable of, Jordyn."

"Yeah, but as of right now, she thinks I'm playing her game," I remind him.

"I know you want to fight for us, baby, but please be safe. Don't piss her off too badly. Not until we have a better handle on things and know what we can use against her to break you free from her."

"Thank you for sticking with me. For staying by my side through all of this. I was scared that night when you knocked on my hotel door. I was certain that would be the last time I ever saw you, yet you're still here."

"Always, sweets. Now, I hear the shower running. Take care of you. Do what your mother asks for now, and I'll be in Atlanta in case you can get away. If not, it's okay. I don't want you feeling guilty. I'd do anything for five minutes with you. An hour's drive is nothing."

"I'll see what I can do."

"Text or call when you can."

"I will."

"Love you, sweets."

"Love you too." The call ends, and I shove my phone into the bottom of a vanity drawer. Not that I expect my mother to come in while I'm showering, but it's not worth the risk. That phone is my connection to the man I love, and I'll protect it, him, and his family at all costs. I just hope the price isn't too high.

I spent the day locked in my room like a moody-ass teenager. My mother didn't grace me with her presence again, not that I expected her to. She issued her demand and to her, that's good enough. I took a long, hot shower, napped, and then took another shower because my hair was a hot mess from falling asleep on it wet. I debated trying to make it work, but Ryder's right. I can be mouthy, but I don't want to push my mother too far.

I know what she's capable of.

My heart squeezes in my chest when I think about my older brother. I miss him something fierce. I hate how he was just wiped from our lives. One day he was here, and gone the next. Suddenly, the pictures are gone, and I'm not allowed to talk about him or acknowledge that I miss him. He was older than me, but I still feel as though a piece of me is missing. I didn't really understand the feeling until I met Ryder. There is twelve years between him and his oldest brother Orrin, but they still have that sibling bond.

Shaking out of my thoughts, I take one last look in the mirror. My hair is pulled up in a French twist, and the little black dress I chose is a classic. I forgo heels and instead slip my feet into a pair of black flats. With a heavy sigh, I turn off the light and make my way downstairs. I'm ready to get this night over with, and if I'm lucky, I can go out after and see Ryder.

As I descend the stairs, I hear voices. One is my father. His deep baritone is not hard to miss. A cackle of laughter that causes chills to race down my spine is my mother. Her laugh is the equivalent of nails on a chalkboard.

There are others. Male voices that I don't recognize, and something that feels an awful lot like a knife twisting in my chest stops me. I breathe through the disappointment. How naïve of me to assume this was a true family dinner. Squaring my shoulders, I steel my resolve and step into the dining room.

"There she is, my little girl." My father boasts a smile as he greets me.

All eyes turn my way, and I smile politely and give a small wave. "Father." I stride over to where he sits at the head of the table and kiss his offered cheek. That's what's expected of me, after all. It's been ages since the man has spoken to me, yet here, in front of his guests, he wants to be the doting father.

It makes me sick, but I swallow down the bile that rises in my throat. "Mother." I smile, as I've been trained to do, just like a puppy. I move to take the seat next to my mother, but she shakes her head, and that's when I go on full alert.

"Your usual seat is fine, dear," she tells me.

Dear? Looks like mother is really laying it on thick tonight. I wonder if the two of them plan their attacks on me before they happen. I glance across the table where I normally sit. The seat is occupied, the one next to it is open, and then the one next to it is occupied. I'm not stupid. I can read between the lines. My mother wants me seated between these two unknown gentlemen.

That's when it hits me.

This is a setup.

My stomach rolls. All I want to do is run away. I want to run to Ryder and stay in his arms for an eternity. Knowing if I cause a scene, there will be hell to pay, I play nice. With a nod to my mother, I step back around the table to take my seat. The guy sitting closest to my dad rises and pulls my chair out for me.

"Thank you," I mumble, trying to be polite. It's not his fault my parents are hateful monsters. I take my seat and place my hands on my lap like the good little daughter they're expecting me to be.

"John, Mike, this is my daughter, Jordyn. She just came back from two years abroad for fashion design."

John, the one who pulled my chair out for me, turns to face me and smiles. "Nice to meet you." He offers me his hand, and I hesitate before taking it and returning the sentiment, even though I don't mean a damn word of it.

"I'm Mike," the other one says, pulling my attention. I turn to face him, and he winks, offering me his hand.

Slimy bastard.

"Nice to meet you, Jordyn. Marvin, you failed to mention how beautiful your daughter is."

"She is lovely, isn't she?" My mother smiles, and I swear even I almost believe this "proud mom" thing she's trying to portray.

Almost. I still know the evil, cold-hearted woman who lives beneath the fake veil of happiness.

Thankfully, our salads are served, and the conversation turns to lawyer talk. I make out that both John and Mike work for my father. Not that I needed their conversation to confirm that. My mother has been very vocal about wanting me to meet a nice lawyer who my father can one day pass the family firm to when he retires.

Dinner drags on. I'm completely ignored. I'm used to it, but tonight it's putting me on edge. I know there's a catch. No way would my mother orchestrate this dinner, and all I have to do it sit through it.

I'm waiting for the other shoe to drop.

Once our dessert plates are removed, my mother's plan is revealed. "Jordyn, why don't you take John and Mike to the formal sitting room and have a chat?"

Fuck you.

Lifting my napkin to my mouth, I wipe gently, and place it on the table, before scooting my chair back and standing. "Of course." The words taste like sandpaper on my tongue.

John and Mike are quick to stand and follow me down the hall and into the formal sitting room of this giant-ass house that is far too large for just three people. Hell, it's not too small for ten people.

"So, fashion?" Mike asks.

I nod. "Yes." I'm not giving them an inch so they can assume they can take a mile. My heart isn't up for grabs, and neither is my body.

"What do you plan to do now that you're home?"

Move to Willow River, marry Ryder, have some babies, and live happily ever after.

"I'd like to open my own boutique." It's not a lie. I would like a small boutique. I don't like the cutthroat business of fashion. My mother encouraged my degree. Claiming that when I'm married, the knowledge would come in handy for charity balls. She goes along with my boutique spiel because she thinks that's never going to happen.

"That's going to be hard, raising a family, and taking over your mother's charity work, while running a boutique." Mike laughs.

"And what makes you think I want to be married, have a family, or take over my mother's charity work?"

"I assumed," Mike says.

I glare at him, and he just shrugs, not the least bit worried that he offended me.

"You didn't know we were coming tonight, did you?" John asks.

"Nope."

He nods. "I guess you don't know about the partner position that we're both up for either?" he offers.

"You'd be right again," I tell him. "So, what? One of you catches my attention and you get the promotion?"

Mike shrugs. "It was implied, but nothing was concrete."

"I'll save you the trouble. Neither of you."

"Oh, it will be one of us," Mike speaks up.

I ignore him, fighting back tears. If I thought I hated my mother before tonight, I don't know what the next step from hate would be, but I feel it right now. The three of us sit in silence. Finally, my father steps into the room.

"How about a drink in my home office?" It's posed as a question, but it's not one. He doesn't wait for either guy to reply. He knows that they'll follow him without question. They are willing to do whatever they need to do to get to the top.

I heave a sigh of relief and slump into my chair. This is so fucked up. We have to do something. That PI needs to dig deeper, hire more help. I don't know, but I can't keep living like this. I can't keep being a pawn in this game.

It's my life.

"Which one?" She doesn't bother explaining what she means. She knows I've figured out what tonight was all about.

I look up to find my mother standing in the doorway. "Neither."

She smiles. "Pick one, Jordyn, or I'll do it for you."

"I don't want to marry someone I don't know."

"I'll choose for you."

"I'm surprised you're even giving me a choice. There is nothing in my life that I've chosen for myself."

"That's not true. I'm allowing you to be friends with Gianna when we both know that she's beneath you."

"Do you hear yourself? Do you care that you're tearing down good people? Gianna is one of the nicest, most loyal people I've ever met."

Mother tosses her head back in laughter. "Loyalty? Come on, Jordyn, I raised you better than that. Life isn't about loyalty. Life is about getting to the top and staying there. You are an Astor, and the man you marry will take over the firm when your father finally pulls himself away from his work. You will rise to the top, and you are expected to represent this family as you've been trained to do."

"You can't make me."

"Oh, I believe I can. You see, I know you still care about that Kincaid man. I still have my files on his family, on him. You will do as I say, or I'll make sure they're all ruined."

"I ended this with him. You promised to leave them alone."

"I did no such thing. I don't make promises I can't keep, Jordyn, but let me say this. If you defy me, if you choose to make this arrangement difficult, I promise you, the Kincaid family will fall. Not just them, but anyone connected to them. That's a promise." She smirks. "Decide, Jordyn. You want some control over your life, or to pretend like you do, so decide. Mike or John? If you don't decide, I'll do it for you." With that, she turns on her heel and walks away.

I rush upstairs, tear out of my clothes, throwing on shorts and a T-shirt. I grab my keys, my purse, both phones, and rush out the door.

I need Ryder.

I tear out of the driveway and wait until I'm several miles away before pulling into a parking lot. My hands shake as I dig for my Ryder phone and dial his number.

"Hey, sweets."

"Ry." My voice cracks.

"Where are you?"

"Headed toward Gianna's."

"Call her. Tell her I'm going to be knocking on her door."

"Someone might see you."

"Call her, Jordyn. Let me worry about the rest. Are you okay to drive? Are you hurt?"

"Not physically."

"Make the call, baby. I'll be there when you get there." The line goes dead, and I do as he says and call Gianna.

When this all blows over, I owe my best friend one hell of a payback. When she needs me, I'll be there. No questions asked.

Chapter 15

Ryder

I was already parked at the gas station down the street from Gianna's place. Why, I don't know. Something just told me to stay close, and I'm glad I did. Pulling my truck into her lot, I park several spaces back and climb out of the truck, pulling my hat down over my eyes. I'm sure I look like a criminal, but fuck it. Jordyn needs me.

My hand is raised to knock, but the door swings open, and Gianna steps back, allowing me inside. "Thanks," I tell her.

"She should be here soon." Gianna takes a seat on the couch next to Calvin, who nods in greeting.

"I'm sorry that we're barging in on you like this. The two of you have done so much for us. Thank you. When you need me, I'm there." I make eye contact with both of them so they can see my sincerity.

"How are you doing?" Gianna asks.

I shrug. "I'm worried about her. She was crying and I don't know why. She assured me she was safe to drive, but fuck, this not being able to go to her is fucking killing me."

"Yeah, she sounded upset. The only thing I was able to get out of her was that it was her mother."

"Of fucking course it's her mother. She's not going to stop until she destroys her spirit," I spit out angrily.

Before I can say more, the door bursts open. I stand and barely have time to brace myself before a sobbing Jordyn launches into my arms. I catch her, holding her tightly. She buries her face in my neck, and I feel as though my heart is cracking wide open.

I hate seeing her upset.

Seconds, minutes, hell, hours could pass, but I'm not worried about the time, as I hold the love of my life in my arms. Eventually, she lifts her head and unwraps her legs from around my waist. I help her stand and then guide us to the chair. I sit, pulling her onto my lap.

"Tell me what's going on, sweets."

"Dinner."

I nod. "You said your mother insisted that you have a family dinner tonight. What happened?"

"It wasn't just a family dinner. There were two other guests."

"Okay?"

"Two men. They both work for my father." She goes on to tell me how she was ambushed and then sent to a room to be alone with the two of them together. My anger simmers, but I fight like hell to hide it. I don't need Jordyn thinking my anger is because of something she did. It's all for her parents, and those two jackasses who think they have a chance with my girl.

Not happening.

"She told me that I'm always complaining I have no control, so she's letting me pick one. If I don't, she and my father will choose for me."

What. The. Fuck?

"I need a few days," I tell her. "Give me a few days to get things figured out. I need to talk to my family. Pack a bag and be ready to leave." I'm already forging a plan in my mind. I'd hoped it wouldn't come to this, but I can't let her go. I can't let her marry some asshole who will use and abuse her. Fuck that. We're leaving.

Heaviness fills my chest when I think about leaving my parents, my brothers, and their families, but it's what I have to do. Maybe it won't be forever, and we can figure out a way for them to come and visit.

I squeeze Jordyn tightly and she winces, which forces me to loosen my grip.

"What are you talking about?"

Lifting one hand, I rest my palm against her cheek. "We have to go, sweets. I can't let you stay with her and force you into a marriage you don't want."

"No. Not yet. There's still time."

"Jordyn." My voice cracks. "I'm not fucking losing you again. Do you hear me, baby? Never again."

She nods, tears once again streaming down her face. "I hear you, Ry, but we have some time. Let's not make rash decisions. We have the PI looking into her background. My father's too. Something has to show up. They're evil, Ryder. They can't hide that forever."

"We still need to be ready."

"Wait. Hold up. What are you talking about? Be ready?" Gianna asks.

"Leaving. This time, if it comes to that, we'll go together." I look my girl's best friend in the eye and her shocked expression tells me she didn't expect that.

"You can't leave." Gianna sounds panicked. "There has to be another way."

"We're working on it," I assure her. "But it will be a cold day in hell before I let her mother or anyone else force her to do something she doesn't want to do. If she's marrying anyone, it's going to be me."

"Dude, did you just propose?" Calvin asks, and I laugh. It breaks the tension in the room, which I am sure was his goal.

"No, but this isn't new information for either of us. We're end game, and I'll be damned if her parents are going to stop us."

"What about the PI?" Gianna asks.

"He's searching, but nothing yet. Nothing that's illegal that we can use to blackmail either of them. They've covered their tracks well over the years."

Gianna nods, and her sad expression tells me she knows about Jeremy. Good. I'm glad Jordyn has someone to talk to that's not me. Not that I don't want to be that person for her, but it's important that she realizes there are people in her corner. She no longer has to be the puppet.

My phone rings. I ignore it, but Jordyn turns to face me. "It could be your family."

Her heart is so fucking big. How she turned out to be the incredible human being she is raised by those assholes, I'll never know. Then again, she did say that she spent most of her time with her nanny or locked away in her room.

Thank fuck she didn't turn out like them.

Shifting to pull my phone out of my pocket, I smile when I see Declan's face. I'm sure Blakely wants to talk to me. "Hey, Dec," I answer.

"What's going on?"

"Nothing. I'm in Atlanta visiting Jordyn."

"Good, put me on speaker."

"We're at her friend Gianna's."

"Trust her?"

"Yes." I don't hesitate. Gianna has helped us so much since Jordyn has been back to town.

"Put me on speaker."

"All right." I pull the phone from my ear and tap the screen. "You're on speaker, Dec. I'm here with Jordyn, her friend Gianna, and her boyfriend, Calvin."

"Hey," Declan greets everyone. "I have a crowd too. We're all here."

"All as in?"

"Everyone. I'm out in the garage, because all our brothers, their wives and kids, our parents, and my family, we're all here."

"Did I forget something?"

"No. It was impromptu, and once we started talking about it, the Kincaid family phone tree started, and well, we're all here."

"So, what's up? Is something wrong?" It's not unusual for us to get together, but this... something feels off.

"Deacon and Ramsey stopped by on their way home from Mom and Dad's. We started talking, and the conversation turned to you and Jordyn. I asked about the PI and Deacon said there was still nothing. That led to Kennedy and Ramsey being pissed that this was happening to the two of you." He pauses, and a deep chuckle flows through the line. "You know how my wife can be. She's determined as hell."

"That's all our sisters-in-law," I agree with a smile. Those ladies love just as fiercely as my brothers do.

"Right, so they started chatting, and called Palmer, Crosby, Alyssa, Jade, and Scarlett. Then they decided Mom should be here as well, and you know how we are. If our wives are going, so are we. The kids are here because everyone we use to babysit is here too. Well, except for you, that is."

"And you have a plan?" I ask. I can't help but smile. I don't care what the plan is. It's the fact that my family is rallying around us. Their support means everything.

"We have a plan. I'm going back into the house now, because the ladies want to be the ones to present it to you."

"Okay." There's shuffling, a door opening, and the quiet time is over.

"Ry?"

"I'm here?"

"Jordyn?"

She freezes in my lap and turns to look at me. I nod, encouraging her to speak up. She clears her throat. "I'm here."

"Good," Declan replies. "Who wants the floor?" he asks my family.

"Ramsey," all the ladies in the room speak up.

"Aw, I feel like I'm in high school again and being voted for prom queen." My cousin's sassy reply comes through the line. "I'll gladly explain because we are a group of fu—freaking geniuses." She clears her throat, and the room quiets down.

The fact that she can get them to all be quiet, kids too, tells me this isn't just an off-the-rails idea. No. This is "we have a plan, and we are going to do what Kincaids do, and we're going to rally."

"Okay, so, I'm sure Dec has filled you in on how this even started, but we've all talked about it, and we think we have a solid plan. This is going to work."

I can hear the smile in her voice and the conviction in her tone.

"What's going to work, Ramsey?" I ask. I'm ready to hear what they've come up with. Is it possible they've actually found a solution that won't result in me jetting off to hide in another country? It sounds extreme even to my own ears, but desperate times call for desperate measures.

"It's so easy. I think that's why we didn't think of this before."

"Are you going to tell us?" I ask my cousin.

"Right." She chuckles. "It's simple, Ry. We beat them to the punch."

"I'm confused."

"Jordyn's mom is threatening to ruin our businesses, our family name. She's holding that over your head, over Jordyn's head. Jordyn, I assume you have proof of this threat?" Ramsey asks.

"Y-Yes. I have all of her messages saved to a cloud account that's under a fake name."

"You do?" I ask Jordyn.

She nods. "I confided in one of my classmates when I was abroad, and she's a big true crime junkie. She suggested I save all the messages and threats because you never know when they might come in handy."

"Yes!" Ramsey cheers. "That's perfect."

"We expose her," Palmer chimes in. At least I think it's Palmer. My mind is a little scrambled at the moment as I try to process what they're saying.

"So, what? We release the text messages?" I ask, still trying to wrap my head around how this is going to work.

"We do, only on a much grander scale. Jordyn's family is well-known. So, I'm sure if she were to launch a video, live or recorded on her socials, and on all of ours, the word would get out. At first, we thought about going to the media, trying to get them to report on the story, but that's tricky. We don't know who she has in her pocket. We don't want her to get wind of this before it hits the public."

"That's—genius." Jordyn turns to look at me, and the smile on her face lights up the room. Her eyes are still red and puffy from crying, but they take nothing away from the effect her smile has on me. "I don't know why I didn't think of the messages before now."

"Right?" another female voice says. I think it's Kennedy, but I can't be sure. "And don't worry, you've been through a lot, and it's easy to forget something that happened a couple of years ago. I'm just glad you saved them."

"How do we do this?" I ask my family.

"We need a plan. A date where we all point our phones at the two of you and go live on our social media accounts. You tell your story, and appeal to the heartstrings of the public. I have no doubt this is going to spread like a wildfire with Jordyn's family's reputation. This is better than the blackmail because she's going to be exposed to the world. Maybe even brought to justice for her part in your brother's accident."

"Count me in," Gianna says.

"Who's that?" someone asks.

"That's Gianna. My best friend," Jordyn answers, smiling over at Gianna.

"Nice." I think that's Jade. "The more the merrier."

"Jordyn, when can you meet up?" Ramsey asks her.

"Um, I'm not sure. I left the house after a confrontation with my mother. I can try to get away next weekend. I'll need some time to gather the few items that mean something to me, the rest they can have. A small bag at most."

"Great. We'll keep brainstorming. In the meantime, gather your thoughts, make notes. When we meet, we'll help you both with what you're going to say and pick a date."

"I don't know what to say," Jordyn tells them. "I can't thank you enough for this."

"We're family," Ramsey assures her. "There's no way this won't work. She'll no longer be a threat because all eyes will be on her. No one will believe a word she says about any of us after hearing the lengths she'd go through to control Jordyn. The queen of Atlanta is about to be knocked off her high-society pedestal."

"You really think so?" I ask her.

"Yep. Think about it. We have proof. Jordyn's mother doesn't have a leg to stand on when we have it in black and white. The PI might not have been able to dig up any skeletons, but we don't need him to. Jordyn's had the best of what we need this entire time."

"I didn't even think about using them." Jordyn blows out a heavy breath. "It's so simple, but I really think it's our best option, and you're right. I think this will work." I meet her gaze and nod. The smile that I get in return lights up the entire room. This is it. We're going to tell the world about her mother's threats, and the past two years will be nothing but an afterthought.

"We do have another course of action," a male voice speaks up. "I'm an attorney."

Deacon.

"We could compile a gag order. She'll have to agree to never doing anything to the family, or we'll release what we have."

"I don't know. I kind of want to expose her. I know that sounds bad, and please don't think less of me, but she's put me through hell. Put Ryder and all of you through hell as well. I want her to pay for that." Her body is rigid as if she's worried my family is going to attack her for speaking her true feelings.

"This will ruin your relationship with your family." It's one of my sisters-in-law, but I'm not sure which one. I think it's Crosby. We really should have done a video call for this.

"I have no relationship with my family. I was raised by nannies and after my brother died...." She pauses, and I wrap my arms around her a little tighter. "After Jeremy died, it was as if I was just there. I can't ever remember getting a hug from my mother or my father. I've never told them I love them. They've never told me they love me. I have no happy memories from my childhood. If this saves the reputation of each of you, your businesses, your family, and if I get to be with Ryder, to be in the presence of each of you, I'm all in."

The room is quiet, and there is silence on the other end of the line. I hate that she's going to sever any kind of relationship with her parents. However, from what she's told me, there wasn't much of one there to begin with.

"Jordyn, it's Raymond." Dad pauses. "Welcome to the family, sweetheart."

Jordyn covers her mouth to try and stop her sobs from escaping, but it's no use. They heard them, and I feel them as her body shakes.

"It's Carol," my mom speaks up. "When you need one of those hugs, sweet girl, you come on over. I can't make up for what you missed out on, but I can promise you that I'll do my best."

"Thanks, guys," I say, my voice cracking.

"We'll let you go," Declan says, and I can tell he's taken the phone off speaker. "Take care of her, and we'll do some more brainstorming. We got you, brother. It's all going to work out."

"Love you, Dec."

"Love you too, Ry. Jordyn. We'll see you soon." The call ends and I drop my cell to the chair next to me and hold Jordyn as tightly as I can, considering the position we're in.

"Hell yes!" Gianna stands. Before I know what's happening, she's pulling Jordyn from my lap and is wrapping her in a hug.

"Sounds like we have a plan." Calvin grins from where he's casually sitting on the couch, watching as the ladies hug and cry, with blinding smiles on their faces. "Count me in for whatever you need."

"Thanks, man. I appreciate that."

"Text your mom and tell her you're not coming home. I'm going to order pizza. We're celebrating!" Gianna's smile is infectious.

Her eyes find mine and I nod and mouth, "Thank you."

She nods and gives her attention back to Jordyn. "This is it, Jordyn. You've got her, and this deserves a celebration."

"Not yet. We don't know if it will work."

"Oh, it's going to work. Ryder has an army of brothers and their wives. The social media reach is going to be out there, and we'll be sure to tag some news outlets. Even if your mother has them on her payroll, they won't be able to not report on the scandal with how big we're going to blow it up."

"Are you sure you don't want to let Deacon handle this through the law?" I ask.

"I'm certain. She doesn't deserve that kind of grace from me." Jordyn is quick to answer.

"All right then." I reach into my back pocket and pull out my wallet. Grabbing my card, I hand it to Gianna. "Let's celebrate."

"I knew I liked you." She laughs and gets to work ordering way too much food.

Jordyn texts her mother that she won't be home. A courtesy she doesn't deserve, but for the time being, it's a necessary evil.

Soon this will all be over, and I can move my girl to Willow River.

Forever here we come.

Chapter 16

Jordyn

It's been one hell of a week. I've been trying to covertly gather everything I'll need to take with me, like my passport and my birth certificate, to name a few. Turns out they are locked in the safe in my father's office. It's going to take some finesse to get them. My goal is to get them this coming week. Once I have everything, we can move forward with the plan to expose my mother.

Gianna and Calvin are going out of town this weekend. Translation: Gianna and I are going out of town this weekend. At least that's what my mother thinks. Gianna offered to keep my cell on her during their trip. That means I'm spending the next couple of days in Willow River with Ryder. We're supposed to meet with his family, and to say I'm nervous is an understatement.

It's early Friday afternoon, and I'm pulling into Ryder's driveway. I know he's still at work and won't be home until later, but Gianna and Calvin are on the road. I'd much rather be here at his place than anywhere else.

Hopping out of the car, I go to the keypad outside of the garage and type in the code. The door squeaks as it opens, and I rush back to my car to pull inside. I stopped at the store to pick up a few things to make dinner. I'm sure Ryder's going to be too exhausted after all the hours he's put in this week to go out and grab dinner. Besides, I like to cook for him. I can put all those days sitting at the kitchen island with our cook to good use.

I'm taking the last bag out of the back of my car when a car pulls into the driveway. I freeze before turning to glance over my shoulder. Ramsey waves, and I find myself lifting my hand to wave back. Her smile is wide and comforting, and I feel myself relax.

Ramsey climbs out of her car and makes her way toward me. "Hey! I didn't know you were coming home this weekend. Ryder said there was a delay."

Home.

Tears burn in the back of my throat, but I refuse to let them fall. "Hi, yeah, it was a luck kind of thing."

"Well, I'm glad. We've been brainstorming. I really think this idea is going to work, Jordyn."

"I hope so. I hate the threats that my mother has made toward your family because of me."

"Not because of you." She reaches out and takes one of the two remaining bags I'm holding from my hands. "Come on. We should chat."

Closing the back of my car, I follow her into the house, hitting the button to close the garage door on my way in. "Sorry, I just need to put these away and get the chicken in the Crock-Pot."

"No worries. I'll help."

"Oh, you don't have to do that."

"I don't mind. I just dropped Brynlee off at my in-laws'. They called me and claimed they were having granddaughter withdrawals." She laughs. "Anyway, I was off today, so I took her over."

"That's great that you let her spend time with them. I didn't have that growing up, so I know it's a memory she'll cherish."

"How much has Ryder told you about me?"

"Not much. Just that your parents were assholes, and you came to live with them after you turned eighteen."

She nods. "You and I are not that different." She tells me her story. How her mother married into money, how controlling her father was, and the disinterest from her mother.

"Reversed, but yeah, very similar. I'm sorry for all that you went through."

She nods. "Aunt Carol and Uncle Raymond took me in, no questions asked. Yes, I was an adult, but they still welcomed me into their home as if I'd always been there or belonged there even. Then I met Deacon, and my life changed again. Love will do that to you, I guess." She grins.

"I wasn't raised in a small town. I was raised with wealth, and I'd give it all up a million times over for the life I have now."

"Thank you."

"For what?"

"Sharing your story with me. Accepting me so freely as a part of Ryder's life after the hell I put him through."

She waves me off. "We know why you did it, Jordyn. We liked you before, but now you're stuck with us for life. You sacrificed yourself and your needs to protect not just Ryder, but the entire family. We understand that this was all out of your control.

There's nothing for us to forgive. The past is the past, and we need to focus on the present, on your future with Ryder."

Tears well once more in my eyes, and this time there's no hiding them. "I want that. So much."

"Good. Now, tell me all the things. Did you go through what you have on your mother as far as the threats go? Are you ready for Deacon to write something up legally?"

"I have, and I am. I have them with me to give to you. Remind me, and I'll email them to you before you leave."

As we talk, I get dinner going in the Crock-Pot. I tell her everything I have and even pull the documents up on my computer to show her. She grins, and we start to talk about the timeframe, and what Ryder and I are going to say.

"My mother, she's trying to marry me off," I tell her. "We had a family dinner last weekend that consisted of me, my parents, and two lawyers from my father's firm. My mother told me to pick one, or she would pick one for me. Thankfully, she's been busy with a charity ball at the country club, so I've been able to evade her and the topic all together."

"Ugh, okay, well, we're going to have to consider that and build that into our timeline. We don't want her to have the time to do something crazy like announce an engagement before we have a chance to out her."

"Shit," I mutter. "I didn't think about her just picking and announcing. However, I know my mother. She's all about attention, so she'll want to plan a party and announce it. I think we have a little time."

"We'd better not risk it. Besides, Ryder will blow a gasket if it gets that far." She winks, and I feel the corner of my mouth lift into a smile.

Everything is going to be okay.

I can feel it.

Ramsey's phone rings, and as she answers it, I take out the trash and unload the dishwasher. I try not to listen, but when she mentions what I'm making for dinner, my ears perk up. I can't hear the other side of the conversation. Maybe she's just telling whoever it is that I'm taking care of Ryder. My chest swells. I want to take care of him, and our home—our kids. The life I've always dreamed of is within reach, but I'm still too afraid to be excited.

Soon.

We'll expose my mother soon, and then we can live not only for the present but also for the future.

"See you then." She ends the call, and when I turn to face her, she's grinning. "That was Palmer."

"Is everything okay?"

"Yes." She nods as she says the word. It's almost as if she needs to convince herself. "She's on her way over. Well, in about an hour or so."

"Oh. Okay." I know that Ryder and his family all have keys to each other's places. I assume he'll be okay with two of his sisters-in-law being here.

"With Kennedy and Alyssa," Ramsey adds.

I nod. "I made plenty." I nod toward the Crock-Pot.

"Crosby is picking up Jade and Scarlett." She flashes me a toothy grin.

"That probably means that husbands and kids will be here as well?"

"Yep."

"So, I don't have enough food."

She waves me off. "The ladies are on it. They're all bringing something."

"Ryder?"

"This is how we roll, Jordyn. You're a part of this family now. You'll get used to it."

Overwhelmed with appreciation for Ramsey, and this entire family, I walk around the island and wrap my arms around her in a hug. She hugs me back with a fierce grip that once again brings tears to my eyes. Not from the pain, but from the comfort.

I feel like I belong.

All my life I've wanted this. I've wished for a family, and thanks to Ryder sharing his with me, I have that. Not a day will pass that I don't thank whoever will listen for bringing Ryder and his family into my life.

"What can I do?" Ramsey asks when I release her.

"Nothing. I was going to clean up for him and do some laundry."

Ramsey looks around the open floor plan of the house. "It's not bad—something you can thank Carol for. She taught the boys to cook and clean."

"It's so weird to hear you call them boys."

"They're man-children." She winks. "I'm just teasing. I like to give them a hard time, but they're all great guys."

"I know."

She nods. "You do. Come on. Let's go take a load off while we wait for everyone else to get here."

I follow her into the living room, where we sit on the couch facing each other with our legs tucked beneath us. We talk like we've been friends for years, and it's the same companionship I felt with them before I left. Before my mother dropped a bomb on my life.

Hope fills my chest. This is going to work. Everything is going to be just fine.

Ryder's house is packed full. Everyone is laughing and cutting up, having a good time. I'm standing in the kitchen holding Caden, Rushton and Crosby's son. That's how Ryder finds me when he walks into the house from the garage. He doesn't know I'm here. He thought we postponed and that I couldn't get away, so he's confused, and then his eyes light up. He tosses his keys and phone on the counter and stalks toward me. He wraps me in his arms and kisses me soundly.

"I don't know how you're here, but fuck me, am I glad to see you." Caden coos and waves his arms in the air, and Ryder takes him from my arms. "Hey, little man. Did you miss your favorite uncle?" he asks the baby.

Caden giggles when Ryder kisses his belly, and I see a moment of what our life is going to be like. This is our life, our future, and I'm so ready to get started on carving our place in this sleepy, little town.

"Not that I'm not happy to see y'all, but what are you doing here?" he asks the room.

"Well, I was driving by and saw Jordyn, so I stopped to chat. Then Palmer called, and well, here we are." Ramsey shrugs.

"What smells so good?"

"All the things, brother," Merrick speaks up. "You know, these ladies know how to feed us. Now that you're here, we can eat."

"Dig in. I'm going to grab a quick shower." He hands Caden to Merrick and laces his fingers with mine, pulling me down the hall to his room. As soon as we're in his room, he closes the door, turns the lock, and pushes me up against it. His lips find mine in a kiss that's much softer than I was expecting.

When he finally pulls away, we're both breathing heavily, and his forehead is resting against mine. "I hope it's okay that I'm here."

"How long?"

"Until Sunday."

He pulls his head back and the love and hope I see in his eyes has my knees going weak. "Yeah, Gianna and Calvin took a last-minute weekend trip. She called and asked me to go along, well, to take my phone along."

"We owe them dinner and something special that's for sure."

"Yeah, she's the best."

"I'm glad that you have her."

"*We* have her. You're sharing your family with me, and well, Gianna is the closest thing I have as far as someone to support and love me."

"Gianna used to be all that you had. I have a house full of people that proves that's no longer the case."

"Sorry about that. Ramsey stopped when I was bringing in groceries, and then it kind of just took off from there, and the next thing I know, everyone was coming over. I should have called you."

"You have nothing to apologize for. They're family. They all have keys to get in and they know they're welcome. However, if you're not okay with that, I can talk to them about calling first, and not ambushing you."

"No. I... kind of love it. I've never had this, and it's nice to feel so... welcome."

"You're so welcome," he says, pressing his lips to mine. "Legs around my waist, sweets." He lifts me, and I do as he says, and he carries me to the bed. He lays me down and stares down at me. "I get you all weekend?"

"All weekend."

His gaze heats. "Pants off."

"What?" I laugh.

"You heard me, sweets. I'm having dessert before dinner."

"Ryder! Your entire family is just down the hall."

"Then you better be quiet."

"We—can't."

"Oh, we can and we will. Get naked, Jordyn. Pants off, baby." He reaches behind his neck, pulls off his T-shirt, and tosses it to the floor. He's quick to remove his jeans and boxer briefs. He's standing before me, his hard cock in his hand, and eyeing me expectantly.

Heat pools between my thighs. "You have to be fast, and we can't make any noise."

He grins, shaking his head. "Trust me, baby, they know what we're doing. Being quiet and fast isn't going to keep them from that knowledge." He leans over me, and his nose brushes mine. "I've missed you, sweets."

I'll never be able to say no to this man. My shoes are already by the door, so I unbutton my jeans, lower the zipper, and lift my hips. Ryder takes over, pulling them down to my ankles. He then drops to his knees, slides beneath my jeans, and pulls me to the edge of the bed.

"This will make getting dressed faster, and I'm starving." That's all he says before his mouth is on me, his head buried between my thighs.

I grip the sheets as his tongue strokes my clit. I grasp the comforter and manage to pull it loose and bring it to my face to help me stay quiet. I bite down on the fabric to muffle my cries of pleasure.

Ryder moans, and my orgasm hits me out of nowhere. I writhe beneath him, only for him to move at lightning speed and tear my jeans off the rest of the way.

"I thought I could wait, but fuck that. You ready for me, sweets?"

I nod. I will forever be ready for this man for anything and everything he's willing to give me. With his cock in his fist, he guides himself inside me. "So tight," he mumbles.

"We have to be fast."

"You want me to fuck you, sweets?"

"I want this to be fast, so I can get myself together and go back to join your family and pretend it didn't happen."

He laughs. "Hold on tight, baby."

I do as he asks, and he fucks me hard and fast just as I asked him to. He's relentless with every push of his hips into mine. "Touch yourself, Jordyn. I'm not going to last."

"Just... come for me."

"Fuck," he groans as his body stills and he releases inside me. "That's not how that's supposed to go. You go first."

"I got mine, Ry." I smile up at him as I run my fingers through his hair.

"Twice. You go twice before me."

"We're both walking out of here satisfied. That's a win, Ryder."

"I'm far from satisfied, Jordyn. I'll never have enough of you. Never."

"Well, that's going to have to hold you over for now. Now, go shower."

"Wait for me. I'll be quick." He slides out of me and rushes off to the shower. I lie on this bed, smiling up at the ceiling like a fool.

Have I ever been this happy? I don't think I have. Before I left, I was happy with Ryder, but now, knowing what life is like without him, it's a different kind of happy. It's a deep-seated contentment in my soul.

It's home.

Pulling myself from the bed, I step into the bathroom and clean up. By the time I'm finished, Ryder is out of the shower and drying off. I wait for him to get dressed and together, hand in hand, we head back to his family.

As soon as we reach the living room, everyone starts to clap, and I feel my face flush. "I'm deducting points for speed," Maverick calls out.

"Told you." Ryder laughs, kissing my lips. "You good?"

"I'm good." We head toward the kitchen and make ourselves a plate of the hodge-podge collection of food that everyone brought over.

"You know," Palmer says, coming to stand next to me, while Ryder gets us something to drink, "that ovation you just received? That means they like you. We all do." She bumps her shoulder into mine. "He's missed you, Jordyn. We're all glad you're back. We not only get you back, but we get our Ryder back too. Thank you for that."

"I love him," I blurt.

She nods. "You wear that love on your sleeve, my friend." She grins, rubs her pregnant belly, and makes her way back to Brooks, who wraps his arms around her, resting his hand on her bump.

My face hurts from smiling, but that's a small price to pay for this moment. Life has a funny way of working out. We have a plan, and that plan will stop my mother, and bring me more happiness than I ever could have dreamed of. A normal life surrounded by love.

That's all I've ever wanted.

Chapter 17

Ryder

"Where are we going?"

"It's a surprise."

"Can I have a hint?"

"Nope. We're almost there." I glance over at Jordyn. She's sitting in the passenger seat of my truck, staring at the front window with a smile on her face. It's as if the stress of our situation has been lifted from her shoulders. We haven't made a move against her parents yet, but we have a plan, one we're all certain will fix the issue.

It's so damn good to see that smile on her face.

We talked as a family last night, and we're going to do it next weekend. We're all going to get together at the Willow Manor, an event venue in Willow River that Kennedy helps her grandmother run. Kennedy said there's not an event booked on Friday night, so we're going to bring food and have an open space that's not anyone's house for when we go live.

One more week, and this is over.

"The animal shelter?" Jordyn asks, sitting up a little straighter in her seat. She glances over at me as I park. "What are we doing?"

"You once told me that you got to volunteer at an animal shelter as a part of a charity event your college was doing. You said that you loved every minute of it." I shrug. "I thought we could spend our day volunteering."

"When did I tell you that?" Her brow furrows as if she's trying to remember.

"Right after we met."

"And you remember that?"

Reaching over, I tuck a loose strand of hair behind her ear. "I remember everything about you, sweets."

Her eyes light up. "Do they know we're coming?"

"Yeah. The woman who runs the shelter is good friends with my mom. I texted her while you were in the shower. Come on. Let's go love on some dogs and cats."

The smile she hits me with is so damn bright, it has my chest feeling tight.

Jordyn scrambles out of the truck and I do the same. By the time I get to her, where she's waiting at the front of my truck, she's bouncing on the balls of her feet. She grabs my hand and leads me up the sidewalk to the front door.

"Ryder!" Dorothy exclaims. "I was so excited to hear from you." Dorothy opens her arms for a hug, and I oblige her.

"How you doing, Miss Dorothy?"

"Fine as frog hair." She laughs. "Oh, aren't you just the sweetest?" Dorothy pushes me out of the way and wraps Jordyn in a hug. "I'm Dorothy," she says, once she finally releases her.

"It's a pleasure to meet you, Miss Dorothy. Thank you for letting us come in today."

Dorothy waves her hand in the air. "These animals can always use some extra loving. Come on back. I'll introduce you."

Jordyn's eyes find mine, and she shakes a little as she grins before turning to follow Dorothy down the hall. I hang back, not because I don't want to be involved, but because I love watching her like this. She's carefree and happy, and damn, I've missed that look on her.

Dorothy goes through where the treats are located, shows us the fenced-in play area, the water, and how to work the cages. She explains that all the animals are friendly, and their fears are listed on the cards outside of their cages, if there are any.

"This little guy could use some extra loving today. He's the last of a litter that was dropped off a couple of weeks ago. The family lost their job and couldn't afford to take care of them. Full-blooded golden retriever." Dorothy points to a cage where a little fur ball is rolled up in the corner.

"Hey, little one." Jordyn places her palm against the cage, but the puppy doesn't move. "Male or female?" Jordyn asks.

"Male. We've been calling him Tucker, because he likes to tuck himself into a ball when he sleeps."

"Tucker, aren't you just the cutest guy?" Jordyn looks up at Dorothy. "Can I take him out of his cage?"

"Of course. They all get along great. Just be sure if you go outside, that the gate is closed so we don't have an escape."

"Thanks, Dorothy."

"You're welcome, young man. You two enjoy. We're here until four today." With that, she turns and heads back to the front desk.

"I want to get him out," Jordyn says, nodding toward Tucker's kennel.

"Yes, ma'am." I unlock the cage and when I start to reach in to get him, Jordyn slides beneath my arm and shimmies her body in front of mine.

"Hey, buddy," she coos. "Do you want to come and see me?" she asks him as if she expects him to answer.

The puppy lifts his head but makes no other attempts to move.

"Come on out and play," she says, slowly reaching into the cage. I place my hands on her hips, holding on to her.

The puppy scrambles to his feet and takes small steps to sniff her hand. "See, I'm nice," she tells him.

I'm glad that I'm standing behind her, because she'd think I was making fun of her the way I'm smiling. I'm not. I'm just really fucking happy that she's happy.

"Oh, goodness." She lifts Tucker, and we collectively step back. "You're so soft," she coos. She moves to the corner and sits on the floor with the puppy in her arms.

"You good here, sweets? I'm going to take some of the older dogs outside to run off some energy."

She barely spares me a glance as she nods and gives her attention back to the fur ball in her arms. With a shake of my head, I check the notes on each dog, then open up the kennels of the older ones. They bounce around and bark, more than ready to run off some energy. They're trained, so as soon as I move toward the door, they follow behind me, and rush out as soon as I push it open.

I spend the next two hours playing fetch with four dogs. I'm tired as hell, and I'm starving. I wrangle them back inside, get them a drink and a treat before putting them back.

I find Jordyn in the same spot. The puppy curled up on her lap, and two baby kittens in her arms.

"Having fun?"

She glances up and nods. "This has been the best day, Ry."

I crouch down in front of her and take the kittens out of her arms. "You ready to head to the party?"

"We just got here."

"Sweets, we've been here for over two hours."

"No." She shakes her head, then turns to glance at the clock on the wall. "Oh."

"I'm going to put these little guys up while you say goodbye."

"Tuck, I've gotta go, buddy. They're closing up soon, and we have a birthday party to go to."

I chuckle when I hear her talking to the puppy like he actually understands everything she's saying. Hell, maybe he does. The way he's looking up at her almost makes me believe that he does.

"We'll come back."

"But what if he's not here?" Her lips jut out in a pout, and I lean in for a kiss.

"That means he's found a good, loving home."

"What if they don't love him like he deserves to be loved?"

I can see it in her eyes. She's worried that Tucker will end up with a family like hers. "Dorothy has a very rigorous process, and they have to pass background checks."

The look she gives me tells me that she knows that doesn't mean Tucker will end up in a good home. "How about we come back next weekend to check in on him?"

Her eyes light up. "Hear that, buddy? I'll be back next weekend to see you." She kisses his fuzzy head and hands him to me to put him back in his cage.

"Be good, Tuck," I tell the pup. He moves to the corner and tucks himself into a tight ball and closes his eyes. It's damn good to already be making plans for our future. If all goes according to plan, next weekend my girl will be a resident of Willow River.

We stop at the counter to say goodbye to Dorothy, telling her we'll be back next weekend, and then I lead my girl to my truck and head toward my parents' place for a birthday party.

Caden, Rushton's son, turned one last week, and Beckham, Declan's son, turned one this week. Crosby and Kennedy decided to combine their parties. I'm stoked that Jordyn gets to be here for this. She hasn't stopped smiling since I walked through the door last night.

"You keep smiling like that your face might crack," Deacon says. He stops next to me and takes a sip of his punch.

Birthday party punch is the best. It brings out the kid in me, and from the looks of the close-to-empty punchbowl that I know for a fact has been refilled a few times, I'm not the only one.

"Thank you for all that you've done with the PI. You and Ramsey. I appreciate the help you've given us."

Deacon nods. "You're family. I'm glad you didn't fight her on it. You know my wife will do anything for the people she loves."

"Yeah, they're all like that."

"It's a Kincaid thing." He chuckles. "Maybe we should get T-shirts."

"Shh. Don't say that in front of Maverick. He'll make it happen."

Deacon's deep laugh tells me he knows I'm right.

"What are you doing after this?" I ask.

"No plans. Bryn is going to be exhausted, so bath time and then bed. You know, dad life."

"You love it." Deacon, just like my brothers who are now dads, love the hell out of being a father. He couldn't wait for Ramsey to tell him she was ready to start trying.

"I want more. Bryn is almost a year old."

"Does your wife know about this?"

"Yep. I told her so the day we brought Brynlee home from the hospital."

"Dude, give the woman some time to recover."

"Yeah." He grins. "We're thinking after her first birthday, we'll start trying again."

"Why don't you let me and Jordyn watch her tonight? You can have a night with your wife."

"Man, you don't have to do that. Your time with Jordyn is limited as it is."

"Not anymore. After next weekend, she'll be living with me. Come on. Let us take her."

"Take who, where?" Ramsey asks, slipping her arm around her husband. Deacon pulls her into his chest and presses a kiss to her temple.

"I was just telling Deacon that you two should go have a night out. Let me and Jordyn have Brynlee tonight."

"You two barely see each other."

"Not after next week."

Ramsey nods. "How about this? How about you all come over to our place, and I'll get this one to take me out for a drink, oh, or ice cream? We won't stay out long, and that way you get your girl all to yourself tonight."

"Either way."

Jordyn joins us with Brynlee in her arms. "She is such a sweetheart."

"She loves to snuggle."

"I'll take all of your snuggles," Jordyn says, swaying a little as if she's rocking Brynlee to sleep.

"Did you ask Jordyn about your plan?"

"No, but she's not going to care."

"Care about what?" Jordyn asks.

"I told these two to go out after this for some adult time and that we'd watch her."

"Yes," is her immediate reply.

We all laugh.

"Are you sure?" Ramsey asks.

"Positive," Jordyn and I reply at the same time.

"Okay, well, our place then? She'll be ready for a bath and bed, so it should be easy. She's worn out after a day of being passed around and playing with her cousins."

"We'll leave when you do," I tell Ramsey. I pull her out of her husband's arms and into mine. "Thank you for everything."

"Love harder," she whispers.

"Every damn day."

"You want me to take her?" I ask Jordyn. We're downstairs at Deacon and Ramsey's, sitting on the couch. Brynlee is asleep on Jordyn's shoulder. After Jordyn helped Ramsey with her bath, she fed her a bottle while Deacon and Ramsey slipped out. She fell right to sleep, and Jordyn has been holding her ever since.

"No. She's fine."

"She won't wake up if we put her in her bed, if that's what you're worried about."

"I'm not worried about waking her up. I just like to snuggle her."

"We need one." The words are out before I can think better of them, but I'm not taking them back.

"How many?"

I shrug. "As many as you want."

"Don't you think we should be married first?"

"Then marry me."

Her mouth falls open. "Ryder Kincaid, I know that was not your marriage proposal."

"No, but it's coming." I wink, and her cheeks flush a slight shade of pink. "Next weekend you move in, engaged by Christmas, and married by what? Valentine's Day?"

"That's pretty fast." Her smile and the tone of her voice tell me she's not the least bit worried about how fast it is and saying what she thinks she needs to say.

"I've loved you for a lifetime. It's fast, but we spent two years apart, and the love we share only grew even when we both thought there was no hope. I don't want anyone but you."

"You're it for me too."

"Great, so move in next week, get engaged by Thanksgiving, and get married by the New Year."

"Ryder." She grins, and that sound reminds me that the old Jordyn is back. The one who smiles and laughs, and just wants to live and love life.

My Jordyn.

"What?" I play innocent.

"That's not what you said the first time."

"Right." I nod. "So engaged by Veteran's Day, married by Christmas."

"What am I going to do with you?"

"Love me, take my name, have my babies, make me the happiest man on earth."

She's quiet as she smiles down at a sleeping Brynlee in her arms. When she lifts her head and locks her gaze with mine, and whispers, "Yes," my breath stalls in my lungs.

"Jordyn."

"I want to take your name. I want to be a part of your family. I want to have your babies. I want nights just like this. Snuggling on the couch, birthday parties. And I want to make you happy. Not because I feel obligated to but because you are the greatest man I've ever known. You loved me when there was little hope. You fought for us and kept that love alive. When being together felt impossible, you never gave up. I love you, Ryder Kincaid, and it would be my absolute honor to be your wife, take your name, have your babies, and live happily ever after with you."

Leaning over, I kiss her softly. "I love you." I kiss her nose. "I love you." I rain kisses all over her face, telling her I love her in between each one. This woman is my future. She's my everything. This wasn't the plan. Hell, I didn't know the words were going to come out of my mouth, but I don't regret them. It felt right. This is our moment, and you can bet your ass I'm taking her yesses and promises to heart.

We're getting married!

"How about we put her to bed so I can kiss you like I want to?" Translation, I want to fucking devour her.

She said yes.

To all of it.

Holy shit!

"We can't get caught making out on your cousin's couch."

"Oh, but we can. You can bet your sweet ass Deacon would do the same. Jordyn, you just agreed to be my wife. That deserves some kissing. Some fondling, and at least five orgasms."

"Shh, not in front of the baby."

"She's sleeping." I grin at her.

"Fine, we'll put her to bed, but just kissing. Everything else is just going to have to wait until we get home."

Home.

"Deal."

Standing from the couch, I carefully lift Brynlee into my arms and carry her upstairs to her room. We've barely gotten her bedroom door shut when the front door opens. With Jordyn's hand wrapped around mine and the baby monitor in the other, we head downstairs.

"That was not a night out," I tell them.

"This one decided grocery shopping was what she wanted to do." Deacon acts irritated, but I know damn good and well he'd do anything for his wife.

"I'll help you unload." I hand Jordyn the baby monitor, drop a kiss to her lips, and get to work helping Deacon carry in everything from the car.

"Whenever you need a sitter, call us," Jordyn tells Ramsey as we're getting ready to leave.

"Be careful what you sign up for," Ramsey teases.

"She's perfect. Really, we're happy to help. After everything you've done for us, that's the least that we can do."

Ramsey pulls Jordyn into a hug. "It's what we do, and don't worry, I'm totally taking you up on the babysitting."

Another round of goodbyes, and we're on the road headed home. "I love your family."

"*Our* family."

"Our family." She closes her eyes, and she's sound asleep when we get home.

I carry her into the house and help her sleepily get ready for bed before crawling in next to her and wrapping her tightly in my arms.

We have a lifetime for nightly orgasms. We have forever.

Jordyn's barely out of the driveway when I pull my phone from my pocket and make a call. It rings three times before she answers.

"Hello."

"Miss Dorothy, it's Ryder Kincaid."

"Oh, Ryder, what can I do for you?"

"I want to adopt Tucker."

"Oh, goodness, that's wonderful news. I'll start the paperwork tomorrow."

"Thank you. Let me know what I need to do."

"Well, I know you work a lot. How about we meet at the shelter and get the paperwork done tonight?"

"I'm on my way." Shoving my phone back into my pocket, I jog inside to grab my keys and lock up. Jordyn told me today she always wanted a dog but was never allowed to have one.

What my girl wants, my girl gets. Tucker will be here next weekend as a surprise welcome home gift. I'll need to get a ring before next Friday as well.

Finally, we're working toward our future.

Chapter 18

Jordyn

"I need your help today at the country club," my mother announces as she enters the kitchen.

"What for?" I don't bother looking at her; instead, I keep my eyes glued to my phone. I'm not seeing anything riveting, just scrolling social media, but my phone, and what a girl I graduated from high school with had for dinner last night, is better entertainment than my mother.

"We're leaving at noon."

"Fine," I mutter.

"I expect you to be put together, Jordyn. You will look and act like an Astor, just as you were raised to be."

"Yep." I make sure to pop the *p* because I know it will piss her off. It's my favorite pastime these days. Especially knowing that her control over me is about to come to a complete halt.

"Yes," she fires back. "I won't settle for your disrespect."

I glance up to find her glaring at me. "Yes," I amend. It takes everything I have inside of me to not roll my eyes.

Two more days, I keep reminding myself. It's Wednesday, and on Friday, I'm going to Ryder's and we're going to expose my mother and her threats against the Kincaids. This will all be over. Well, over as in her threats will no longer be a concern.

My mother is a monster, but she's not dumb enough to pay someone to hurt Ryder and his family after she's been so publicly exposed for threatening to do so.

"What do you need my help with?"

"Does it matter? You'll whine regardless."

She's not wrong. I'm not a fan of the country club. It's not the club itself that bothers me. It's the stuck-up assholes who frequent the place. You know, my mother, her friends, and their offspring.

"I need to know how to dress." That's a lie and we both know it. I'm to dress to impress always. Especially moments when I'll be with my mother.

"You dress like a damn Astor, Jordyn. Can you handle that? Do I need to lay your clothes out for you as I did when you were a toddler?"

Again, the urge to roll my eyes is strong. "I'll figure it out." What I want to do is remind her she's never in my life laid out my clothes. She's instructed my nanny, or the housemaid, to tell me what to wear, but she, herself? Nah, that's beneath Margaret Astor.

Two more days.

"Have you thought any more about the choice you have to make?"

"No."

"You have until the end of the weekend, or we decide for you. Your father wants to announce the new partner soon."

"I don't want to marry either one of them. I want to marry for love."

She laughs. It's humorless and full of malice. "No one marries for love, Jordyn. It's always about what you and your partner can do for one another."

"Are you telling me you and Father didn't love each other when you got married?" This is the first I've heard of this. I guess I just assumed they were married, and it was for love. I assumed they were a perfect match. She's evil, and he's uncaring.

"My parents had a law firm that was in direct competition with your grandfather's. Your father was young and eager. He approached me. He suggested we marry and merge the two. I convinced my parents, and your father was handed the firm on a silver platter."

"Why would you do that? Your family had money. You didn't need his."

"You're right, but I also had a vision of how I wanted my life to be. My parents were on board with that vision. My family had money and reputation. Not near as much as the Astors but enough that I was an acceptable companion for your father. On paper we were perfect."

"Do you love each other now?"

"Your father and I are fond of one another. We have the same goals and aspirations. We want the same things out of life."

"Wow." I'm speechless. I didn't think there was ever anything my mother could drop on me that would shock me after everything she's already done, but I guess I was wrong.

"Be ready." She turns on her heel and stalks out of the kitchen.

Quickly, I finish breakfast and rush up to my room to text Ryder. He's working, but he always replies when he gets the chance.

> **Me:** *Mother of evil is requesting my presence at the country club this afternoon. She claims to need my help but won't tell me what with. I'm probably going to be picking out napkins or something as equally boring. Two more days, Ry. Two more freaking days and this is all over.*

Throwing my phone onto the bed, I toss the blanket over it and head to the shower. I'm dreading today. Spending any kind of time with my mother is torture. I just need to keep reminding myself that this is it. I'll never have to go somewhere with her again. I'll never have to visit the country club again.

I quickly tie my hair up in a bun, as expected by my mother, and pull on a dress. I'm not putting in a whole lot of effort, just enough to keep her off my back.

Just a few more days.

Life is about to change in the best of ways, and I cannot wait. I'd love to say that my mother will see the error of her ways and want to be a better person and be a part of my life, but that's not who she is. I don't think she shed a single tear when Jeremy died.

I'm still floored about what she revealed. I shouldn't be surprised. It's not like they're overly affectionate with one another. Now that I think about it. I don't think I've ever seen them kiss. Nothing more than a peck on the cheek, and that's usually for show. Damn, I feel sad for both of them. To never know love is a tragedy. Just something else I have to thank Ryder for.

> **Me:** *I just realized that you taught me love. Taught me to give and accept love freely. I can't wait to spend forever with you.*

Tossing both of my phones into my purse, I give myself a quick once-over. I look like a younger version of my mother. She'll be so proud. I roll my eyes and smile.

Two more days.

Two. More. Days.

"Why are you driving?" I ask my mother. I can't remember the last time I saw her behind the wheel of a car. Hell, I didn't even know she had her driver's license.

"Your father needed Mario today, and Angelo is on vacation. His wife is having *another* baby."

"Aw, good for them." She ignores me, keeping her hands at ten and two on the steering wheel. It appears that the emotionless Margaret Astor is nervous. "Want me to drive?"

"I'm capable," she spits.

"Okay," I say under my breath as I type out a reply to Gianna, who asked me what I was doing today. She's off and wanted to get together for a late lunch.

> **Me:** *Headed to the country club with my mother. She claims to need my help but refuses to tell me what she needs help with.*

I don't bother to put my phone back into my purse because I know Gianna will be texting me right back. Sure enough, my phone beeps, and I look at her message.

> **Gianna:** *Ugh. Call me later. Maybe we can do dinner.*

I'm typing out my reply when a message notification comes from my purse. I freeze. So does my mother, who just pulled up to a Stop sign.

"What's that?"

"Gianna." I hold up my phone as the other one alerts me to another message.

"Do you have another phone?"

"What? No. Why would I have two phones?"

She studies me for several long heartbeats, and I pray that she starts to drive, and the notification doesn't sound again before I can pretend to dig in my purse for... something and turn it on vibrate or clear the messages.

Finally, she starts driving again. Once we get on the other side of town, I reach for my purse and pretend to be looking for something.

"Want some gum?" I ask, still digging. I can't find the other phone. I knew I should have cleaned my purse out when I thought about it earlier today. Finally, my hands grip the other phone. I'm working on hitting the buttons blindly on the side of the phone to silence it when my mother reaches over and grabs my purse.

I yank it back on instinct, and the car starts to swerve. "Mom!" I scream, but it's too late. We're rolling down an embankment.

We're both screaming.

The car continues to flip over and over down the hill.

When we finally stop, and thankfully, we're upright after all that turning, I look at my mother, and she's sloped against the wheel. She's covered in blood.

"Mom." There's nothing but silence. As I reach over to check for a pulse, the sudden movement makes the car rock, and I realize we're not stable. Sudden movements could have us dropping further.

"Mom!" I yell—still nothing. My heart hammers in my chest. The frantic rhythm reminds me I'm still alive.

"Mother! Wake up." Silence greets me, and my fear multiplies. Fear grips me. Why won't she wake up?

"Margaret!" I shout as loud as I can, but my throat is raw from the screams that left me as we rolled down the hill. I move my arm to shake her awake, and the car rocks. I immediately pull back, holding still as the rocking motion settles. I expel a heavy breath as my hands start to tremble.

Shit. This is bad. I don't know how far down we dropped, and I was so distracted I don't know if there were any other cars around us at the time. It could be hours before someone finds us down here. We rolled several times, and if no one was on the road, around us, we might be too far down for anyone to see us here.

All I see is vast trees and a valley down below. I try not to think about what that means. One simple move could send us further down this damn hill.

I take a minute to survey the situation. My mother is unconscious. At least I hope that's the case. I can't let myself think about the alternative. The car isn't stable. In my hands, I'm gripping my purse. The purse I ripped from my mother's grasp and caused this accident.

Tears prick my eyes as panic wells in my chest.

My legs are trapped beneath the dash. I don't dare try to move for fear of what that could do. I know enough that I could injure myself further, or even worse than that, send the car further down the hill.

I finally take stock of my injuries. There are scrapes and cuts on my arms. My head is killing me. I touch my forehead lightly, and when I pull my hand away, it's covered in blood. Hence, the cracked side windshield. If I thought my hands were trembling before, it's nothing compared to the sight of fresh blood on the tips of my fingers. Closing my eyes, I try to take a calming breath, but it doesn't work. My heart feels as though it could bounce right out of my chest.

Stay calm, Jordyn.

Shit. Shit. Shit.

Slowly, I pull in a breath, count to ten, and exhale before repeating the process a second, third, and fourth time. I'm finally calm enough to think about what I need to do.

Carefully, I place my hand in my purse.

"Please," my voice cracks. "Please let it be in there." I dig around, careful not to jolt, so the car doesn't go for another roll down the embankment. When my fingers clutch my Ryder phone, I sob. I can't stop the tears, and I keep glancing at my mother, waiting for her to tell me to shut the hell up and make the call.

She doesn't.

I repeat my breathing exercise until my tears calm. My hands shake as I swipe at the screen and see replies from Ryder. I don't bother to read them; instead, I hit his name to call him. It rings four, five, six times before going to voicemail.

"Shit." Panic starts to surface again, but I push it back. "You have to stay calm," I mutter to myself. My throat is raw, and my voice doesn't sound like my own.

Thankfully, Gianna's number is also programmed. I hit her name, and she picks up on the second ring. "Jordyn? Why are you calling me on this phone?" she answers.

"G." I can't say her name. I barely got out what I did before my tears took over yet again.

"Jordyn. Where are you? Are you safe?"

"W-We had an accident."

"Breathe for me, Jordyn. In and out. In and out." I can hear the fear in her voice, but she's calm as hell, and I need that right now. "Good. Now, there was an accident. You and your mother? Is anyone there yet?"

"We rolled. Down the hill," I add. I'm not explaining well enough that I know she can understand what the hell happened. I need to so she can send help. Swallowing back my tears, I try again. "We rolled. We were on our way to the country club, and we wrecked. I don't know if there was anyone else around us. As far as I know, it was just us."

"Are you hurt?"

"I-I don't know. My legs are trapped. My mo—mother, she's not answering me. She's unconscious. She was driving."

"Have you called for help?"

"I called Ryder, and he didn't answer. Then I called you." I see now that I should have called 9-1-1 first.

"Okay. I'm going to hang up and call for help. I'll call you right back."

"Thank you."

"I've got you, bestie. Hang on for me. I'll call you right back."

I grip the phone in my trembling hands as I wait for her to call me back.

"Mom?" I ask. I stare at her, and nothing. I don't see any movement from her. I don't think she's breathing. *No. No. No.* This cannot be happening.

My phone rings, and I struggle to swipe at the screen. "Hello," I finally answer.

"Help is on the way, Jordyn. I need you to keep talking to me until they get there."

"Okay."

"I'm on my way to you. I'm in the car."

"Be safe. W-We should hang up so you can focus."

"I'm on hands free, Jordyn. I'm fine. You just keep talking to me. Can you tell me what happened?"

"I had my other phone in my bag and forgot to turn off the sound. Ryder texted me back from earlier, and I was holding my phone in my hand, texting you, and she freaked out. She grabbed my bag, and I grabbed it back, and she swerved, and the next thing I knew we were rolling over and over down the hill." I suck in a breath. I need to calm the hell down. Gianna will make sure she sends help. I just need to sit here and be patient, and not freak out.

It's all going to work out.

It has to.

"Keep talking," she tells me. "Help is on the way."

I close my eyes and rest my throbbing head back against the headrest. "I don't think she's breathing, G. I—I killed my mother." Panic takes flight again, and it feels as if there's an elephant sitting on my chest.

"No. No. Don't think that way. I can't speak to her condition, but you did nothing wrong. She was driving and was distracted."

"I should have let her have my purse. I never should have jerked it back."

"This is not on you, Jordyn. You hear me. This is not on you."

"I hate her, but this... not this, G. I didn't want this."

"Shhh," she soothes. "Tell me about Ryder."

"I love him."

"He loves you too. As soon as help gets there, I'm going to try to get ahold of him for you. He and I will be at the hospital as soon as we can."

"I didn't want this."

"This is not your fault, Jordyn."

"I hear sirens."

"Good. Hang on with me."

"I'm here."

"Does anything hurt?"

"My head, my elbow, and I don't know about my legs. I'm afraid to move. When I did, the car rocked. I don't think we're stable."

"Yes. Stay still. They'll get you out of there. You're going to be okay."

"G?"

"Yeah?"

"Thank you. I love you. You're the best friend a girl could have."

"I love you too."

"Can you—just in case, can you tell Ryder I love him? Tell him I'm sorry we never got to live out the dreams we had for us."

"Stop. You're going to be just fine."

"Just in case. I don't know. I feel really tired."

"Jordyn. Stay with me. Jordyn."

"Ma'am. Can you hear me? Don't move. We're going to stabilize the vehicle and get you out of there."

My head feels fuzzy, but I need to tell her. "They're here, G. Thank you. I love you. Tell Ryder. Please tell Ryder he's everything."

"I'm going to hang up now. They're going to take good care of you. I'm almost there. I'll follow you to the hospital, and I'll get ahold of Ryder."

"I love you both," I whisper before everything goes black.

Chapter 19

Ryder

My phone keeps vibrating in my pocket. I'm in the bucket working on a line. I hope everything's okay. It doesn't stop, so I radio down to the guys that I'm coming down. When I get to the bottom, I pull my phone out of my pocket. I see a missed call from Jordyn and several from Gianna.

"I have to take this," I say, tearing out of the bucket and calling Jordyn back. The call goes directly to voicemail. "Fuck." Ending the call, I quickly dial Gianna.

"Ryder. Thank God," she breathes.

"What's wrong?"

"There's been an accident."

"What kind of accident? Where's Jordyn? Is she okay?" My heart is beating so fast, I fear it might jump right out of my chest.

"Car accident. They took her to Atlanta General. I'm here in the emergency waiting room. They won't tell me anything because I'm not family."

Atlanta General.

Emergency room.

Jordyn.

"Is. She. Okay?" The words are strained, and my voice doesn't sound like my own.

"She was alert and talking to me. She called me, and I called for help. I followed the ambulance here. She was unconscious when they brought her in."

"*Fuck!*" I roar. "I'm on my way." My feet start moving toward the guys on my crew. "Stay there, please, and keep me updated. I'll be there as soon as I can."

"I will. Ryder. Please be safe. She's going to need you."

"I've got her. Always." Ending the call, I lock eyes with my foreman.

"What's going on, Kincaid?"

I swallow back my emotions. "My girl—she was in a bad accident. I need to go." I don't ask for permission because there is nothing and no one that will stop me from getting to Jordyn.

"I'll drive," he says.

"No, I know you're needed here on the job. I can manage."

"Nope. Hawkins, you take the company truck. I'll drive Kincaid in his, and you can bring me back to the job site."

I nod. "Thank you."

I'm grateful that I don't have to focus on driving because if I'm being honest, all I can think about is my girl being hurt. I have to get there to her. I don't give a fuck what her mother says. She's not going to keep me away. If we have to go live from her hospital room, we'll do it. I don't give a fuck what she threatens. I will not be kept from her.

She needs me.

I don't remember much of the drive to the hospital. Again, I'm grateful to my foreman for getting me here safely. My hand is on the door handle as soon as we get close to the entrance of the emergency room. "Thanks," I say, my voice gritty.

"Let us know what you need. Take the time you need to take care of your girl."

I nod, because I can't say more.

We were so close. So damn close to having it all. To blowing her mother's threats up and disintegrating them into a cloud of dust, and now, she's in this hospital, and I don't know how badly she's hurt. I don't know what I'm walking into, and that has me almost immobile with fear.

Almost.

"Thanks," I mumble as I hop out of the truck and make my way inside the emergency room. My eyes scan the room until they land on Gianna. She's sitting in a chair rocking back and forth, tears rolling down her cheeks.

My gut twists.

"Gianna." My booming voice has her lifting her head. She stands and rushes toward me, wrapping her arms around me. I do the same, offering her comfort, even though I'm numb myself. "Tell me," I croak. She steps back and heads back to where she was sitting in the corner of the waiting room.

My knees are knocking as I follow her, desperate for any kind of information she can give me about Jordyn. What happened? What did she say when she was talking? Is she going to be okay? Who is with her? Can we see her? I have so many fucking questions and no answers.

She goes on to explain what she knows about Jordyn and her day, and the fight with her mother. I grip my phone and finally allow myself to look at her messages. I read over her telling me that she had to help her mother with something at the club. However, it's the message that comes after that that has me choking on a sob.

> **Jordyn:** *I just realized that you taught me love. Taught me to give and accept love freely. I can't wait to spend forever with you.*

I choke back a sob.

Stay with me, baby.

I send up a silent prayer to anyone who will listen to save my girl. We've fought too hard. We've been through too much, come too far to not be able to live out our happily ever after.

"I can't lose her."

Bending forward, I rest my elbows on my knees and bury my face in my hands. I need to call my family. I need them here with her. She needs them too. We're Kincaids and we love harder, and my girl, she needs that love. This might be the hardest we've ever had to love, but we'll do it.

"G." I look up to find Calvin rushing toward us. He drops to his knees and hugs Gianna, and I find anger twirling in my gut. He has his arms around her, holding her. I need to see Jordyn. I need to wrap my arms around her. I need to hold her and tell her I'm here and that everything is going to be all right.

Fuck.

I need Jordyn.

Jumping to my feet, I race to the counter. "Jordyn Astor, my fiancée, can you tell me how she is?"

It's not a lie. She might not be wearing my ring, but she agreed to marry me. Sure, I'm going to do better, make it official and all that, but I'll say what I have to say to get to her.

"And your name?" the lady behind the desk asks.

"Ryder Kincaid." I'm waiting for her to tell me that Jordyn's mom has forbidden me to have access to her. I'm ready to fight, but when she speaks again, I realize I don't have to.

"We've been trying to reach your future father-in-law. Would you happen to have a way to contact him?"

I nod. "I'll let him know." *Eventually.* I'll let him know, eventually.

I know he's a big shot attorney here in Atlanta. I don't have his number, but I can find him. After I check on my girl.

"Come with me. I'll put you in a room and have someone come and update you on your fiancée and her mother."

"Thank you." It never occurred to me to worry about Jordyn's mother's injuries. That makes me sound cold-hearted, but after everything she's put Jordyn through, I can't seem to find it in me to care. I don't want her hurt, but she's not my priority.

"Gianna," I call, and she and Calvin stand and walk toward me. "They're taking us to a room for an update."

"How? I've been trying."

"They can't deny me access to my fiancée."

She smiles through her tears. "I knew I liked you, Kincaid."

"It's not a lie," I find myself saying.

The nurse appears and leads us down the hall. She opens her mouth. I'm sure to say Gianna and Calvin can't be back here, but I beat her to the punch. "We are her family. All three of us." I dare her to argue with me. I must look like a man ready to lose his shit, because she nods and motions for us to enter the small room.

"The doctor will be with you."

Just like that, she's gone, and we're in this tiny little room, waiting yet again to hear.

"What did you mean? It's not a lie?" Gianna asks me.

"We talked about it. She said yes." That's kind of how it happened. It's the gist of it, anyway. I'm sure if Jordyn wants to give Gianna all the details, she will. It's not my place.

"She loves you."

"I love her," I reply as the doctor enters the room.

"Family of Jordyn Astor?"

"I'm her fiancé. Ryder Kincaid." I stand and offer him my hand.

"I'm Dr. Jackson. I'm the attending physician who worked on your fiancée and her mother when they were brought in."

"How is she? They? How are they?" I correct, because she might be a hateful bitch, but I still want her to be okay.

"Mr. Kincaid, your fiancée is in surgery. Her right leg was broken in two places and required surgery. She's got a lot of cuts and bruising. There was a laceration on her spleen and her liver, but we expect her to make a full recovery."

"Thank fuck," I say, feeling some of the heaviness in my chest release. "And her mother?"

I can see it in his eyes before he speaks the words. "I'm sorry, Mr. Kincaid. Mrs. Margaret Astor didn't make it."

The heaviness is back. I stumble, and reach for the chair, and fall back into it. "Does Jordyn know?"

"She doesn't. She was in and out of consciousness when she was brought in. We ran tests and took her straight to surgery."

"Thank you."

"Jordyn's still in surgery. They were finishing up, and she did perfectly. Once she's out of recovery, we'll come and get you. You're welcome to stay here until then. I'm sorry for your loss." He stands and leaves just as quickly as he arrived.

"She blames herself."

"What?" My head whips around toward Gianna. "What do you mean she blames herself?"

"When I was talking to her, before the paramedics got there. She said her mother wasn't moving, and that she wasn't sure she was breathing. She said that if she hadn't tried to pull the purse back out of her arms, they never would have wrecked."

"No." I stand and start to pace the room. "That's not true. It was instinct. She didn't do this. Her mother was distracted."

"I know that. You know that, but Jordyn, she was already blaming herself."

"No," I say again.

"She's going to need us to be strong for her."

"I've always been strong for her. I'm not going to stop now." Which reminds me. "I need to call my family. She needs us. All of us." Pulling my phone out of my pocket, I decide to text in the group chat with my brothers. I have one that has the entire family, but I can't deal with double the questions. My brothers can tell our parents and their wives.

> **Me:** Jordyn was in an accident. I'm at Atlanta General. She's in surgery. Just talked to the doctor. He said she's going to be okay. Her mom didn't make it.
>
> **Maverick:** What do you need?
>
> **Merrick:** On my way.
>
> **Brooks:** I'm on shift. I'll find someone to cover me, and I'll be there.

Orrin:	*Getting in the truck now.*
Declan:	*How are you?*
Rushton:	*I'll call Mom and Dad, and head that way too.*
Archer:	*I'm working on the new school not far from there. I'm headed your way now, Ry. I'll be there soon.*
Sterling:	*Just told the boss man I was headed out. I'm on my way.*
Deacon:	*Closing the office now. Hang in there, Ry.*
Me:	*Please be safe.*
Orrin:	*Love you, brother.*

A string of texts from the others telling me the same blow up my phone. I slide it back into my pocket and close my eyes. Tears threaten to fall, but I hold them at bay. Not because I'm too embarrassed to show my emotions, but because Jordyn needs me to be strong for her.

I need to be her rock. I can't break down.

Feeling a hand on my arm, I peel open my eyes to find Gianna watching me intently. She nods toward the door and there stands Archer. I climb to my feet, and we meet each other halfway. He pulls me into a hug, and I choke back a sob.

"We've got you, brother. Both of you," he says, his own voice showing his emotion.

I wrench out of the hug, wiping at my eyes. "Did you have any trouble getting back here?"

"Nah, it's busy out there. She told me where to find you and waved me off."

"Thanks for being here."

"Jordyn's family. Do we know anything?"

I repeat what the doctor told us, and he's quiet while he listens, his eyes filling with sorrow.

"Damn," he mutters.

"I'm going to go grab some drinks. You two want something?" Calvin asks.

"Nah, I'm good."

"Me too," Archer says.

"I'm going to stay. Is that okay?" Gianna asks me.

"You're her best friend, her chosen family. You have just as much right to be here as I do."

Tears glisten in her eyes. Calvin kisses the top of her head, whispers something, and walks out of the room.

Now we wait.

Closing my eyes, I rest my head back against the wall. I am trying to be patient, but I need to lay eyes on her.

What feels like several hours later, but it's only been an hour and sixteen minutes since the doctor talked to us, a nurse steps into the waiting area. "Jordyn is in a room. Only two at a time."

I stand and look over at Gianna, offering her my hand. She stands as well. "We'll go first."

"She's on the third floor." The nurse goes on to rattle off the room number and explains that there's a much larger waiting room.

I can only imagine what she's thinking. Gianna, Calvin, Archer, Deacon, Orrin, Rushton, Merrick, and I are squeezed into this tiny room.

"What can we do, Ry?" Orrin asks.

"Just hang out. I know that's a lot to ask, but until I see her—yeah, if you don't mind."

"That goes without saying, brother. The rest are on their way."

"Palmer and Kennedy are staying back with all the kids," Rushton says, looking down at his phone. "Everyone else will be here."

There's that fucking lump again. "Thank you." I manage to push the words past my lips. I start toward the door but realize I never tried to call her father. "Deacon?"

"Yeah?"

"Can you try to get a hold of her father? Marvin Astor."

"I have a contact at his firm." He nods. "I'll take care of it."

"Thank you." I turn toward Gianna. "Ready?"

She nods. Calvin kisses her on the cheek and tells her he's going with my brothers to the waiting room and will be there if she needs him.

The walk to the elevator and the ride up to the third floor seems to take years, when I know, in reality, it's a matter of minutes. The nurse shows us to the room and walks away.

Gianna reaches over, grabs my hand, and we walk in together.

The moment I see her, my heart cracks. I feel it, the shattering in my chest. Jordyn's face is covered in cuts and bruises. Her arms are bandaged, and her leg is wrapped from her surgery. The slow beep of the monitors tells me her heart is beating strong and steady. Dropping Gianna's hand, I move to one side of the bed while she takes the other. Pulling the chair as close as I can get it, I drop down into it and carefully slide my hand beneath Jordyn's. I place my lips on her knuckles.

"Hey, sweets," I say, my voice trembling. "I'm here. Gianna too. There's a waiting room full of people who love you who are waiting to see you open those big brown eyes for us." I kiss her knuckles again. "I love you."

"Hey, J," Gianna speaks up. "You gave us all a scare, but you're going to be okay."

We both grow quiet as the door opens and a man in scrubs walks in. "I'm Dr. Maynard. I'm the orthopedic surgeon that repaired Jordyn's leg. Six weeks in the cast, and then we'll reassess from there. No weight bearing for six weeks."

"And her liver and spleen?" I ask.

He nods. "Not my area, but it looks here as if they're expected to heal on their own. My guess is they'll have her back for MRIs in a few weeks to check them, and subsequent scans as needed until they're certain she's healed." He keeps scrolling through the tablet in his hands. "They had plastics stitch up the laceration on her face, so there should be minimal scarring over time. She's a very lucky woman."

"Thank you, Doctor."

He nods and turns and walks out of the room.

"You hear that, sweets? Everything is going to be just fine." I kiss her hand.

"I'm going to step out and update everyone. Is it okay if I send your family back?"

"Yeah, that's fine. Thank you, Gianna."

She smiles. "Thank you for loving her like she deserves to be loved." She doesn't give me time to reply before she's out the door.

Leaning forward, I rest my head on the bed, careful not to hurt her. The emotions of the day catch up with me, and this time I don't try to hide them. I can be strong for her when she wakes up. Tears run freely as the fear and the worry bubble over.

"R—Ry?" a deep, croaking voice asks.

I lift my head to see those brown eyes that bring me to my knees. "Hey, baby." I wipe at my cheeks.

"W—" She starts, and I jump to pour her a glass of water.

"Small sips."

She nods and takes a few small sips before pulling her mouth away from the straw. "Why are you crying?"

"I could have lost you."

"My mother?"

I shake my head. "She didn't make it, Jordyn. I'm so sorry."

Tears well in her eyes. When she squeezes her eyes closed, they cascade over her cheeks. "It's my fault."

"No. It's not your fault." I reach over and press the button for the nurse. "Are you in any pain?"

"Not really. Sore, I guess. What's the damage?"

Before I can answer her, a nurse walks in and does it for me. She asks about her pain and pushes something into her IV. The door pushes open, and in walks a man in a suit, his face void of any emotion.

"Father," Jordyn croaks.

He nods and turns to the nurse. "What's the outcome of my daughter's injuries?"

The nurse goes through the same spiel. "She'll need assistance for the first six weeks and won't be able to climb stairs."

"Fine. I'll hire a nurse."

"No." I stand up and cross my arms over my chest.

"Who are you?" he asks.

"I'm the man who's going to marry your daughter."

He shows no emotion. "As I said, I'll hire a nurse."

"No," Jordyn's meek voice speaks up. She stares at her father, then her gaze finds mine. I nod and mouth, "I love you." Something flashes in her eyes. "Father, I'm not going back to the house. I'm moving in with Ryder. We're getting married."

The nurse looks worried, no doubt afraid there's about to be a brawl, but instead of anger, her father shows nothing but indifference.

"Fine." He looks down at his phone. "You're on your own."

"No, she's not. She never will be again." My voice is firm and commanding.

Her father doesn't spare me a glance. He stares at Jordyn for several long beats of a minute before turning and walking out of the room.

"Did he really just fucking walk out on you?"

"That's how he is. That's how he's always been," Jordyn says softly.

I lean over the bed. "You are not alone. You hear me? You are my fucking heart and soul, and I've got you. We're going to get you healed up, and we have a plan. A plan for our future, and we're moving forward with that. I'm sorry you lost your mother. I'm sorry your father is an uncaring asshole, but I can assure you, sweets, from here on out, you will be surrounded with nothing but love and acceptance. You're going to be smothered in it."

Tears well in her eyes. She carefully lifts her hand and places it next to my cheek. "I feel so much guilt. I—I'm going to need some help with that."

I can tell the words are hard for her.

"Whatever you need. Professional help. My love smothering you. Gianna's love smothering you, my family's love smothering you," I say, and she smiles. "We've got you, baby. You are not alone."

She nods. "Stay present."

"Yeah, baby. Stay present and look forward to the future."

Chapter 20

Jordyn

I spent a week in the hospital. A week of which I was never alone. Ryder's family took turns sitting with me, Gianna, too, and there was never a moment when I felt alone. I got to know his family again and made a point of apologizing to each of them.

I know I didn't have to, but it's what I need to do to heal.

I haven't seen or heard from my father since he walked out of my hospital room. He must have decided I wasn't worth the effort. Not that I'm surprised. He did, however, take care of my medical bills. One final parting gift. I assume it was to save face. Heaven forbid he be dragged through the mud for not paying medical bills for his daughter. My mother always seemed to be the driving factor, and after her "we're not in love" admission, I didn't expect him to be all emotional over the events of the accident.

Honestly, I'm not sure he's capable, and that's very, very sad. My heart hurts for him, and the lonely life he's living. I was on that path, and Ryder saved me. I've never been so glad to detour my life.

I've been home for almost a week, and Ryder and his family have been in rotation to sit with me during the day. Me and Tucker. That was a huge surprise. We got home Monday, and I heard barking. Ryder just grinned, got me settled on the couch, and walked out of the room. He came back with Tucker in his arms, the tiny fur ball licking at his face.

I cried. Happy tears. I was too overcome with emotion to speak. He explained that the Sunday after our trip to the animal shelter, he called Miss Dorothy and set up the adoption. Tucker was supposed to be my welcome home surprise the following weekend. He still was. There was just a delay. In a way, it's better. The comfort that this little fur ball brings me is immense.

Apparently, Maverick and Merrick, who still live together, took care of him while I was in the hospital. Ryder barely left my side. Just long enough to come home and shower before picking me up whatever food I was craving that day, and rushing back to sit at my bedside.

"Yo, J! Where are you?" I hear a voice call out.

"Kitchen!" I call back. Heavy footsteps head my way.

"Woman, what in the hell are you doing up?" Brooks eyes me—I'm standing next to the patio door in the kitchen.

"I have my scooter." I nod down to the scooter that lets me place my knee on the seat and push off with the other to get around the house.

"You knew I was coming over. You could have waited." He scowls at me.

"I'm fine. I just needed to let Tucker outside. Besides, I can't just sit on my ass for the next several weeks. I'll turn into a bloated couch potato."

"You can and you will. It's called healing." He gives me a stern look that I'm sure he's perfected dealing with difficult patients being an emergency room nurse.

"That's the nurse in you." I smile so he knows I'm teasing him.

"Maybe a little, but it's more the brother in me." He winks, returning my smile.

My heart melts at his words.

I miss my brother so much, but I've gained eight, nine if you count Ramsey's husband, Deacon, to help stand in for the brother I lost. "Oh, no, you don't, Brooks Kincaid. You cannot pull that wink on me. I'm immune."

"Riiiight." He laughs. "That's what my wife says too. I know it's the hair." He runs his hand through his locks, which I admit is sexy. However, I still roll my eyes. The ladies have warned me. You give these Kincaid men an inch and they'll take fifty miles.

"Come on, you. Let's get you settled, and I'll wrangle fluffy into the house."

"Tucker," I remind him.

He grins and places his hand on the small of my back as if he's afraid I might wreck my scooter and walks with me back to the living room. I'm surprised to see Palmer and a grinning Remi on the love seat.

"Hey," I greet them. "I get the whole family today?"

Brooks lifts me into his arms and transfers me to the couch. I huff and he shrugs.

"I wanted to see how you were feeling," Palmer explains.

"You saw me two days ago when it was your turn to watch me."

"We're not watching you, Jordyn. We're taking care of you. You need the help, and we have enough people to do it. We care about you."

"I know. I'm sorry. I'm not used to having so many people who care."

"We're a lot," she agrees. "But we mean well, and we'll have your back, always. Now, how are you feeling?"

"I feel good. Not as sore. My leg doesn't hurt much, unless I bump it or something."

"Which is why you need to stay on the couch." Brooks gives me a pointed look.

"This is nice," Palmer says, kicking her feet up on the table.

"What's nice?" Brooks asks her.

"You fussing over someone who's not me." She rubs her very pregnant belly.

I burst out laughing, which makes Remi laugh as well. "I'm going to grab the groceries and make lunch. You ladies, all three of you, behave." He points at each one of us, trying to be stern and failing before he walks back outside.

"Real talk. How are things?" Palmer asks.

I nod, because I know what she's asking. I've been open with all of them about my guilt over the accident. "Okay. The guilt is still heavy." I rub at my chest as if I can feel the responsibility of the accident that took my mother like it's a real tangible being.

"You didn't cause the accident, Jordyn."

"Yeah, I know. I think it's because I hated her. You know? I feel guilty because I didn't want her to die. Even after everything she did to my brother. She was still my mom. Not a good one, but the only one I had."

Palmer nods. "We're here for you. Have you thought about talking to a professional?" She runs her fingers through Remi's hair, as she is lying with her head on her mom's lap, looking at a book.

"I have. I know there are resources, and Ryder has encouraged me to do so as well. Honestly, I think I just need some time."

"That makes sense. However, please don't suffer in silence. It's okay to ask for help. You can call any of us at any time, and we'll be here for you."

"Thank you." My voice is full of emotion. "I'm tired of crying." I wave my hands in front of my face as if it's going to keep the tears at bay.

"It's healthy," Brooks says, coming back into the room. "You ladies okay while I get started on lunch?"

"You mean since the last time you checked ten minutes ago before you packed in the groceries?" Palmer asks.

He leans down and kisses her belly, kisses Remi on the forehead, and then presses his lips to Palmer's. "Yes, since then." He taps her nose with his index finger, and she smiles up at him adoringly.

"We're fine. Thank you." Palmer finally relents.

He points at me, silently asking if I need anything.

"I'm all set. Thank you for taking such good care of me."

"Family, J. You're family."

He stalks off toward the kitchen to make lunch.

The rest of the afternoon is spent talking and laughing and watching Remi play with Tucker. It's another good day surrounded by great company. I don't have time to let the guilt take over, even though it's lingering, always making itself known. Instead, when Ryder gets home, I'm still laughing and smiling, and when I tell him I've had a good day, I mean it.

I'm still struggling with the loss of the woman who gave birth to me but had no feelings toward me. Even the police ruled it as an accident. I know some of my guilt comes from my hatred for her and what she did to my brother. But I'm going to give myself some grace, and if I can't get past it, I'll ask for help. I have so many people in my corner now. I know they'll be there if and when I need them.

"What did we get him?" I ask Ryder. We're in the truck on the way to Orrin and Jade's house for Orion's second birthday. "That box is huge." I take another look over my shoulder to glance at the giant box in the back seat of his truck.

"Right?" Ryder glances over at me, and the smile on his face is almost as big as the box wrapped in toy trucks. Almost. "It's this huge-ass semi. It's got lights and horns and sirens, and a huge trailer on the back. When you open the trailer, there are three side-by-side UTVs in the back that he can pull out and play with."

"Sounds great. I could have wrapped it and pitched in." I don't have a job, but I do still have some money in savings. I need to start thinking about my next move once the cast is removed.

"Sweets, my money is your money, and besides, I'm an expert gift wrapper. Eight brothers, and lots of littles running around and you get good at it."

"Are you saying your gift-wrapping skills are superior to mine?" I pretend to be offended.

"I mean...." His voice trails off, and I swat playfully at his arm.

Instantly, I freeze. My breath stalls in my chest.

"I'm so sorry."

He glances over at me.

"No. Look at the road. Please, Ryder, don't look at me."

He nods and checks his mirrors before signaling to turn into the parking lot of the grocery store. He puts the truck in Park, climbs out of the truck, and comes to my side. He pulls open the door, unbuckles my seat belt, and turns me carefully to face him, being mindful of my leg. I close my eyes, not wanting to see the disappointment in his for my actions. I could have caused another accident.

I could have lost Ryder.

"Look at me, baby." His tone is gentle and full of patience.

I shake my head. I don't want to look at him. I don't want to see.

I feel his lips press to my forehead. "Jordyn, baby, I need those pretty brown eyes."

Forcing myself to face the moment, I peel my eyelids open. "I'm sorry." Tears prick the back of my eyes.

"You did nothing wrong, Jordyn. Nothing. That simple touch on my arm was featherlight, and we were safe the entire time. That touch, your touch, was not going to cause anything bad to happen to either of us."

"I pulled back on my purse. I should have just let her take it from me. She might still be here if I had."

"Maybe, but she was the one who allowed herself to get distracted. She took her eyes off the road. The car was already swerving before you pulled back. You read the police report of the eyewitness. You did not cause that accident, Jordyn."

Tears roll down my cheeks as I stare at the man I love.

He's here, and he's fighting this battle with me. I can see it in his eyes that he wants to take this burden from me. I wouldn't let him even if he could.

"I think I need help." I can't go on like this. I know I said I needed time, and I do, but this goes deeper. I'm still that ten-year-old little girl who lost her brother in a car accident caused by her mother to the now twenty-four-year-old woman who just lost her mother in the same manner. I know I need more than just time, and I need to face that truth.

"Name it."

"I think I should talk to someone."

"We'll talk to Brooks at the party and see if he has any recommendations."

Just like that. No hesitation, and he still looks at me like I'm his favorite person.

This isn't coming between us. Our bond, the love that we share, can withstand anything. I truly believe that.

"Can I ask you for a favor?"

"Anything, sweets."

"I could really use a hug right now."

He steps in closer, mindful of my leg, and wraps me in his arms. He doesn't care how we look or if people are watching as we hug it out here in the parking lot of the grocery store. He only cares about getting me what I need.

I have no doubt that I'm going to get through this. Ryder and his love will make sure of it.

The party has been so much fun. I'm soaking in every moment. I never got to experience anything like this growing up.

The large family is something I've always craved, and now I have it. I'm surrounded by endless love and support. I've had the best day. So much so that my face hurts from smiling. I've been catered to by everyone and welcomed with open arms.

My heart is full. A twinge of guilt seeps into the cloud of happiness, but I push it back.

Earlier, Brooks gave me the name of a therapist at the hospital he works for and says he's highly recommended. I'm going to call on Monday to make an appointment. I don't want this grief of losing my mother the way I did to overshadow moving forward, living my life for me. Luckily, I'm still on my father's insurance. I don't know for how long, but we'll cross that bridge when we get there. I only have another year before I needed my own anyway; by law, I wouldn't be able to stay on theirs. That's probably why they wanted to marry me off so soon.

"Aunt Jordyn, this is for you." Blakely skips over and hands me a picture.

"Did you draw this?" I take the drawing from her hands.

"Yep," she says proudly.

I read what she wrote above it and bite my lip to keep from laughing.

"It's for you. We've all been bothering you lots, and my mommy says sometimes it's okay to need space. So, you can put this on the front door when you want space."

"What you got there?" Ryder asks.

"Oh, well, Blakely drew me a picture."

Blakely pipes up and explains what and why she drew what she did.

"Don't cum in her," Ryder reads. He smirks, and I see him bite down on his cheek to get his laughter under control. "It's my favorite," he says, giving me a heated look.

"You have to give her space if she needs it," Blakely says, hands on her hips, sounding much older than her seven years.

"Yo, Dec, Kennedy, your daughter drew a picture. You should come and look at it," Ryder calls out for them.

Blakely takes the picture from Ryder and presents it to her dad when he gets closer. "Look, Daddy. I made Aunt Jordyn a 'don't come in here' picture to hang on her front door when she wants space, 'cause we've all been bothering her a lot lately." She smiles, proud of herself.

I watch as Declan's eyes scan the page, and his face goes red. He hands the paper to his wife, and she gasps and covers her mouth.

"Wow," Kennedy breathes.

"I know. I'm a good artist," Blakely says. She turns to walk away and shrieks. "Uncle Mav! You have a golden ticket!" She scurries off to Maverick, who is standing just a few feet away.

Maverick holds his hands up to catch her, but she stops and crouches down, lifting his foot. "See, a golden ticket." Maverick's face goes white and then red. "It's a ma—mag—magn—um. Magnum golden ticket!" She waves it in the air, and Maverick is quick to snatch it out of her hands.

"That's—a candy wrapper, kiddo," he tells her.

"Oh, do you have anymore? What's it taste like? I've never had that kind," Blakely rambles on.

Raymond is laughing but saves his youngest—well, one of his youngest, since he is a twin—from his granddaughter. He lifts her into his arms, and tickles her belly, taking her to the kitchen, luring her with the temptation of another cupcake.

Everyone is laughing and giving Maverick a hard time about his "candy" while I sit here laughing so hard there are tears streaming down my face.

"You good, sweets?" Ryder asks, still recovering from his own laughter.

"Yeah." I wipe under my eyes. "I've heard so many Blakely stories, but this, this is my first live experience. I love that little girl. She's the best."

"Yeah, she is. As the oldest, we're all in for some crazy times if she's leading the pack."

"So, you're telling me that our kids might turn out just like her?"

"Yep."

"Perfect. They can be whoever they want to be. They're free to love whoever they want to love, and I'll stand beside them no matter what."

"We both will." He leans in for a kiss.

I have a long road ahead of me, but everything is going to be just fine. I'm going to work hard, and love all of my new family harder. I am going to be a Kincaid after all. I think I'll adapt to the family motto just fine.

Chapter 21

Ryder

I go over my list once, twice, three times, making sure we have everything. Jordyn has complained all morning that I'm not letting her help, but I just smile, and kiss her soft lips and refuse her offer. She's still healing from the accident, and that's her primary job. Well, to heal and to love me. I'm selfish like that. And yes, I have zero shame in admitting it. She's finally home with me, where she belongs permanently.

Life is fan-fucking-tastic.

"I think that's everything," I say, stepping back into the house.

"Phone chargers?"

"Got one for both of us."

"Are you sure I packed enough clothes?"

"Sweets, it's a camping trip. We're only going to be there for two days. Trust me when I tell you no one is going to care if you wear the same hoodie two days in a row."

"I know." She sighs. "I'm nervous, and before you tell me I have no reason to be, I know that too." She smiles at up at me. "Ryder, this is my first ever family anything where I'm not being shown off. I get to hang out with a lot of really amazing people and just be me. I don't have to worry if I'm dressed appropriately, if my hair and makeup are on point, or if someone caught me sneaking an extra cream puff from a passing server."

I sit on the couch next to her, and, careful of her leg that's still in a cast, pull her onto my lap. "And that makes you nervous?"

"Yes! What if I don't know how to be—normal?"

"Baby, you just have to be you. Any version of you that you want to be. That's who we want to see. Not someone you think you have to be. Be the you that lounges around the couch with me and watches movies. Be the you that fawns all over my nieces and nephews. Just be my Jordyn, and everything else will fall into place."

"I really, really love you, Ryder Kincaid."

"Yeah? That's good because you already agreed to marry me."

She snuggles into my chest, and even though we need to get on the road, neither one of us moves. Jordyn didn't get snuggles growing up, and I'll never pass up the chance to give them to her now.

She starts therapy next week, and she's nervous. We've been talking about making an additional Kincaid family camping trip—a tradition to include the ladies and the kids—and we're making it happen this weekend. One text to the group chat and my brothers were in. However, Brooks was leery since Palmer is due to have their second baby in six weeks. He insisted we stay somewhere close. Luckily, we have a local campground about thirty minutes from us. It's in the opposite direction of Harris, and there's a hospital ten minutes away.

What's even more incredible is that we were able to get enough cabins to house all of us. We're pairing up. Two couples per cabin, leaving the twins with Mom and Dad. They are the babies, after all.

"We should get going." She tries to move, but I stand with her in my arms and place her back on the couch.

"Let me make a quick run through, make sure the house is all locked up, and I turned everything off. I'll be back to get your walker and take you out to the truck."

"You know the walker is here for a reason, right? To help me walk."

"Not on my watch, sweets." I bend to press a kiss to her forehead and dart off to make my rounds.

I check the back door, turn off all the lights, and move to the bedroom. I grab a pair of my sweats and a hoodie, shoving them into a backpack. She packed her own stuff, but I want to make sure she's warm and comfortable. With the cast, it will be easier for her to wear my clothes as layers. Besides, there is just something about your girl wearing your clothes. Luckily for me, we're rooming with Archer and Scarlett, and they're still in the honeymoon phase. They'll be too busy at night to worry about what we are or are not doing.

At least, that's what I'm going to tell Jordyn.

When I make it back to the living room, she's no longer on the couch and her walker is gone. I turn my head and see her standing at the door in the kitchen that leads to the garage. There are two steps there. Steps I never thought much about until my girl's leg was in a cast.

"I got you." With the backpack slung over my arm, I lift her bridal style and carry her down the steps and to the passenger side of my truck. She pulls open the door, and I set her gently inside. Leaning over, I buckle her seat belt.

"Ryder." She sighs.

"I know what you're going to say. You can buckle your own seat belt. I know you can, sweets, but I can do it for you too. I want to spoil you, Jordyn. You've been through so much, not just with the accident but in life, and I want to show you every single day that you are loved beyond measure. I'm never going to stop doing these things for you. Not as long as there is breath in my lungs."

Her eyes shimmer with tears. She lifts her hands to cup my cheeks. "There are not enough words in the English language to tell you what you mean to me, Ryder. I feel helpless with this bum leg and your family watching over me. I don't want to be a burden."

"You're family, Jordyn. Not a burden. This is what it means to be a part of a family. A group of people who love you unconditionally and will drop what they're doing to help you. You have that now, baby. I know it's going to take you some time to get used to it."

"Thank you for your help." She smiles sweetly, and I grin back at her.

"There you go." I drop a kiss to her lips. "Let me go lock up and grab your scooter." Back in the house, I do just that before loading her scooter into the back seat, and we're on the road.

"Wow, it's beautiful here," Jordyn says as I carry her into the living room of our cabin. Archer is right behind me with her scooter. "Thank you both. I'm sorry you have to wait on me like this."

"*Pfft.*" Scarlett waves her off as she takes a seat next to her on the couch. "Let them use those muscles for good. You heard the Blakely arm porn story, right?"

"Yes!" Jordyn laughs. "That girl is something else."

"She gets it honest," Scarlett replies.

I hand Jordyn her phone, a bottle of water, and kiss her sweet lips. "You good for a few minutes?"

"I'm fine, babe."

My heart trips over in my chest at the term of endearment.

"She's got me," Scarlett speaks up.

"Thank you." I nod to my newest sister-in-law. "We're going to go start gathering firewood for the weekend."

"What can I do?" Jordyn immediately asks.

"Nothing. We already decided the Kincaid ladies and the kids get a relaxing weekend while us guys handle the rest," Archer answers before I can.

"I can cook or something," Jordyn offers.

"Nope. You two sit there looking pretty, and let us do our thing." Archer bends to kiss his wife.

"I was warned on the way here that this is how the weekend was going to go," Scarlett tells Jordyn. "Since the guys are making the new tradition, they decided they get to make all the rules." She playfully rolls her eyes.

Jordyn's eyes find mine. "What are we supposed to do all weekend?"

"Nothing. Talk, nap, read a book, whatever you feel like. Camping is all about slowing down."

"Go on." Scarlett waves us off. "We have girl talk to start."

"Love you, sweets." I kiss my girl one more time, while my brother kisses his wife, and we head outside to start gathering firewood.

I want to capture every second of this night and brand it in my mind. Just as I knew they would, my family has welcomed Jordyn into the fold, as if she's always been a part of us. My girl hasn't stopped smiling since we got here.

When Archer and I came back from gathering wood, we found Jordyn and Scarlett sitting on the back porch of the cabin. It's still warm during the day here in Georgia, growing colder at night. The two of them were laughing and cutting up as if they'd known each other for years. We left them there and headed off to see what we could do to help with dinner.

Speaking of dinner, I'm stuffed. We had burgers and hotdogs on the grill, baked beans, chips, and macaroni salad. It was delicious, but tomorrow night, Orrin is making campfire chili, and damn if my mouth doesn't water just thinking about it.

Currently, there isn't a single place I'd rather be. Jordyn is on my lap with her leg propped up on her scooter. There's a blanket over her to keep the chill of the night air at bay.

I watch as my brothers help their kids roast marshmallows, and I admit I can't wait until that's me. I love holding Jordyn in my arms, being here with everyone that I love, but I'm also looking forward to that being me.

Sterling helps Blakely, while Declan handles Beckham. Orrin is laughing at Orion, and Brooks is letting Remi feed him hers, which means he has melted sticky marshmallow all over his face, but he smiles at his daughter, anyway. Deacon offers Brynlee a bite, but she crinkles up her nose, and shakes her head before resting on his shoulder. Caden squeals with laughter when Rushton lets their marshmallow catch on fire.

My brothers are happier than I've ever seen them.

I chance a look at Sterling and Archer, and something tells me I'll be getting more nieces or nephews soon. Hell, maybe if I'm lucky, it will be Jordyn and me who are adding to the Kincaid clan.

Maverick and Merrick are being their goofy selves while roasting marshmallows for the ladies of the family. And the ladies, they all look happy and content. All of them wearing smiles much like Jordyn's the entire day.

This is what life is about.

Working hard and loving harder.

I always thought I knew what my dad meant by that, but it wasn't until Jordyn that I truly understood. I can't help but grin when I think about my little brothers and watching them find their happily ever after. They're always the loud, funny ones, and it's hard for me to imagine them settling down, but I know it will happen, and like the rest of my family, we'll be with both of them every step of the way.

"You need anything?" I ask, my lips next to Jordyn's ear.

She shakes her head and turns to look at me. "Nothing. I can't think of a single thing I need that I don't have right here around this fire."

"I can think of one thing."

"Yeah?" There's disbelief in her tone.

Shifting her on my lap, I reach into my pocket and pull out the ring I bought for her. I don't make a big to do about it. We've already talked about this, and she said yes. The ring? It's just a symbol of my love for her. Carefully, I slide the ring onto her finger.

"Now," I say, kissing her temple, "everything is perfect."

"Bro!" Maverick calls out. "Did you just slip something sparkly on J's finger?"

"Yep," I call back.

"What?" Everyone talks at once, and we get several hugs of congratulations.

I see Jordyn wiping at her eyes. "You good, sweets?"

"Better than good. Thank you for loving me, Ryder Kincaid. Thank you for sharing your family with me." She then turns her face to the fire. "Thank you," she says, loud enough to capture the attention of our family. "Thank you for helping us get here. For your never-ending support and love. Thank you for being there for Ry when I couldn't be. Thank you for letting me be a part of this moment."

"You're family, sweetheart. That's what we do," Mom replies.

"I've never had a family. Not one like this."

"Oh, well, there are plenty of us to go around." Dad laughs.

"I love you. All of you," she says, her voice cracking.

Not gonna lie. That's not the smoke of the fire making my eyes water. I swallow thickly and hold my fiancée tightly as my family returns her sentiment of love. "Engaged by Halloween," I say to break some of the tension. Halloween is next week; I barely made the cut.

Jordyn sits up straight and pulls her leg from where it rests on the scooter so that she can look at me better. "Married by Veteran's Day."

"You trying to steal my thunder, baby?" I tease. My heart is thumping like a drum against my ribs. That's less than three weeks from now. Three weeks and she will finally be Jordyn Kincaid.

She'll be mine.

My wife.

"Um, Jordyn," Alyssa speaks up. "That's just a little over two weeks away."

She nods. "I know. It's not the wedding that's important, or the date. It's the man. It's the future. I've never wanted to be a part of something more." She pauses and twists her hands together in her lap. When she finally looks up, she squares her shoulders and takes her time going around the fire and making eye contact with every single person. "There's this man. He's strong, and hardheaded, and he loves so damn hard." She swallows. "He once told me I could be anything I want to be. You all keep telling me that I'm family, and I love you for it. However, I want that to hold true. I don't want to be an Astor anymore. I don't want to be a part of what that represents. I'm starting therapy next week because of the guilt I feel about the way my mother died. I feel that guilt, but that doesn't change who she was. That doesn't change that I hate her for what she did to me, to all of us, and then that causes even more guilt. I know I have to work through all of that, but I know what I want."

She turns now and gives me her full attention.

"I want to be your wife. I want our kids to grow up having moments just like these. I want Sunday dinners and babysitting for date nights. I want the chaos and the love. I don't know what I'm doing with my life as far as my career goes. That's something I'm hoping to decide in the coming weeks and can work on that once this comes off." She points to the cast on her leg. "However, whatever I do, I want it to be with you by my side."

"Damn," Merrick mutters. "I kind of just fell in love with your fiancée, bro."

Jordyn's head falls back in laughter. The sound surrounds everyone here like a blanket of love and happiness. Something I wasn't sure I'd ever get to witness from her again.

"Well, that settles it," my mom speaks up. "Ladies, we have a wedding to plan."

"Really?" Jordyn asks.

"We can start now. Let's go back to a cabin and get to work."

"No." I wrap my arms tightly around Jordyn, making her laugh. "Not tonight. Start tomorrow. Give me this tonight."

"Tomorrow," Jordyn agrees. "Carol? Can we really do this in that amount of time?"

"What kind of wedding do you want?" Kennedy asks.

"One with all of you and my best friend, Gianna. I don't care about the rest."

"Dress?" Palmer asks.

"I never really put too much thought into my wedding because I knew my mother would control every aspect."

"Then we'll figure it out together. We'll talk about what you want and pick a date based on making it your special day."

"That would be wonderful. Thank you."

"Of course." Mom smiles kindly.

Everyone starts talking about anything and everything, while I sit quietly and bury my face in Jordyn's neck. Soon, this incredible woman will be my wife.

All of the hurt, the pain, and the worry brought us to this moment. It was hell, but as they say, nothing worth having comes easy.

Chapter 22

Jordyn

I'm bouncing with excitement. Ryder just smiles over at me because I am literally bouncing in the passenger seat of the truck. "Can this thing go any faster?" I ask him.

"Relax, sweets. Palmer and the baby will still be at the hospital when we get there." He chuckles.

"I know, but I can't wait to meet him."

"It's pretty cool that our nephew was born on your birthday, huh?" He glances over quickly before turning his eyes back to the road.

Our nephew.

My grin grows even wider. "So cool. I'm an aunt."

Ryder laughs. The sound is deep and throaty, and it does things to me. Things that I should not be thinking about as we are headed to the hospital to meet Brooks and Palmer's new baby boy.

"I hate to break it to you, sweets, but you were already an aunt."

I don't know how to describe this… melting feeling in my chest. It's warm and comforting and feels like home. I have a home. A happy one, where I can be me, and I'm loved for it.

It's still something I'm getting used to. I've been in therapy for a couple of weeks now, and it's helping me. It's only been a short time, but I feel, dare I say, better? I'll always harbor some form of guilt, but I'm getting there.

"I know, but this is the first one I get to be there for from the beginning. It feels different."

"I promise we'll still celebrate you."

I whip my head around to look at him. "Are you kidding me? This is the absolute best birthday present ever. *Ever*," I repeat with conviction, being honest. I can't remember a birthday I've ever been this smiley for.

"It's still your day, Jordyn."

"You're right; it is my day, and I can't think of anything better than celebrating the birth of our nephew." Tears cloud my eyes because my heart is so fucking full, I can't help it.

"I don't know how that heart of yours fits inside your chest, future Mrs. Kincaid."

I smile over at him as we pull into the parking lot of the hospital. The truck is barely in Park before I'm tearing off my seat belt and pushing open my door. "Grab the bag," I call over my shoulder to Ryder.

"Woman, you better not try to get out of this truck on your own." He gives me a stern look.

"Then hurry up, slowpoke. We have a baby to snuggle." I turn back around, slipping my purse over my head, and wait impatiently for him to come and help me out of the truck.

"Maybe I should get a wheelchair," he muses.

"Ryder!" I laugh. "Stop. Grab the scooter and help me down. I don't need a damn wheelchair."

He winks and reaches into the back seat to grab my scooter, then lifts me out of the truck, placing me on my feet. I don't wait for him. Instead, I start my trek to the hospital entrance.

"What took you so long?" I ask when Ryder jogs to catch up with me.

"I had to get the gift bag. How in the hell did you get so fast on that thing?"

"I zoom around the house all day while you're at work."

"You're supposed to be resting."

"If I keep resting, my ass is going to leave a permanent indention on the couch. I can't just sit around all day. I can't wait to get this cast off."

"Next week, sweets."

Originally, it was only supposed to be six weeks, but when I went in for my checkup, the doctors decided I need a little more time. They then put me in an air-cast-boot-looking thing and advised me to limit the weight I put on the leg for two more weeks. And Bossy Mc-Bosserson is sticking to the rule to the letter. Hence the reason I have the damn scooter still instead of the crutches they gave me to use as well. Ryder doesn't think they're safe.

I love the man, but he's driving me crazy. I don't say anything, though, because I've been on the other side. Where there is no one there to fuss or drive you insane. I'll take the former all day long.

When we reach the waiting room, it's filled with family. Our family. I tear up again, but blink it back. Now is not the time. This is my new normal. It's going to take some getting used to, but I'm definitely up for the challenge.

"Hey." Carol, my future mother-in-law, comes over and hugs me. "Happy Birthday, Jordyn."

I lose the battle as I smile back at her and wipe the tear from my eye. "Thank you."

"Sweetheart, are you okay?"

I smile. It's not fake or forced. It's one-hundred-percent percent genuine. "I'm more than okay."

She pulls me into another hug, and this time, I hold on a little longer and squeeze her a little tighter, but she doesn't seem to mind.

"Go on back," Orrin tells us. "We've all already had our turn. Everyone except for the twins, but they're on their way."

"Thanks." Ryder turns toward me and winks. "Let's go, sweets. We have a baby to snuggle."

I barely contain my urge to let out a squeal of excitement. I wasn't kidding when I said this is the best birthday I can ever remember.

Ryder pushes open the door, and I slowly scoot my way inside.

"Hey," I whisper. Brooks is sitting on the edge of the bed with their new baby boy in his arms while Palmer looks at both of them with a blissfully exhausted yet happy look on her face.

"Hi, guys." Palmer smiles. "Come meet your nephew."

"Congratulations," I say, wheeling over to the side of the bed opposite of where Brooks is sitting. "He's so handsome." I swallow over the lump in my throat.

"Thank you," they say at the same time.

"You did good, Momma," Ryder says as he leans over the bed and kisses Palmer's cheek.

"Thanks, Ry. Do you want to hold your nephew?"

"Yes," we say at the same time. Brooks and Palmer smile at one another before Brooks stands and walks around the bed, placing his son in his brother's arms.

"Hey, little man," Ryder coos. "Has Mommy and Daddy given you a name yet?" he asks the baby.

"Leo," Palmer speaks up.

"Hey, Leo. I'm Ryder, your favorite uncle."

It's funny as hell, but also so damn sweet. I cover my mouth to hide my emotions. I feel a hand on my arm and look over to see Palmer smiling at me. She nods and mouths, "I know," before her eyes go back to her son.

"All right, baby hog." I offer Ryder a watery smile. "Can I have a turn?"

"Okay, little man, it's time to meet your aunt Jordyn."

A soft sob falls from my lips as Ryder places him in my arms. "Hey, Leo," I whisper, just for him. "I'm your aunt Jordyn. I never thought I'd be an aunt, let alone share my birthday with my nephew. I won't tell you I'm your favorite because you have a group of aunts who are all badass, but I'm honored to be one of them."

I hear a throat clearing and a sniffle. I look up to find three sets of eyes, all wet with emotion, smiling back at me. "I'm sorry, I just—this is so much more than I ever imagined my life would be blessed with." I swallow hard. "When I lost my brother, I just—" I stop talking, because I can't seem to get the words out.

"He's lucky to have his aunt Jordyn," Brooks speaks up. "We all are."

I nod and turn my gaze back to the sleeping baby in my arms, trying to get a handle on my emotions. When I finally feel like I can speak without my voice cracking, I look up to find Ryder watching me. "Can we have one?"

His reply is a slow, sexy smile accompanied by a nod. He reaches out and tucks my hair behind my ear. "Yeah, sweets. We can have as many as you want." He leans over and kisses me, and if there was ever a chance of a heart bursting with love, it would be mine in this moment.

Ryder spins me around the dance floor at Willow Manor as our family watches on. It's the first Saturday of December and my wedding day. My mother-in-law and my sisters-in-law joined forces, and this day couldn't have been more perfect.

"How's the leg, Mrs. Kincaid?" Ryder asks.

I smile up at my husband. "Perfect, Mr. Kincaid."

Ryder stops moving and rests his forehead against mine, not giving a single fuck that every member of our family, and my best friend and her boyfriend, are watching. "I'll never forget this day, Jordyn. Never."

"You're not supposed to make me cry on my wedding day."

"It's the moment, sweets. I'm gonna need you to stay present." He winks.

"The present is nice, but I kind of like the outlook for the future as well."

"Did you toss them?"

"Toss what?" I know what he's asking, but I'm feeling a little mischievous.

"You know what. Did you stop taking your birth control?"

"Yep. I didn't take last night's pill either."

His hand slides down to my belly. "So, tonight, we might be working on another piece of that future?"

"I don't think it works that quickly, but we can definitely practice."

"Oh, sweets, we'll be practicing. Not that we need it. We're pros."

My face heats. Before I can reply, Maverick appears, pulling me into his arms.

"You have to share, Ry."

"She's my wife."

"Well, she's my sister." He smiles down at me. "Love ya, sis."

"I love you too."

"I'm watching you, little brother," Ryder warns with absolutely no heat. He leans in and kisses me softly. "Love you, wife."

"Love you too."

He walks away and lets me dance with Maverick. Little did he know, all of his brothers, Deacon, Calvin, and his father, would all request a turn before he got me back into his arms.

I used to count the good days. Now, there are too many to count. Too many to memorize. So many moments I'll cherish for a lifetime.

It's the week before Christmas and I'm packing up supplies to head to my in-laws' to meet all of my sisters-in-law for a baking day. I'm so damn excited. I've been working here and there for the family businesses. I've watched the photography studio for Scarlett while she works and Palmer is on maternity leave. I've done the same at Orrin and Declan's shops. I'm hoping something more permanent comes soon. I want to contribute to our family. However, a degree in fashion really isn't doing much for me here in Willow River.

Just as I'm about to leave, my cell phone rings. I don't recognize the number, but I answer anyway. I no longer dread incoming calls. "Hello."

"Jordyn Astor?"

"It's Kincaid now," I tell the caller. "Who is this?"

"I wasn't aware. I apologize. This is Harold Matthews. I was your grandfather's attorney."

"Okay?" I ask cautiously.

"Mrs. Kincaid, you just turned twenty-five."

"That's right."

"I'm calling to make arrangements for your trust fund."

"I don't have a trust fund." My mother always said I'd be married off and my husband would be able to take care of me. There is a pang of sadness anytime I think about her, but I'm getting better every day.

"Your grandfather set up a trust for you. The rules were you couldn't have access to the funds until your twenty-fifth birthday or at the time of marriage."

"A trust fund?" I repeat, because I'm having a hard time believing this is real.

"Yes. When is a good time for us to meet to get the transfer taken care of?"

"Um, can we do it on a weekend so that my husband can be there?"

"Yes. He'll be required to sign off, since he gets a portion in his name as well."

"Okay. Yes. Um, a Saturday, please."

"How about this Saturday?"

"This Saturday is Christmas Eve."

"Yes, but the sooner we get this taken care of, the better." He sounds so much like my father. Cold. Emotionless. Working on holidays, not a care for his family. Part of me wants to say no, but I know his type. Me refusing this weekend won't keep him from the office.

"Saturday works fine."

"Great. Can you give me your email address, and I'll send you our address?"

I rattle off my email address and confirm Saturday morning at nine for our meeting and end the call.

Shaking out of my stupor, I head to my car. It's on the way to my in-laws' that I realize I didn't ask him how much money.

"I'm sorry. Can you repeat that?" Ryder says from his seat next to me.

"Ten million dollars. Five is to be issued in your name, Mr. Kincaid, and the other five to your wife."

"Is this a joke? Is my father here somewhere?"

"No. In fact, your father doesn't know about the trust. Only your grandfather and myself. Should something have happened to me before this meeting, an associate of mine would have taken over the account."

"They didn't know?"

"No. Here." He hands me a small envelope. "From your grandfather."

Taking the note with shaking hands, I pull out a small notecard.

My Dearest Jordyn,

I worked too much. I didn't make time for my family, and I see that in my son, your father. It's at the end of a man's life where he can truly see the error of his ways. I know my son and the greed that lives inside him and his wife. I never want you to have to struggle. Take this money and live your dreams. Find your passion and be happy.

All my love,

Grandpa Mathis

Tears track my cheeks because he was always so cold and distant growing up, and this is completely unexpected.

Mr. Matthews gives us each what feels like a million papers to sign, and sends us on our way.

Ten million dollars richer.

In the car, we're both quiet. Ten million dollars is a lot of money, but I know what I want to do with it. "We have to pay Ramsey back. I don't know if we can figure out how much she paid the PI, but I want to pay her back."

"Okay," Ryder agrees.

"I want to buy a boutique. I saw there was some space next to Palmer's studio. I want to open up my own space to sell clothes."

"Okay," my husband says again, with a huge smile on his face.

"I want to build a place. A home for us, but I also want to build another building. I want a place with a huge kitchen, play and nap areas for the kids, and a kitchen table big enough for all of us to sit and have family dinners. A barn or something that's finished on the inside."

"What?" Ryder asks.

"Our family, Ryder. We're growing leaps and bounds and we're all adding babies. I want a place where we can all sit on a couch, or at the kitchen table and a place the kids can be kids, and the adults can be adults. Can we find enough land for our house and that space? I want them to be separate. That way, our family can use the other anytime they need it."

"Are you sure?"

"Yes. I don't care if we use every dime. I want that space for our family."

"I fucking love you. Every piece of that big heart of yours, Jordyn Kincaid."

"I love you too."

Jordyn

It's amazing what money can do. I shouldn't be surprised by that with the way that I was raised, but this is different. This is using money for good. For a growing family who opened their hearts and their homes to me and made me feel as if I was one of them long before I was.

Here we are two weeks shy of six months from the day I found out about my trust, and Kincaid Central, as the twins like to call it, is complete. Ryder and I found some land not far from his parents' place, and we decided to build the family building first. Our home is next. We don't want anything over the top. Just a nice three-bedroom ranch with a basement. We meet with the builder to finalize plans next week.

Ramsey wouldn't let us pay her back. Instead, she told me to put the money into the family building. Everyone loved the idea, and for me, it was my way of giving back to the people who have given me so much. So, just as Ramsey suggested, I put it into the building.

I added a theater room. One that will house all of the adults and room for the kids to camp out below. It's over the top, but I know the kids are going to love it.

Money isn't a new concept for me, but I know it is to my family. The Kincaids have busted their asses for everything they have, and while I didn't work for this money, it was given to me by my grandfather, and his wish was for me to live my dream.

This is it.

I'm living it.

"Aunt Jordyn!" Blakely comes rushing toward me. "This is the bestest birthday ever!" She cheers.

"I'm so glad, sweetie." I pull her into a hug. She releases me and she's off to play with her cousins and a few of her friends, who are here to celebrate her eighth birthday.

"You did good, sweets," Ryder says, wrapping his arms around me from behind. I lean into him, taking in the moment.

"We did good. This place has your influence all over it."

"I love that we have a place where there is more than enough room for everyone. No matter how many kids are added to the next generation, this is where we'll be for birthdays and holidays and everything in between. Thank you for giving this to us."

"It's your money too," I remind him.

"We did good," he says, kissing my neck.

"Yeah, we really did."

We stand together, watching our family laughing and having a good time, and this is another one of those moments, the ones that far outweigh the bad that I want to memorize.

This family loved me when I was at my worst, and this is how I show them that I'm going to love them harder.

Epilogue

Ryder

She did it. It took a little longer because her focus was on Kincaid Central, but my wife finally opened her own boutique. Today is opening day for family only, and I swear that smile she's wearing could light up the entire fucking town of Willow River.

Not that we need a family opening day. They've all been here over the past several months to check in on the progress and lend a hand. But Jordyn insisted that she wanted to share this with the family before she opened her doors to the entire town.

She bounces over and wraps her arms around my waist. I kiss the top of her head and hold her tightly in my arms.

She peers up at me under long lashes. "Thank you for this life."

"Stop thanking me for loving you, sweets. It's as easy as breathing."

"Speech!" Merrick calls out.

"Is Maverick close?" she asks.

"Let me call him."

"We're waiting on Mav," Jordyn calls back.

Pulling my phone out of my pocket, I call my brother. He wasn't supposed to work today, but it rained three days this week, and his paving crew is already behind schedule.

"Yo," he answers.

"Hey, man. You headed home?"

"Yeah, I'm walking to my truck now."

"All right, be safe. Come straight to the boutique."

"I will. Aw, shit," he mumbles.

"What's up?" I ask.

"Nothing. It looks like a woman might be broken down. Flat tire from the looks of it now that I'm closer. I will handle this, and then I'll be on my way."

"Be safe."

"Always."

"Is he on his way?"

"Yeah, he's helping a woman change her tire, and then he will be. He's working in Harris, so it won't be too much longer."

"Perfect." There's a sparkle in her eyes as she winks and saunters off to steal Leo from Brooks.

I sit back and watch my family and shoot the shit with my brothers, and love on my nieces and nephews. Finally, an hour later, Mav shows up. He's not alone. There's a woman holding a little girl in her arms.

"Hey, everyone." Maverick waves. "This is Stella, and this little cutie is Ada. Their car broke down, and I gave them a ride into town, after calling Dec's shop to tow their car. I told her the more the merrier."

"Of course," Kennedy speaks up. "How old is your daughter?" she asks.

"She just turned one."

"Come on in. Let's get you something to eat."

I look on as Maverick watches them walk away before he makes a beeline for my wife, lifts her in his arms, and spins her around. She laughs and swats at him as he places her back on the floor. She motions to the table of food before her eyes meet mine. She nods, and I make my way toward her.

Once I reach her, I lace her fingers through mine.

"Thank you all for coming. I couldn't have done this without each and every one of you. Thank you for helping make my dream come true."

"Pull the sheet!" Sterling calls out.

Jordyn smiles as she turns to me and nods. I pull the sheet, revealing the lit sign that reads Kincaid's Boutique.

"I wanted it to be a piece of all of us. Our kids can work here when they need a job after school, and our family name will be displayed proudly in town. Thank you for showing me what it means to be a part of a loving family."

"You said our kids," Palmer calls out.

Jordyn looks at me, and I know that look. She wants me to give them our good news.

"We're having a baby!" I shout, and the room erupts. We're hugged by every single person, and perhaps more than once; I lost count.

Eventually, it's just the two of us, and my wife is back in my arms where she's supposed to be.

"You once told me to stay present. I was stuck living in the past, unable to see beyond the fear and the hatred to look forward to anything else."

"So glad you listened to me," I tease.

"Me too."

"Love you, baby momma."

"Love you too, baby daddy."

Thank YOU

for taking the time to read **Stay Present**.
I hope you loved Ryder and Jordyn's story.

We have two Kincaid brothers left! You can preorder Maverick
and Merrick's story now.

Stay Anyway – Maverick
kayleeryan.com/books/stay-anyway/

Available June 11, 2024

Stay Real – Merrick
kayleeryan.com/books/stay-real/

Available August 27, 2024

Did you know that Orrin Kincaid has his own story?
Grab **Stay Always** for free here

kayleeryan.com/books/stay-always/

Start the Riggins Brothers Series for FREE.
Download **Play by Play** now.

Never miss a new release:
Newsletter Sign-up

Be the first to hear about free content, new releases, cover
reveals, sales, and more. kayleeryan.com/subscribe/

More from KAYLEE RYAN

With You Series:
Anywhere with You | More with You | Everything with You

Soul Serenade Series:
Emphatic | Assured | Definite | Insistent

Southern Heart Series:
Southern Pleasure | Southern Desire
Southern Attraction | Southern Devotion

Unexpected Arrivals Series
Unexpected Reality |Unexpected Fight | Unexpected Fall
Unexpected Bond | Unexpected Odds

Riggins Brothers Series:
Play by Play | Layer by Layer | Piece by Piece
Kiss by Kiss | Touch by Touch | Beat by Beat

Out of Reach Series:
Beyond the Bases | Beyond the Game
Beyond the Play | Beyond the Team

Entangled Hearts Duet:
Agony | Bliss

More from KAYLEE RYAN

Standalone Titles:

Tempting Tatum | Unwrapping Tatum | Levitate

Just Say When | I Just Want You | Reminding Avery

Hey, Whiskey | Pull You Through | Remedy

The Difference | Trust the Push | Forever After All

Misconception | Never with Me

Cocky Hero Club:

Lucky Bastard

Mason Creek Series:

Perfect Embrace

Kincaid Brothers Series:

Stay Always | Stay Over | Stay Forever

Stay Tonight | Stay Together | Stay Wild

Stay Present | Stay Anyway | Stay Real

Everlasting Ink Series:

Does He Know? | Is This Love?

More from KAYLEE RYAN

Co-written with Lacey Black:

Fair Lakes Series:

It's Not Over | Just Getting Started

Can't Fight It

Standalone Titles:

Boy Trouble | Home to You

Beneath the Fallen Stars

Co-writing as Rebel Shaw with Lacey Black:

Royal | Crying Shame

Watch and Learn

Acknowledgments

There are so many people who are involved in the publishing process. I write the words, but I rely on my team of editors, proofreaders, and beta readers to help me make each book the best that it can be.

Those mentioned above are not the only members of my team. I have photographers, models, cover designers, formatters, bloggers, graphic designers, author friends, my PA, and so many more. I could not do this without these people.

And then there are my readers. If you're reading this, thank you. Your support means everything. Thank you for spending your hard-earned money on my words, and taking the time to read them. I appreciate you more than you know.

Special Thanks:

Becky Johnson, Hot Tree Editing.

Julie Deaton, Jo Thompson, and Jess Hodge, Proofreading

Sarah Book Cover Boutique – Cover Design (Guy Cover)

Emily Wittig Designs – Special Edition Cover

Wander Aguiar – Photographer (Main Guy Cover)

Chasidy Renee – Personal Assistant

Jamie, Stacy, Lauren, Franci, and Erica

Bloggers, Bookstagrammers, and TikTokers

Lacey Black & Kelly Elliott

Stacy - Graphics

The entire Give Me Books Team

The entire Grey's Promotion Team

My fellow authors

And my amazing Readers

Much love,

Kaylee Ryan

AUTHOR